SHIKHANDINI

WARRIOR PRINCESS OF THE MAHABHARATA

ASHWINI SHENOY

ISBN: 978-93-52018-91-8

Layouts: Hitanshi Shah
Cover design: Boomranng Studio
Printing: Thomson Press

Published in India 2019 by
PLATINUM PRESS
An imprint of
LEADSTART PUBLISHING PVT LTD
Unit 25/26, Building A/1, Wadala (East),
Mumbai 400037, Maharashtra, INDIA
T +91 96 99933000 **E** info@leadstartcorp.com
W www.leadstartcorp.com

To my parents

Ramachandra & Rekha Shenoy

About the Author

ASHWINI SHENOY is an electronics engineer by profession and a writer by passion. Though born in the coastal city of Mangalore, Ashwini had her schooling in various parts of India, travelling to wherever her father's postings took the family. She grew up fluent in Konkani, Kannada, Hindi and English, while having studied Sanskrit and Marathi as well.

In addition to a Master's degree in Technology, Ashwini holds a diploma in creative writing. A fervent reader with an abiding interest in Indian mythology, historical fiction and stories with life lessons, she wrote her first story at the age of eight and has been writing ever since, experimenting across genres and drawing into the limelight some of the most underrated yet pivotal characters of Indian mythology and history, retelling their stories from a more logical and balanced modern perspective. *Shikhandini* is her first full length book.

Apart from her passion for writing, she is a keen photographer and an avid painter in oils. She can be reached at:

ashwinishenoy.wordpress.com
ashwini.shenoy.m@gmail.com

Contents

Author's Note

The traditional tale goes something like this: Shikhandini was the Princess of Panchala. Born a girl, she was believed by many to be the reincarnation of Princess Amba of Kashi, who vowed vengeance on *Maharathi* Bheeshm of Hastinapur, before ending her own life. Shikhandini thus lives her life with the sole purpose of slaying the Maharathi. She finally has the opportunity when a war is declared between the Pandavas and the Kauravas.

As per most retellings of the ancient Indian epic, when Shikhandini realises she will not be permitted to participate in the Kurukshetra war because of her gender, she undertakes penance for several days. Pleased by her single-minded dedication, a mythical Yaksha named Sthunakarna agrees to swap his body with hers. Thus Shikhandini becomes Shikhandi. She goes into battle and fights heroically against the Maharathi, defeating him, thus playing a pivotal role in the victory of the Pandavas.

It is believed that the Kurukshetra war was fought 5000 years ago in the land of Bharatha, modern India, for the restoration of *dharma* or righteousness. The epic *Mahabharata,* in which the Kurukshetra war in the climatic denouement, is one of the two great Indian epics and continues to be told and retold centuries later.

There have been innumerable retellings of the Mahabharata, both oral and written, some with changes of perspective and interpretation, focussing on the life of one, often under-rated, character in the story. There have been books written on the life of Karna, the *suthaputhra* turned brilliant warrior, Duryodhana, the anti-hero Kaurava prince, Draupadi, the common wife of the five Pandavas, and so on.

But surprisingly, not a single book has been written on the life of Shikhandini, the lesser known Princess of Panchala, an exceptional warrior, an unparalleled swordswoman, and a key character in the victory of the Pandavas in the Great War. The reason for her part in the story being under-rated is not because of her lack of character or skill, but because of her gender, an obnoxious reason undoubtedly. When Shikhandini realised that being female would obstruct her from fulfilling her purpose in life, she decided to make the ultimate sacrifice of her womanhood – probably the greatest sacrifice made by any character in the epic, for to live neither as a woman nor a man, was unaacceptable in society, then as now.

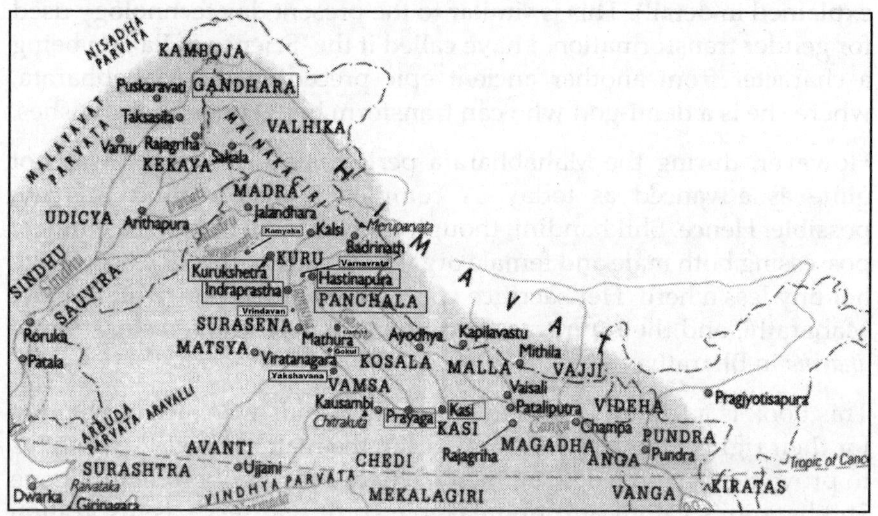

DISTRIBUTION OF KINGDOMS IN THE MAHABHARATA ERA

Now we come to my interpretation of her story: It is irrational to the modern mind to suggest that two humans can actually swap bodies. Nor can one believe with any conviction that the ancients were magical beings with supernatural powers. However, it is now accepted that science was far more advanced during the Mahabharata era than we had earlier imagined, hence the mention of nuclear weapons, flying chariots and the mesmerizingly beautiful concept of *ksitigarbha* or the artificial womb, through which a hundred Kauravas were born. It is thus possible the ancients were not oblivious to the concept of gender transformation either.

But it is unlikely that Shikhandini was changed into a man overnight. She had known of the impending war a decade before its commencement, when the Pandavas, accompanied by her sister, Draupadi, were sent into exile. During this period, Shikhandini lived in Yakshavana, the village of the Yakshas. The Yakshas, in my retelling, are intelligent beings who harnessed science and technology. They were known to have secretly worked on several groundbreaking scientific experiments, revealing them to the outside world only when most needed.

With the aid of the Yaksha leader, Sthunakarna, Shikhandini undergoes a stage by stage transformation, starting with *antahsraava* being injected into her body periodically, and then undergoing several *shashtra chikitsas* needed for her physical transformation (these stages are explained in detail). This is similar to the present day technology used for gender transformation. I have called it the 'Science of Ila', Ila being a character from another ancient epic preceding the Mahabharata, where she is a demi-god who can transform her gender as she wishes.

However, during the Mahabharata period, surgical science was not quite as advanced as today. A complete transformation was not possible. Hence, Shikhandini, though transformed, remains a eunuch, possessing both male and female organs. However, this does not make her any less a hero. Her sacrifice was essential for the downfall of the Maharathi, and the Kauravas, leading ultimately to the restoration of *dharma* in Bharatha.

This book is a tribute to all those beautiful souls who strive each day for their rights, doing everything within the realm of their capabilities to prove their mettle, despite the injustices heaped upon them. I hope Shikhandini's valour and unbreakable spirit will serve as inspiration to many.

PART I

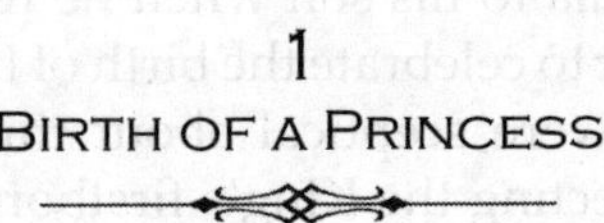

1
Birth of a Princess

Ahikshethra, Kingdom of Panchala

Om Namah Shivaya... The chant seemed to merge into the rippling waters of the sacred Ganga. It was the first prahar of the day. King Drupada stood offering prayers as the magnificent river, born in the mighty Himalayas, flowed on across the plains of northen Bharatvarsha, towards its meeting with the ocean. The river flowed through Panchala, dividing the kingdom in two. To the north stood the capital city of Ahikshethra, where King Drupada's royal abode rose to meet the sky.

O Lord Surya, the Great Sun! The eye of the Virat-Purusha. You who are all-energy, all-strength, all-powerful, bless me with health, strength, vigour and vitality...Drupada, son of King Prishata, was thirty-five years of age. His lower body was covered in a white *antariya* that extended below his knees, like a *dhoti*. A white *angavastram* covered his torso. His shoulder-length, wavy hair was freshly washed and left open to dry in the morning breeze. His routine included fourteen *suryanamaskars* at sunrise, followed by prayers to his personal deity, Lord Shiva. His prayers generally included *mantras* praising Shiva and recitation of the *Shiva-Sahasranama*. In this way he offered up his gratitude to the Lord, for he believed his health, fame and prosperity had been bestowed upon him by the great Lord.

Today, however, he had yet another reason to thank his Lord. He had been blessed with a beautiful baby girl. He and Queen Kokila Devi had been married for ten long years and as year followed barren year their yearning for a child became ever more desperate. Kokila's inability to bear an heir to the throne had led to a strained relationship with her husband for several years. Drupada and Kokila, both devout worshippers of Mahadev, had spent years performing austerities and *yagyas* in his name. And finally their prayers had been answered. They named their beloved daughter after the Great Lord – Shikhandini – a name they had chosen from the Shiva-Sahasranama, which Kokila and Drupada recited every day.

In the royal palace at Ahikshethra, Prishata, having handed over the kingship of Panchala to his son when he reached the age of sixty organised a grand feast to celebrate the birth of his first granddaughter. The common people were sceptical about this unusual celebration, for they had been expecting the King's firstborn to be a boy, and heir presumptive to the throne of Panchala.

In the royal chambers, Drupada and the *Raj Jyothishi*, the royal astrologer, watched as Prishata bent over the newborn and placed a tilak on her small forehead."This child shall live to avenge my humiliation at the hands of Bheeshm. Her name shall go down in history as the one who slayed the invincible warrior from Hastinapur!" Prishata said softly.

Five prahars after the Princess' birth, her destiny had been ordained.

Kokila recalled the incident her husband had once narrated to while they sat on the palace terrace, watching a summer moon rise over Ahikshethra. Many years ago, Maharathi Bheeshm, the great warrior of Hastinapur, had set out on a military expedition to expand the reign of his step-brother Vichitravirya, then King of Hastinapur. In this quest, he had attacked the kingdom of Panchala. Bheeshm's vast, trained army had outnumbered the small Panchala force and quickly overrun the kingdom. The Maharathi had spared King Prishata's life in a gesture of mercy, but ever since, the proud Panchala King had lived a life of self-flagellation and humiliation. As a result of his self abasement, the kingdom of Panchala had suffered greatly, both economically and socially.

When Drupada returned from his *gurukul* after twelve long years of study and military training, he was immediately installed as Crown Prince, and then King. Under Drupada's administration, Panchala recovered its prosperity, but not everything was as it had once been.

A few years later, travelling bards told of a strange prophecy – that Bheeshm would meet his end at the hands of a woman. The prophecy had travelled from Hastinapur to all the neighbouring provinces, including Panchala. Now, Prishata saw in Shikhandini's birth, the promised fulfilment of that prophecy.

"Raj Jyothishi-ji, pray tell us what destiny has in store for Shikhandini," Prishata said, a faint smile of anticipation on his lips.

The Jyothishi replied indifferently, not much interested in a mere female, even one of royal birth. It mattered little what the stars foretold. "The child was born during the second hour of the second prahar, in an hour influenced by Rahu."

Kokila glanced at Drupada, her eyes moist with unshed tears. She was aware of the consequences her little girl would have to face if Panchala decided to avenge itself against the great Bheeshm and Hastinapur's mighty army. Drupada stood in silence beside his father, his head bowed in respect. Prishata signalled for the Jyotishi to continue. His face showed no sign of either anxiety or sympathy for the child. Kokila wondered if the destiny of her beloved daughter would simply be as an *astra*, a weapon of destruction, to be nurtured in secrecy and summoned at the right time to avenge her royal blood.

"She will, without doubt, succeed in fulfilling her goals, but the path to success will not be smooth. She will have to face innumerable hurdles and lead a life full of hardship and adversitiy."

The Jyothishi's words fell on Kokila's ears like the rumblings of war drums. Anxiety filled her heart. Drupada glanced down at his daughter, sleeping peacefully in her mother's lap, oblivious alike to the dictates of duty and destiny.

"Adversity is the best teacher", Prishata said, his face calm and free of emotion. "Fear not, for she is a boon from Lord Mahadev himself. I will personally train and prepare her to destroy that arrogant Maharathi when the time comes."

The Gurukul of Sage Bhardwaj, several yojanas from Panchala

It was the day's final prahar when Drona entered his private quarters at the gurukul, where he lived with his wife Kripi, and their two-year-old son, Ashwathama. He was dressed in a saffron dhoti and brown uttariya, tied across his upper body, accentuating his wide shoulders and broad chest. A single chain of one hundred and eight Rudraksha beads adorned his neck. His beard was shaggy and long, matching in length the unruly locks that spread over his back. His forehead bore three horizontal marks and a red oval in the centre, indicating he was a follower of Lord Mahadev.

It was the same humble abode where the great sage, Maharishi Bhardwaj, scion of Lord Brahma, had once lived with his disciples. The gurukul was one of the finest in Aryavart (the noble land of the Aryas), and tutored princes from the kingdoms of northern Bharatha. It was here that Drupada and Drona had become friends. Under the tutelage of the Maharishi, both Drupada and Drona, the adopted son of the sage, had mastered advanced military arts and the skilful use of powerful astras.

The gurukul extended over several acres of land, in the midst of the dense forest of Prayaga. The area was divided into several sectors, each serving a particular purpose. One quarter was used for domestic purposes, and included a cowshed and stable. Several small huts were built in this area, which served as residences for both the Guru and his pupils. A slightly larger area, containing a huge banyan tree at its centre, was used as the classroom. The Guru sat under the tree on a raised platform while the students sat on the ground below. It was here that most of the important discussions and debates between the Guru and his students took place. The rest of the land was used as a battleground for training in combat and horse riding.

During their twelve-year stay at the gurukul, the students led a simple and disciplined life. They were divided into groups, based on age. Those below the age of ten were taught the basics of mathematics, physics and philosophy, along with the *Vedas* and *Smrithis*. The older students, having completed their basic courses, were trained in advanced military arts and warfare.

Three modes of learning, *Shravana* (Listening), *Manana* (Deliberation of the topic taught), and *Nidhidhyarama* (meditation), were followed under the classic style of the *Guru-shishya parmapara*. The Guru was not only responsible for imparting knowledge both religious and secular, but also in moulding the character and personality of his students. Apart from this, the students, irrespective of their social status, had to learn to cook, clean and look after the cows and horses in the *ashram*.

Following the death of Maharishi Bharadwaj, the gurukul had been shut down. Drona, young and inexperienced, with insufficient resources, had been drowning in self-doubt. He did not feel ready to be the Guru, yet. However, he ensured the maintainence of the gurukul in as pristine a fashion as in Maharishi Bharadwaj's time. Drona and his wife survived on what they found in the forest around the gurukul. Occasionally, travellers and sages, en route on various pilgrimages, would stop to rest. Pleased with Drona and Kripi's hospitality, they would leave behind some small portion of what they had. It would last a few days and then Drona would go into the forest again. Strong believer in *karma* that he was, he believed that if he did his duty truthfully, he would be rewarded sooner or later.

As Drona entered the hutment now, he looked around for Kripi. He found her sitting on the charpoy at the far end of the hut, beside a sleeping Ashwathama. As he walked towards her, he heard her sobbing quietly.

"What is the matter, my dear?" he asked in his low hoarse voice, looking into her eyes.

"We will never be able to give him the life he deserves," she sniffed, placing a gentle hand on their son's head. It had taken her two and half hours to put a hungry, fretting Ashwathama to sleep.

Drona chose to remain silent. His inability to provide a life of happiness and comfort for his family, gnawed at him each day. In the years before the birth of their son, they had enough to feed themselves and tend to the needs of the gurukul. Over the years, their resources had diminished, leaving them in dire poverty.

"How much longer are you going to pretend everything is alright?" asked Kripi, her voice louder than usual. It was the first time she had openly expressed her frustration over their financial situation.

"I know it is my fault," admitted Dronacharya helplessly. This quiet acceptance of vulnerability was unusual in one feared for his quick temper. The evening sky changed colour from shimmering gold to inky blue, as though reflecting Drona's life.

"I cannot understand why you will not open the gurukul again. The princes from the surrounding kingdoms would be happy to have you, the son of the great teacher Maharishi Bhardwaj, as their Guru."

"Kripi, please understand that I will not use my father's name to attract students. I still have much to learn before I can take on the role of Guru."

"I do understand your dilemma, Drona," Kripi sighed. She said more calmly, "But we have little to live on. We need more resources. If not, the day is not far when we will have to give away Ashwathama, since we are unable to feed him."

"Do not say such a thing, Kripi!' Drona's voice was tinged with a spak of his famed temper. "I am sure Lord Parashuram will show us a way out of our difficulties."

"The way is right in front of you, husband, but you are not ready to acknowledge it."

Drona stood still, closing his eyes as he tried to calm his mind.

"Drona, the time has come to approach your friend, King Drupada. I am sure he still remembers what he owes you," Kripi said, reminding him of a long lost memory.

THE FOREST OF HASTINAPUR, 125 YOJANAS FROM PANCHALA

Maharishi Vyasa, one of the greatest scientists of the age, was on the verge of yet another ground-breaking scientific experiment.

"*Pranam* Maharishi!" said Pavaki, greeting her teacher. She was one of Vyasa's most ingenious students. A Brahmin by both birth and *karma*, she wore the *Janivara* or auspicious thread that marked the acceptance of a student by the Guru. Dressed in a long white anthariya with a matching blouse and angavastram, Pavaki, like all Vaishnav followers of Vishnu, had a u-shaped mark on her forehead.

"Pranam, Pavaki. Is it ready already?" asked Guru Vyasa, looking into her still childlike eyes. Vyasa, who was unusually tall and lithe, towered over the short and plump Pavaki, as he stood up. His attire reflected his character. His dhoti and angavastram were a rare shade of saffron that complimented his dark skin. His long unruly mane was tied into a neat bun, while his white beard flowed freely, covering most of his upper torso. Though simple in appearance, brilliance radiated from his eyes.

"Yes Gurudev, we can now proceed to the final step." Pavaki smiled with pride. Having begun as a young student, Pavaki was now one of the best *Vyeds* or doctors in northern Bharatavarsha. Having excelled in fields like *Ayurveda* and *Panchakarma*, her knowledge of medicines and their effects on the human body was second to none. Vyasa, who was well aware that his new invention would be impossible without Pavaki, had sent for her a year ago. Pavaki and her team had immediately left for Hastinapur to join the project. Vyasa began walking towards the back of the cave.

"But you have not answered my questions, Gurudev," frowned Pavaki.

Vyas turned around, chuckling in amusement as he recalled her days at the gurukul. Pavaki, an enthusiastic learner, would shower her Gurudev with questions whenever he started a new topic. Vyasa, not wanting to overwhelm her tender mind with too much information, would delay his answers. Pavaki, however, would not let go without a promise from her Guru to answer all her questions at a later point in time. Vyasa would gladly agree. Over the years, this had set a pattern in their *Guru-Shishya* relationship.

"Why will you not tell me who is it for?" Pavaki asked, exasperated.

"You will know soon enough, my child. Have patience," answered Vyas with a warm smile.

"You always say that!" Pavki rolled her eyes. Like a daughter to him, she was one of the privileged few who could get their way with the otherwise strict and feared Maharishi.

"I promise. You will have your answers by the end of the day."

Pavaki grinned in reply. For the last year, she had yearned to know the reason Vyasa had taken up such a challenging yet sensitive task. She was well aware of the consequences if the experiment failed, but her confidence in her Guru kept her going.

The Last Prahar

"*Namaste,* Veda Vyas Ji" Vidura, Prime Minister of Hastinapur, said as he walked into the cave Vyasa had made his home for the past year. Vidura always addressed him as Veda Vyas, acknowledging the vivid contribution the Maharishi had made to the intellectual development of mankind.

Maharishi Vyasa was popularly known as the man who had categorised the primaeval Veda into four canonical collections – the *Rigveda,* the *Yajurveda,* the *Samaveda,* and the *Atharvaveda*. This splitting of the Vedas had enabled people all over Bharatavarsha to learn, understand and absorb the cryptic knowledge embedded in these scriptures. Possessing a deep and thorough knowledge of the Vedas, the Maharishi was always keen on converting some of the mesmerising theoretical concepts they contained, into reality.

"Namaste, Vidura. How have you been, my child?" Vidura was also Vyasa's godson.

"I am well, Maharishi" Vidura replied. "Can we take a look at it now?" he asked, unable to contain his excitement. "Their Majesties will be here any minute."

"Yes, it should happen any time now," smiled Vyasa.

"Have you decided on a name yet, Gurudev?" asked Vidura, gazing at the incredible sight before him.

Just as the final prahar of the day had been struck on the massive brass gong in the palace, a messenger had arrived in Hastinapur, carrying Vyasa's summons to the royal family. Vidura, as always, was the first to arrive. It was part of royal protocol for the Prime Minister and a small group of bodyguards to reach a particular place before the King's arrival.

"*Kshitigarbh,*" answered Vyasa now, without hesitation.

"What does it mean, Maharishi?"

"Kshitigarbh, my son, is what we can call an earthly imitation of a mother's womb. *Kshiti* means 'earth' and *garbha* means 'womb'. In essence, are we not all born of Mother Earth's womb?"

Kshitigarbh was Vyasa's latest contribution to the perplexing field of genetic engineering. To the layman, it was nothing short of a miracle. Kshitigarbh was a secluded spot inside a cave in the depths of the forest that surrounded Hastinapur. Vyasa's unparalleled knowledge of the Vedas and Smritis, and his passion for *Vignyana,* had facilitated the creation of this remarkable 'womb', which was about to bring forth the birth of a hundred Kauravas. No one that day knew that Vyasa's marvel would also deliver the nemesis of the Kuru clan.

"It is the perfect name, Maharishi," said Queen Gandhari graciously as she climbed the few steps into the cave, her hand on King Dhritarashtra's arm. Gandhari, regarded throughout the kingdom and beyond as the epitome of virtue and ultimate *pativrata,* had a cloth tied over her eyes. Following her marriage to the blind King of Hastinapur, she had resolved to lead the rest of her life as a sightless woman in order to share the debility and pain of her husband.

"Pranam Maharishi," Dhritarashtra said in his rich deep voice. "I cannot believe the day has finally arrived!"

Even at a distance of 20 feet, the King appeared to look right into Vyasa' eyes as he spoke. Vyasa felt pride swell his heart. His second godson, Bheeshm, had done a splendid job, he thought. Bheeshm, the King's step-uncle, was also his Guru. He had personally trained the King and his two brothers, Pandeshwar and Vidura, for over 12 years. It was Bheeshm's training and faith that had helped Dhritarashtra overcome his disability and rise to the throne of Hastinapur.

"Yes, indeed, my son." Vyasa said more gently than was his wont. He could sense the pain in the King's voice.

A year ago, Satyavati, the *Rajmata* of Hastinapur, along with her grandson Dhritarashtra, and his consort Gandhari, had approached Maharishi Vyasa with a problem; Gandhari's inability to carry a child to full term had rendered the throne of Hastinapur heirless. Gandhari, a devotee of Lord Shiva, believed that, pleased with her selfless devotion, Mahadev had himself, in a dream, blessed her with the ability to bear a hundred sons. Dhritarashtra, a rational thinker, knew it to be humanly impossible for a single woman to deliver a hundred children in a lifetime, no matter what divine visions had been granted his wife. Satyavati, the Rajmata, aware of her son Vyasa's scientific abilities, decided to visit him with the royal couple.

Before Vyasa became Maharishi, he was known as Krishna Dwaipayana or 'island-born'. Parashara, a travelling sage and renowned astrologer had married a *Matsyakanya* or fisherwoman, who lived with the fisher clan on an island in the Ganga, a few *yojanas* from the capital city of Hastinapur. Soon after their marriage, Dwaipayana was born. Owing to his dark skin, he was given the name Krishna Dwaipayana.

At a very young age, Dwaipayana realised the purpose of his life. He decided to go to the forest and perform *Akhanda Tapas*. He studied the ancient scriptures and tried to use his knowledge for the benefit of mankind. Satyavati had finally let him go, having extracted a promise that he would come whenever she sent for him. Parashara, who had already foreseen this, blessed the boy before continuing his journey across the length and breadth of Aryavrath, the land of the legendary Aryans.

Some years later, when all hope of Parashara's return had been extinguished in the desert of silence, the Matsyakanya, now known as Satyavati, married the then King of Hastinapur, Shantanu, thus becoming Rajmata.

"Pranam Maharishi," said Bheeshm as he walked into the cave, followed by his step-mother, Satyavati.

"Pranam Bheeshm," Vyasa replied with a smile.

Other than being Guru and step-uncle to the King and his brothers, Bheeshm was also the *Senapathi* of Hastinapur. He had remained loyal to the throne of Hastinapur, irrespective of who was King. It was his abilities, dedication and loyalty that had kept Hastinapur steady and prosperous over the eventful decades.

"Pranam *Mata,*" Vyasa greeted Satyavati, the seventy-eight-year-old Rajmata, his palms joined together, his head bowed.

"*Ayushman Bhava,*" Satyavati said, speaking the traditional blessing for a long life over her unusal son's head.

"Wonderful!" exclaimed Bheeshm as he absorbed his surroundings. "Maharishi, only you could have thought of doing something so unbelievable."

"No, the credit goes to the entire team. This would have been impossible had it not been for Pavaki and the others," Vyasa replied humbly.

In the Kshitigarbh, Vyasa and his students had created several sack-like structures that hung from the roof, each containing a foetus. Each foetus was a clone of the one Gandhari had been carrying at the time she visited Maharishi Vyas. The garbhas had been designed to provide oxygen and nutrients to the growing embryos.

Pavaki and her team had studied the structure of the garbha in and out. After several trials, they had developed the right dosage of medicines to be administered into the garbhas. Her highly trained team had taken immense precautions to avoid infection or miscarriages during the development of the foetuses. A set of thin organic pipes ran across the roof, connecting the garbhas and functioning as umbilical cords. Another set of pipes connected from the base of the structures to the ground, and were used for waste disposal. The temperature inside the cave was regulated to provide the necessary warmth essential for fetal growth. Unlike a mother's womb, these garbhas were meant for one-time use only. As the child in the womb matured, the garbha shell turned fragile and the baby eventually broke out of it.

Before Vyasa could explain this to Bheeshm, he heard the first sound. The outer shell of the first garbha, that one that held the original, un-cloned fetus, had cracked. Everyone in its vicinity stood spellbound, marvelling at the sight of the birth of the first Kaurava, descendant of Kuru. Gandhari's eyes welled with tears of joy as she tried to visualise the birth of her son. For the first time she regretted her decision to lead a blind woman's life. Dhritarashtra, known for his stoic calm, trembled with excitement; his hand gripped Gandhari's.

Vyasa, equally mesmerised by the sight, quickly sent for Pavaki and her team. They appeared within minutes. Pavaki had expected her

Guru to send for her as the birth of the foetuses became imminent, but she was taken aback by the unexpected presence of the entire royal family of Hastinapur in the Kshitigarbh. The truth dawned on her as she looked at Gandhari. The popular belief of her delivering a hundred sons, potential heirs to the throne, was no longer just a prophecy. Guru Vyasa had achieved the impossible, and she had unknowingly contributed to this great deed. Realisation struck hard as she recalled one of Vyasa's disciples in the gurukul saying, "Gurudev does not work miracles, his knowledge does."

Pavaki collected her scattered wits and began the procedure. "Gurudev, I believe it is time to disconnect the chords. The baby is almost out," Pavaki said, examining the garbha.

"Yes, go ahead."

"Uddhiran, quickly get me some clean towels. Vrinda, bring some warm water and the antiseptics," Pavaki briskly ordered her well-trained team. Vyasa, Pavaki, Uddhiran and the others completed the final procedure over the next hour and a half. Gandhari, Dhritarashtra and the other members of the royal family waited patiently, chanted prayers to Lord Shiva.

At the end of the final prahar a baby's wail was finally heard. It was the sound the Hastinapur royals had craved for decades. Pavaki cautiously carried the baby and placed it in Gandhari's lap. It seemed to have a soothing effect on both mother and child. Gandhari slowly moved her fingers over the child's body, whispering prayers of gratitude. She then lifted Dhritarashtra's hand and placed it on the baby. Dhritarashtra's eyes welled with tears as the baby's tiny hand wrapped around his little finger. Bheeshm, Vyasa, Vidhura and the others looked on in awe.

"The birth of my son is nothing less than a miracle." Dhritarashtra spoke for the first time since the birth. "He has fought death like a true warrior and emerged victorious. He shall forever be unconquerable! All of Aryavrath shall know him as Duryodhan."

2
The Pandavas

Having endured a two-week journey on horseback along the banks of the Ganga, Drona finally arrived at the royal palace in Ahikshethra. Though exhausted from his travels, he went directly to the palace. He had promised Kripi he would soon return.

"A visitor has arrived, Your Highness, and seeks audience," said the court announcer.

King Drupada sat in the main audience hall with his officials and nobles. It was one of their monthly meetings, held to update the King on social, economic and financial affairs of state in various parts of the kingdom. Following these sessions, Drupada sat and ate with his courtiers in recognition of their service.

"Who it is?" asked Drupada.

"A Brahmin sage from beyond the kingdom. He introduces himself as your friend, Your Majesty."

Drupada immediately realised who the Brahmin was, but wondered why he had come to Panchala after all these years. "Send him in," he ordered, taking a drag at his favourite chillum.

Drona came in with hurried steps, the smile on his weathered face showing his pleasure in seeing his old friend. "Drupada, it is I, your childhood friend, Drona!" he exclaimed. Fifteen years had passed since they had left the gurukul but Drona was sure their friendship would not have quivered one bit, even after all these years.

Before Drupada could acknowledge Drona's presence, a Minister growled, "How dare you address the King by his name, you fool!"

"He is my friend first, then your King," responded Drona, his quick anger rising.

"You, a beggar from the street, a friend of the great Yagyasena?" scoffed another courtier, quick to follow the Minister's lead.

Drona looked at Drupada, silently asking him to intervene. But the King remained silent, merely taking another pull at his chillum.

"Drupada, will you not speak? Will you not tell them of our friendship? Have you forgotten everything?" asked Drona, turning towards the King, who sat on a raised platform, above the others. A short flight of ten steps led to the throne. At the foot of the steps on either side, were two magnificent lions carved out of white stone. Intricately carved pillars graced the entire audience chamber.

"I have forgotten nothing, Drona," replied Drupada nonchalantly and Drona smiled at his words. "Allow me to introduce you to the court in the correct manner," added Drupada. "Drona here is the son of my Guru, the great sage Maharishi Bhardwaj, and an acquaintance from my gurukul days."

"Acquaintance! Is that all I was to you?" asked Drona, surprised.

"What else can there be between a Panchal Prince and the Guru's son, Drona?"

There was a moment of silence as Drona stared at Drupada, his eyes burning with hurt and humiliation. Then he said in a voice that reached every corner of the vast chamber, "You choose to forget your own promises, Drupada, the promises you made before leaving the gurukul? The promise of a friendship that would last a lifetime; the promise of sharing everything we achieved in life. Do you forget I saved your life from the leopard in the forest?"

"I made no such promises," retorted Drupada, his eyes falling away before the burning gaze of the Brahmin. "As for saving my life, my guards protect me every day; that does not make them my friends."

"We spent twelve years together as students, Drupada. Twelve years! It was I who helped you clear the exams when you were unable to do so by yourself. It was I who taught you to use the sword when you were not quick enough to learn from Guruji. It was I who saved your bloody life! You owe me everything!" spat Drona, his anger getting the best of him.

"I owe you nothing, Brahmin! Your teaching would have done nothing if I did not have the skill to learn. I used that knowledge and my talent to build this vast empire," replied Drupada, his voice laced with arrogance and pride. "Leave my court at once or I will have you punished for insulting the King of Panchala."

"Insult! Is that what our friendship is to you? I did not come to ask you for an equal share in your kingdom, Drupada. All I wanted from you was a position in your court so that I and my family could live with dignity."

"Shower him with a hundred gold coins," ordered Drupada. "We do not let any sage leave our kingdom without offering alms."

"I have not come here for alms, Drupada!" scowled Drona, his voice a mix of sadness and anger. "I came here looking for my friend; a friend who promised to stand with me in happiness and in sorrow."

Drupada smirked. "Drona, have you seen how moss grows along with the lotus in the river? Just because they are nourished by the same water and soil, would you say they are of the same worth? You are smart enough to know the worth of each, Drona."

The court roared with laughter at the King's analogy. Drona, who even in the direst poverty had always lived a life of dignity and self-respect, felt shattered. It was beyond imagination that the one he considered his derest friend would spurn him in this manner. As he stood in the Panchal audience hall, surrounded by ribald laughter, Drona finally understood the truth behind this mortal life – friendship, trust and modesty were mere philosophical concepts. The only thing people respected was money and power.

"It is the power and status of the throne that makes you speak thus, Drupada. The day will come when I will be standing where you are today and you will be kneeling before me, your head bowed in shame." Drona pointed to the ground below his bare feet.

"Today, you have not just denied our friendship, but insulted my knowledge and abilities. I promise you that when the day comes, I will not use any weapon. It will be my ability to impart knowledge that will bring you low. It will be my ultimate step in the journey to becoming a Guru," Drona vowed.

Tittering laughter faded away into uneasy silence and fear at the Brahmin's words. The more superstitious among those gathered said a hasty prayer to protect themselves from the evil eye.

"And I do not forget *my* promises!" declared Drona, his unwavering gaze on Drupada. Turning away, he left the great hall as quickly as he had come.

In the valley of Shatashrunga Parvata near Uttarakuru, Pandeshwar, former King of Hastinapur, and his wives Kunti and Madri, awaited the birth of Kunti's second child.

It was the fourth prahar. Sarmishta, the midwife, raced along the dirt track that led to the humble abode in the forest. Kunti was lying on a *charpoy*, writhing in pain and chanting the name of Lord Vayu, Lord of the Winds whose blessings she sought for her unborn child. She had been in labour for over six hours. Madri sat beside her helplessly, waiting for Sarmishta.

Pandeshwar sat outside the hut with their three-year-old son, Yudhishthira, in his lap. He wore a pale yellow dhoti and an orange angavasthram that glowed against his albino skin. His neck, once adorned with the finest jewellery of Hastinapur, now had a single strand of holy Rudraksha beads. His unusually silky hair was tied into a modest bun, held with a hair-tie made of the same beads. His once lithe and muscular body had become flaccid.

It had been over three years since that fateful day when Pandeshwar had decided to renounce the throne of Hastinapur. An exceptional archer, he often wandered into the deep forest to hunt. That day, for the first time, his sharp hunter's instinct had deceived him. The arrow meant for a passing deer, had accidentally pierced the heart of a wandering sage – Rishi Kindama. Pandeshwar, a believer in *Kshatriya Dharma,* was unable to bear the sight of the dying sage. For a Kshatriya, killing a Brahmin sage was considered the ultimate sin that left one marked for life.

Pandeshwar, knowing that no one in Hastinapur would dare punish the King for this deed, decided to impose punishment on himself. He believed everyone was equal before the law. Kshatriya Dharma spared none, whether a lowly foot soldier or the King himself. He no longer felt worthy to sit on the sacred throne of Hastinapur. He renounced the royal title, the throne and all the luxuries of the palace, to go and live in the forest, with his two wives. His elder brother, Dhritarashtra, who had earlier been considered ineligible to be King because of his blindness, now took his place as King of Hastinapur.

"Pranam, My Lord!" Sarmishta said, greeting Pandeshwar quickly before rushing into the hut. Sarmishta, who greatly admired Pandeshwar's skills and contribution to Hastinapur, always addressed him as King. Pandeshwar had restored the supremacy of the Kuru clan over many well known kingdoms of the Sindhu, such as Kashi, Kalinga and Magadha, expanding Hastinapur's sway. He was not only respected but loved by the common people.

"Pranam Sarmishta," he replied to the midwife's retreating form. Pandeshwar silently whispered a prayer to his favourite God, Vishnu, hoping that with Sarmishta's arrival, the birth would proceed smoothly.

As though sensing his father's anxiety, Yudhishthira moved his small hands over Pandeshwar's cheek, grazing at him lovingly, just as his his mother did to soothe him. Pandeshwar smiled in response and kissed his son's broad forehead.

It was the last hour of the day when Vayuputra Bheem was finally born after a long and arduous labour.

"He is unusually large for a newborn child," Sarmishta said, carrying the large child to Madri.

"That explains Kunti's massive appetite over the last few months, then!" Madri laughed. "We kept wondering where all the food went." She playfully nudged the baby's stomach. Little Bheem gurgled acknowledgement.

"Give her these once she wakes up. She will be asleep for another hour or so. It was a long day for her," Sarmishta said, handing over some potions.

"Sarmishta, if not for you, things would have been difficult indeed. It would have been impossible to take her to town in her condition."

"Madri Ma, I merely did my duty" Sarmishta said, smiling.

THREE HOURS LATER...

Pandeshwar and Madri sat beside Kunti's charpoy. She had finally woken and Madri had given her the potions left by the midwife. She had lovingly placed Bheem beside Kunti.

Yudhishthira, sitting in his father's lap, smiled at the sight of a smaller being in the house. He was finally the big brother. "Bheem," he whispered, pointing at the sleeping infant.

Pandeshwar nodded. "Yes, my child, he is Bheem, your brother."

"Can I play with him?" Yudhishtira asked, straining his neck to get a better look at the strange creature.

"He is too young to play now. You will have to wait for a few months, Yudhi," Madri replied, smiling.

Yudhishtira pouted, crinkling his forehead. Madri and Pandeshwar laughed.

Kunti had a faraway look in her eyes. She had not yet embraced the child. Something seemed to be making her anxious. Madri merely thought she was exhausted from the long and painful labour. Madri, who had been present at Yudhishthira's birth as well, knew from Sarmishta that new mothers often felt depressed. It was normal after childbirth and nothing to worry about.

Pandeshwar, however, knew better. Signalling for Madri to take Yudhishthira out, he moved closer to Kunti. "Let it go, Kunti. You can't hold onto the past forever."

Kunti's eyes were fixed on the setting sun outside the window. Her eyes glinted with unshed tears, as she silently asked the Sun God for forgiveness.

When he did not get a response, Pandeshwar placed a hand on Kunti's shoulder and shook her gently. As though on cue, Bheem's hungry bawl filled every corner of the small hut. This seemed to break Kunti's trance.

"Let it go," whispered Pandeshwar again, looking from Kunti to Bheem. "Don't be so hard on yourself. You did not have a choice."

Kunti looked up at Pandeshwar, tears streaming down her plump cheeks. Holding the child in her arms, she sobbed as if her heart would break. Her mind swirled with emotion. The birth of her newborn son reminded her of the unfortunate day, many years ago, when she had consciously committed a great sin; a sin that would leave her scarred for the next seven births.

3
Kingdom of Hastinapur

Hastinapur, Six Years Later

The supreme and omnipotent throne of Hastinapur that had once been heirless, now had a hundred and five heirs – the hundred sons of blind King Dhitarastra, and Pandeshwar's five sons. Among the wealth of sons, Hastinapur also had a young Princess – Dushala, who, like Dhritarashtra and Gandhari's hundred sons, had been born in the Kshitigarbh.

A year after Bheem's birth, Kunti delivered another handsome son – Arjun, whom she believed had been born with the blessings of Lord Indra, King of the Devas, who had ruled millennia ago. It had been a time when the lives of the benevolent Devas and the malevolent Asuras still intersected. The Great War between the two resulted in terrible bloodshed. The Asuras were wiped off the face of the earth, restoring peace and harmony. Indra, fighting with the Devas, thus put an end to the Asura way of life, earning him the title *Devendra*.

A year after Arjun's birth, Madri gave birth to twin sons – Nakul and Sahadev. Kunti's strong beliefs had influenced Madri too, and the twins were considered blessings of the twin-gods, Ashwini-Kumar.

A few years after the Great War between the Devas and Asuras, a dread plague had hit most of northern Aryavrath, leading to the untimely death of thousands of people, even royalty. The twins Ashwini-Kumar, well known doctors of the time, developed a new potion that could not only cure those affected by the plague but work as an antidote to other diseases as well.

Over the years, this potion was learnt to have the power to keep one young and healthy, increasing the average lifespan of people. Some even believed that, if taken regularly, the potion gave one immortality, but there was no proof to validate this belief. The potion soon had a name – *Amrut*, the Sanskrit word for immortality. It earned the Ashwini-Kumars the title of Gods of Medicine. And now Madri, who had always believed in the importance of good health over prosperity, prayed for her children would be blessed by them.

***

The first rays of sunlight had just crept silently into the Hastinapur palace when Rajmata Satyavati's cries of "Bheeshm! Bheeshm!" echoed through its corridors. Her wizened hands quivered as she held the palm-leaf note that had just been delivered by a carrier pigeon. Her eyes welled with tears and her heart hammered like a drum against her ribcage. Grasping the bedpost for support, she slowly slumped onto the bed. *This is not fair! This is just not fair!* she thought in anguish.

On hearing the Rajmata's agonised cries, Bheeshm hurried through the palace corridors, his sword drawn, fearing an attack. Within minutes the palace came to stand still as everyone from bodyguards to maids stopped their work, sensing a great calamity.

"Bheeshm…" Satyavati called, her voice a whisper now. Tears flowed down her cheeks as though an internal dam had burst.

Bheeshm had never seen the stern and prideful Rajmata in such a state, not even when King Shantanu had departed to his eternal rest.

"Mata…what has occurred to disturb you like this?" Bheeshm enquired, his eyes quickly scanning the chamber for danger.

Not trusting herself to speak in that moment, Satyavati held out the palm-leaf note to him.

Bheeshm sucked in his breath and blinked back sudden tears as he read the note. He knew he had to be strong. It was not a time to give way to emotion.

"I will make the arrangements for the journey, Mata. It should not take us more than two prahars to reach Shatashrunga."

Satyavati gazed at him, her heart filled with grief. *Is this man not capable of any human emotion?* she wondered in awe.

UTTARAKURU, TWO PRAHARS LATER…

The second prahar had just begun when Bheeshm, Rajmata Satyavati and Prime Minister Vidura reached Shatashrunga Parvata, the mountain that had earned fame as the abode of the Supreme Power, Lord Brahma. They had not informed the King, or anyone else, of the sudden journey.

While Bheeshm and Vidura rode on horseback, Satyavati travelled in a horse-drawn carriage with ten bodyguards in tow. She had composed herself and was once again her regal self. She knew Hastinapur's destiny was going to change course after this day. She had to find a way to save the future of the Kuru dynasty.

"We have arrived, Rajmata," said Vidura, signalling the *sarathi* to stop the carriage.

As Satyavati stepped down, she felt her senses calm down in the serenity of the surrounding. A cool breeze wafted across her face, leaving behind a mild flowery fragrance. The sight of the vast expanse of sky merging into the endless sea on the horizon was breathtaking. From here she could see the sacred lake of Koti Thirtha, where Lord Ram had performed a great *puja* to wash off the sin of *Brahma Hatya,* the sin of killing a Brahmin – Ravana, King of Lanka.

Satyavati whispered a silent prayer before walking away with Bheeshm and Vidura towards Pandeshwar's hut. The bodyguards remained at a distance, but close enough to afford protection.

"Kunti?" Satyavati called.

Kunti sat in one corner with her five sons around her. "Mata…" she whispered, looking up. For the first time in four prahars, Kunti felt a sense of relief. Her family was here. She no longer had to be the strong one. She rose and ran towards Satyavati, whom she had learnt to love like a mother. As Satyavati embraced her, Kunti began to sob in great gulps, as if the very breath was being sucked from her body.

After a quick glance at the boys, and then at Vidura, Bheeshm walked out to make arrangements for Pandeshwar's last rites. Vidura walked towards the boys, hoping to comfort them, but was amazed to see how the eldest, Yudhishthira, had quietly assumed Kunti's place and was now holding his brothers together.

"Are you afraid, my son?" asked Vidura gently as he walked Yudhishthira towards the door, away from the others. He wished to prepare Pandeshwar's eldest son to perform the last rites. As the eldest, he now had to take upon himself the responsibility for not only his mother, but his four younger brothers. Pandeshwar had been a loving husband and a caring father, but also a righteous guide to his sons. Vidura had not expected a nine-year-old boy to understand how the family's lives were going to change forever. Little did he know that life had taught them things the hard way.

"I am, *Chacha Ji,*" Yudhishthira replied, "but if I let my fear show, my brothers will become weak. I must be strong for them. It is my responsibility now to take care of Ma and my brothers."

Vidura smiled to see the determined look in the youngster's eyes. His nine-year-old nephew was far older and wiser than his years.

***

As Yudhishthira lit the funeral pyre of his father and Mata Madri, who had chosen to follow her husband into the next life, Satyavati, Bheeshm, Vidura and the boys stood silently watching the leaping flames consume their bodies.

Kunti, who had slowly begun to return to harsh reality, looked around and realized that apart from Rajmata Satyavati, Prime Minister Vidhura and Maharathi Bheeshm, no one from the royal family had come to witness Pandeshwar's cremation. Pandeshwar's mother, the Late King Vichitravirya's wife, Ambalika, with her sister, had left for the forest a couple of years after Vichitravirya's death, so her absence at her son's final rites was not unexpected. But Pandeshwar's beloved brother, King Dhritarashtra's absence was unsettling.

"*Bhabhi,* brother Dhritarashtra is not here," Vidura said gently, as if reading her mind.

"Why could he not come?"

"We decided this would be best. Things have changed in Hastinapur since Pandeshwar renounced the throne," Bheeshm interjected, a tinge of bitterness in his words. Kunti, not in any state to read into Bheeshm's words, simply nodded.

"How did this happen, Kunti?" Satyavati asked quietly.

Pandeshwar's untimely death was a big blow not only to the royal family but all Hastinapur. The people of Hastinapur worshipped Pandeshwar and believed he would return to the throne after he had lived a period in exile. Under Dhritarashtra's governace, the once magnificent kingdom was slowly turning hollow as the demons of corruption and greed began spreading their tentacles. Although, to an outsider the city appeared as magnificent as before and its social systems near perfect, the citizens themselves knew it was not so.

"Rajmata, Pandeshwar's death was not untimely," Kunti replied. Her sons were seated in the courtyard outside. The last thing she wanted was for her innocent children to know the cause of their father's death. Fate had demanded they grow up quickly, but Kunti longed to hold back the hands of time for just a little longer and not snatch away their innocence.

"What do you mean?" asked Bheeshm.

"Pandeshwar died six years ago, Chacha Ji, on that fateful day when he became the cause of Rishi Kindama's death. His soul died long ago; it was only his body that we burned today," she replied as fresh tears rolled down her cheeks. "In spite of the punishment he took upon himself all these years, he was never able to put that deed behind him."

Kunti tried to numb her emotions. Life had always been unfair to her. First, the incident at Mathura that had left a permanent hollow in her heart, then the life in the forest, and now Pandeshwar's death.

"On one hand, the guilt of the incident gnawed at him from within, while on the other, seeing his family struggle to meet the basic needs of life in the forest made him feel unworthy. Although we never complained, he blamed himself. He died each day, bit by bit."

Bheeshm took a deep breath, closing his eyes. No one could understand Pandeshwar's agony better than Bheeshm. Being the cause of an innocent man's death, whether intentional or not, was the greatest sin of Kshatriya Dharma.

"And Madri?" questioned Vidura hesitatingly. He wanted to make sure it was a natural death and that she had not fallen prey to the dirty politics that had begun to ravage the capital city.

"Madri could not bear the trauma of Pandeshwar's death. She followed him, leaving our sons behind." Kunti seemed to look into some distant scene that was visible to her alone. She had lost two of the most important people in her life. The only reason keeping her alive was the thought of the five innocent lives solely dependent on her now.

4
The Cursed Garland

THREE MONTHS LATER

Following Pandeshwar's death, Satyavati asked Kunti to return to Hastinapur with her five sons. Bheeshm and Vidura too, considered it wise. It was only right that Pandeshwar's sons be given a royal upbringing and the chance to aspire to the Kuru throne, along with Dhritarashtra's sons. Kunti, having no further reason to remain in the forest, agreed, hoping for a new beginning and a better life for her sons.

Once the Pandavas returned to the city, Satyavati informed the family of her decision to leave for *vanaprastha*. She knew the kingdom was safe in the able hands of Maharati Bheeshm. The end of her life approached and she longed to leave the demands and clamour of the palace behind and seek the solitude of the forest.

As high and low watched in respectful silence, Matsyakanya Rajmata Satyavati left Hastinapur forever.

***

"Pranam, Jija-sa"said Kripacharya, Royal Priest of Hastinapur. He had come to the main gates of the city to welcome his brother-in-law, Guru Dronacharya. Drona had been invited by the Maharathi to a private audience later that day.

"Pranam, Kripa," replied Drona as he walked through the city gates, taking back his ticket from the guard. He has received it along with the invitation, with instructions to show it at the main gate. "Interesting," Drona said, inspecting the palm leaf ticket in his hand.

"I know. It is one of the many security protocols installed by the Late King Pandeshwar. Any non-resident entering Hastinapur must have a gate pass to be allowed into the city. It is used for authentication purposes. Without one being issued, non-residents are not allowed to step into the city, making it impossible for spies of enemy kingdoms to enter the capital," explained Kripacharya.

Drona narrowed his eyes, bringing the ticket closer. The palm leaf had the Hastinapur's royal symbol, the popular Suryavanshi motif with the sun's rays shooting in all directions in a wavy pattern. In the centre was the name 'Hastinapur', in Sanskrit.

"But the ticket looks replicable," said Drona sceptically, inspecting it on both sides.

Kripacharya smiled as he moved Drona's hand that held the pass towards the sky, in the direction of the sunlight. What Drona saw rendered him speechless for some time.

"In the name of Lord Parashuram!" exclaimed Drona when he had recovered from his astonishment. He finally understood the Late King Pandeshwar's ingenuity. To a layman, the pass was nothing but a palm leaf with the commonly used Hastinapur symbol inked onto it. But if one raised it to the light, one could see a tiny symbol embedded into the leaf. It was the same Suryavanshi emblem of the sun, but carried more details. The core of the symbol, which was usually a circle coloured in red, had been replaced with the face of a fierce-looking man representing the warrior form of the Sun God. The original pattern of eight rays, representing the eight prahars, had two shorter rays between the two longer rays, the three spaces representing the number of hours in each prahar. The first civilisation to adopt and use a system that could measure time had been the ancestors of the Suryavanshis, followers of the Sun God.

Drona, who had grown up reading the history of the Suryavanshi and Chandravanshi dynasties, knew that the secret symbol embedded into the leaf was the original Suryavanshi emblem. The one inked on the pass was, in fact, a modified version, brought into use a few centuries ago to make it simpler for official usages.

The hidden logo was carved into the ticket with such delicacy that to an ignorant eye, it was almost non-existent. However, the guards at the gate were trained to identify and authenticate the passes, based on this symbol.

"So, if someone tries to replicate the pass, not only is he denied entry, but is also charged with fraud," remarked Drona admiringly.

"Yes, that was the brilliance of our King."

But Drona was a scholar, details matterd to him. Now he had another question. "Once the information about the hidden symbol is revealed, is it not possible to replicate the symbol then?"

Kripacharya smiled. He had expected nothing less from his brilliant brother-in-law. "Yes, that was a problem when the system was first implemented. So, to enhance security, King Pandeshwar proposed the position of the imbedded symbol be unique to each pass and a copy of each pass remain in the records of the city guards. That way, they had a reference to compare with when anyone arrived at the gate." He pointed to the symbol on Drona's pass; it was placed at the right hand top corner.

Looking closely, Drona realised the palm leaf also had a grid marked onto it, to position the symbol exactly as required. Drona smiled, finally convinced. "Hastinapur is indeed the finest city in Aryavrath," he said, recalling what he had heard from his wife Kripi.

***

The afternoon sun shone over Panchala. The kingdom now had a population of over seven hundred thousand people. Under the shrewd and ambitious King Drupada, Panchala's position and prestige had grown dramatically. It was now one of the most renowned kingdoms in northern Bharata, second only to Hastinapur and Kosala.

While the royal palace was governed by the unquestioned rules set by the King, there was one little girl who believed that the sole purpose of having such rules was to break them.

"Look, what I found, Ma!" she now exclaimed as she hopped into her mother's private chamber.

"I am busy now, *bachhi*. Go and play with your friends in the garden," replied Kokila, continuing with her daily prayers.

"Please Ma, just look. It is so pretty!" pleaded the little girl.

"What is it?" Kokila turned to see what her little one had found so amazing. Her eyes widened in horror as she took in her child's new found interest. Before her stood Shikhandini, her beloved daughter, her doe-eyes twinkling with mischief, her contagious smile almost reaching her ears, her plump cheeks red with glee. But Kokila's eyes were fixed not on the child's face but on something that was to change the fate of Panchala forever.

"What have you done, Shikhandini?" Kokila slapped the little girl. Her

voice was hoarse from the lump that had formed in her throat. A long forgotten fear began to rise in her heart again as she recalled the Raj Jyothishi's words about her little girl's destiny. "What have you done, Shikhandini?" Kokila asked, softly this time, her eyes pooled with tears that formed a shimmering veil to hide her agony and fear.

"Ma..." sobbed Shikhandini, cradling the cheek clearly imprinted with her mother's palm print. Tears streamed down her little face, her eyes wide with shock at her mother's harshness. It was the first time anyone in her family had ever punished her. Being a naughty one, she often teased people in the palace, but they always accepted her pranks with an indulgent smile.

She looked at her mother through her tears, not sure why she was being punished. "Ma, I..." she tried again, her voice cracking. Her little hands became numb with fear. Why was Ma crying? What had she done?

"How many times have I told you not to wander in the palace backyards? Now look what you have done!" Tears streamed down Kokila's face as she realised her darkest fears had come true.

The palace backyard was a restricted area for both the royals as well as the palace workers. Only a few trusted guards were permitted to go there and carried the responsibility of catching any trespassers or ignorants not aware of the rule. Almost three decades ago, the palace back gates, which were then the main gates, had been sealed shut and declared a forbidden area by the King. A new entrance was created in the north-westerly direction. In this way, King Drupada sought to ensure that 'the curse of the abandoned warrior Princess' never touched anyone in his kingdom.

"Shikhandini, go to your chamber and do not come out till I say so. Have you understood?" Kokila said sternly before turning away, back to her interrupted prayers, her mind a prey to the wild buffeting of a thousand fears.

Confused and hurt, Shikhandini ran out of her mother's chamber, not towards her own, but to find her grandfather. Little did she know then that she would pay for such innocent mischief all her life.

***

"These are her favourite flowers, and they are so pretty! So why is Ma so upset?" sobbed Shikhandini, looking down at the garland of blue lotuses she had so merrily flaunted to her mother.

"I know, my child, I know. But it is no ordinary garland. Everyone in Panchala fears it, even your parents. Your mother is worried for your safety, which is why she is angry," explained Prishata as he gently wiped the tears from Shikhandini's plump cheeks.

"Why is everyone scared of it, *Pitamaha*? How can something so beautiful be bad?"

For a moment Prishata contemplated telling her the truth, then thought better of it. She was just a child. It would be too much for her tender mind to absorb. He would have to wait for the right time. For now, he would concentrate on gaining her complete trust.

"You will know soon enough, my child. I promise," Prishata told his favourite child as he cradled her in his lap. When he had seen Shikhandini with the garland of blue lotuses around her neck, his joy had known no bounds. The moment had finally arrived. Lord Shiva had chosen his grand-daughter for the task everyone believed to be impossible! She would be the one to take revenge on the arrogant Bheeshm and bring him down forever.

He wondered how Shikhandini, a naïve six-year-old, had managed to slip past the guards and tight security to reach the cursed garland that had been waiting for her at the long sealed palace gates for three decades; the garland last touched by the abandoned warrior Princess from the kingdom of Kashi. All doubts about the prophecy of Amba's rebirth as Shikhandini, to seek vengeance on the Maharathi of Hastinapur, had been removed by Shikhandini's innocent act. Prishata sighed. With Bheeshm's death, he would finally get retribution and be freed of the curse of bitter hatred. It was the only reason he had lived through all these years of humiliation.

***

As Drona stepped into the city, he was engulfed by its charisma. The city, popularly called 'a paradise on earth', was not only blessed with scenic beauty, but also an abundance of natural resources. With the river Ganga skirting the city, the fertile soil bore enough crops to feed the population twice over. The place had attracted a large number of immigrants in the last century and had expanded into the surrounding regions to accommodate the vast population. Despite the vast population, Drona noticed the place was run in a systematic manner. The city had been built keeping in mind the needs of those who lived there. There were no diseased beggars on the streets or stray animals digging into untreated garbage – a common sight in other cities. Having travelled the length and breadth of the land, Drona could easily see why Hastinapur was considered a model city.

Under the reign of King Pandeshwar, the standard of living in Hastinapur had risen. He had installed several *ayuralayas* or hospitals, *patshalas* or schools, as well as administrative offices, to benefit the poor. He had also tightened the security system of the city through new protocols. Existing laws were revised and made known to every citizen, thereby reducing crime. All damage to public buildings, incurred during the reign of his father, the Late King Vichitravirya, was repaired. The nobles and the commoners of Hastinapur, who had alike led lives of misery and debt during Vichitravirya's reign, became devoted followers of King Pandeshwar. They believed he was the only one who could bring back *Ramrajya,* the reign of Lord Ram, in Hastinapur. They had witnessed such an ideal society during the early years of Pandeshwar's grandfather, King Shantanu's reign.

Hastinapur had been built in three concentric sectors. The outermost sector accommodated the night guards, the soldiers and gate-keepers, along with the war horses and elephants. They were key to the protection and security of the other sectors. The next sector had public buildings such as hospitals, schools, the market area, theatres and public baths. The innermost sector consisted of houses, crop storage buildings, farms and cattle sheds.

The housing units all looked alike, without distinction between rich and poor. Each unit was two-storeyed, built with red baked bricks and painted in a combination of blue and white – the colours of the sky. Roads and walkways made of cobblestones connected the buildings and sectors. Beyond the outermost sector was the surrounded wall that reached a height of a hundred feet, made with several layers of large stone blocks. At the far end of the city, on the bank of river Ganga, stood the Hastinapur palace, the abode of the Kuru dynasty for many centuries.

In the heart of the city was located the sacred Mahadev Temple, dedicated to Lord Shiva. At Drona's request, Kripacharya led him towards it. The temple was believed to be nearly five centuries old. It was the epitome of architectural brilliance of the ancient Suryavanshis. The entire structure was made of grey stone blocks, the walls decorated with paintings from the *Ramayana* and the *Shiva Purana*. Unlike most temples, the *garbhagriha* or sanctum sanctorum, had four entrances in the four cardinal directions. Each entrance was lined on either side with stone pillars that touched the roof at a height of 20 feet. Each pillar was intricately carved with images of the Holy Trinity – Lord Shiva, Lord Vishnu and Lord Brahma. The entire temple structure was crowned with a *gopuram*, a conical tower, over 50 feet high, with the Suryavanshi flag fluttering at its apex.

In the exact centre of the garbhagriha, was a cupola made of black stone, which contained the sacred *Shiva Linga*, the form in which the people in Hastinapur worshipped their Lord. Above the Shiva Linga, a pot of *tamra* metal containing *Ganga-jal* was suspended from the roof. From a small opening at its base, the Ganga-Jal dripped onto the Shiva Linga. Once the Ganga-jal filled the cupola, it flowed out through a carved outlet in the floor to a container outside. The Ganga-jal, having graced the Shiva Linga, would then be distributed to devotees as *prasad*.

In the calming aura of the temple, Drona felt at peace. Kripacharya stood beside him, softly chanting the Lord's name.

The sound of the great bell reverberated through every corner of the city, rousing Drona from his holy trance. "What was that?" he asked.

"It indicates the beginning of the second prahar, Jija-sa. It helps in the coordination and management of events. It also helps to synchronise movements and timings when many people have to work together in shifts, like the watch-guards and gate-keepers, the doctors in the ayuralayas or the teachers in the schools."

Drona nodded his understanding. It was a worthwhile system.

Having offered their prayers and obeisance at the Mahadev Temple, Drona and Kripacharya accepted some *prasad* and then proceeded towards the palace, situated at the far end of the city.

***

"Why do you need so many flowers, Shikha?" asked Sarala, Dai Ma's grand-daughter and the closest Shikhandini had to a sister.

"I am making a *gajra* for Ma," Shikhandini replied. Shikhandini loved her mother more than anyone else. She understood that her mother was upset about something and had not meant to punish her. Shihkandini had easily let go of her anger and was now looking for ways to make her mother smile.

"These flowers smell so good," said Sarala, gently sniffing the freshly picked jasmines and roses. The girls were in the palace garden, seated on the ground beside a flower bed.

"When I give her this, Ma will forget all her anger. She loves flowers!" Shikhandini told her bosom friend as she held the flowers in her hand and inhaled their fragrance.

"But why is she angry?" asked Sarala, her young face puzzled as she helped Shikhandini pluck more flowers.

"I do not know. Pitamaha says it's because of the garland I picked up from the old palace gates," Shikhandini shrugged.

"The one with the blue lotuses?" gasped Sarala dramatically.

"Yes," Shikhandini replied and then almost bit off her tongue. "Oh no! I was not supposed to tell anyone about it!" she lamented.

"Are you mad?" laughed Sarala, her eyes wide with amusement.

"Promise me, Sarala, that you will not tell anyone. Ma says that Pitamaha, my father, and she, are the only ones in Panchala who know whatever the secret of the blue lotus garland is."

"I promise, but…"

"Don't tell me you too think it is bad?" Shikhandini said, annoyed.

"Of course! Everyone knows that! You are not supposed to touch it."

"Do you know why?" challenged Shikhandini.

"Ummm…no…Dadi Ma never tells me anything clearly. She just told me I was too young to understand and I should just do what the the elders said."

"Pitamaha says the same thing," replied Shikhandini despondently.

"I do not think they know the real reason. They simply pretend to know everything, these elders," sniffed Sarala.

Shikhandini giggled, playfully nudging her friend. "I think we have enough flowers," she said, looking into her basket. "Now let's make a pretty gajra for Ma."

Sarala nodded, getting to her feet and dusting off her clothes.

***

Following Shikhandini's misadventure, Prishata, Drupada and Kokila decided to bury the incident within the walls of the palace. Fortunately, only a handful of people had witnessed Shikhandini with the garland of lotuses round her neck. All those who had, were either sent off to some distant place by the King, or sworn to secrecy by Kokila.

5
The Guru

Hastinapur, capital of the Kurus

The Hastinapur palace, which dated back five centuries, epitomised Kuru pride. The early architects had designed it in a wholly new manner. In contrast to the conventional palace architecture of the time, the Hastinapur palace was a conglomeration of three buildings. The central structure had six storeys, while the other two had five each. Every floor had the capacity of housing over five hundred people. The central structure was for the royals, while the other two were meant for the accommodation of ministers and the nobility in attendance at court. The first two storeys of each structure were used as quarters for the servants and guards. The three buildings conjoined at a common entrance, connected together in case of attack.

The entire design had been implemented with crystal-like white stones imported from the far west. In the blazing sun, the palace shone like a flawless pearl. The pathway from the palace gates to the main building was lined with white stone pillars chiselled with intricate representations of the heroic and valourous deeds of the Kuru forefathers. The main structure was crowned with a crystal dome, the Suryavanshi flag at its apex.

From a bird's eye view, one could easily guess what the palace architecture depicted. Set in green gardens with lush green trees on all sides, the palace with its three long structures connected at a common entrance with an array of pillars, gave the illusion of the sacred *Trishul,* the deadly weapon of Lord Mahadev, worshipped by both the commoners and royalty of Hastinapur. Rumour had it that the chief architect had been showered with gold coins equivalent to his weight as a reward for this unique design.

"The Hastinapur palace is indeed a paradise on earth," Drona remarked, looking around. He and Kripacharya had just entered the palace gates after clearing the security checks.

"It is indeed," Kripacharya agreed. "It is believed to have taken twenty-one years to complete this masterpiece. Three thousand workers, masons, sculptors, and some of the best architects, toiled day and night to finish it. The entire project was the brainchild of the great architect, Vishwakarma. He too, like the people of Hastinapur, was a follower of Lord Shiva."

"Vishwakarma appears to me to have been a divine architect. It is unbelievable that a human mind visualised and implemented a complex structure like this with such precision."

"It is not the structure alone that earned him the title of Vishwakarma, but the encrypted message the structure holds."

"And what is the message?"

"From the top of the Sumeru Parvat, the palace, with its long array of pillars, represents Mahadev's sacred weapon," Kripacharya replied, pointing in a north-easterly direction, where the peak of the Sumeru mountain was visible.

Drona narrowed his eyes to scan the structure before him. He imagined how it would look like from high up on Sumeru. With his visual memory, he created a memory map of the palace grounds from a bird's eye view. "The Trishul!" exclaimed Drona. "How is it even possible?"

"Some say Vishwakarma used the *Puspaka Vimana,* flying chariot, to govern the execution of his design from above. Other rational thinkers scoff at the idea of such a chariot and believe he stationed himself on Sumeru and sent instructions to the workers through an advanced communication medium," Kripacharya remarked.

"Either method makes the architect worthy of the title *Vishwakarma,* 'architect of the universe'," said Drona admiringly.

The Kingdom of Panchala

King Drupada was worried. "Are you sure, Vignajit?" he enquired of his Minister.

"Yes, Your Highness. I received the message from one of my most trusted men. The sage has returned from the Himalayas."

Vignajit was one of the King's inner circle of trusted ministers. Apart from being Minister of Diplomatic Affairs, dealing with neighbouring kingdoms, he used his vast network to get inside information from enemy territories. Drupada had assigned Vignajit the task of keeping an eye on Drona following their last fraught encounter at the Panchal court some years earlier.

"Do we know where is he now?"

"He was last seen entering the gates of Hastinapur, My Lord," answered Vignajit.

"What else have you gathered about him, Vignajit?" Drupada tossed aside the palm-leaf scripts he had been reading.

"I am told he spent the last five years in the northern mountains, learning advanced skills of warfare, weaponry and militia from the ultimate warrior, Lord Parashuram himself. His return is the hot topic of discussion among both commoners and the nobility in all of Aryavrath. Having mastered several *daiva astras* and the use of other destructive and uncommon *shastras*, he is believed to be next only to Maharathi Bheeshm of Hastinapur," Vignajit replied in the practised manner of a courtier.

Drupada's forehead creased, absorbing this new information. "Any information on what he is doing in Hastinapur?"

"Although there is nothing confirmed, rumour has it that he has been invited by the Maharathi himself. The Hastinapur royals consider Drona a potential Guru for the Kuru Princes."

Drupada's coal black eyes widened as the truth struck hard. Drona was preparing for his vengeance. His silence these last five years had been the silence before the storm. He has come back, more powerful, and was now preparing to strike Panchala in alliance with the largest empire in all of Aryavrath.

With deep foreboding, Drupada recalled Drona's parting words: *I promise you that when the day comes, I will not use any weapon. It will be my ability to impart knowledge that will bring you low. It will be my ultimate step in the journey to becoming a Guru.*

***

As Drona walked into the palace grounds, he saw boys in the age group of six to ten, playing at various games and sports. A few were busy plucking fruit from the trees while others swam in a small pool;

yet others were playing a ball game. Drona's attention was attracted to a young boy at the far end of the ground, holding a bow. A bunch of arrows lay scattered in front of him. A quiver full of arrows was tied to his back. Drona walked in the direction of the boy, to get a closer look, without making his presence known. Kripacharya watched keenly.

The boy, who seemed to be about six years old, was trying to shoot a mango that hung from a tree at a height of nearly fifteen feet, at a distance of ten metres. It was clearly an impossible shot keeping in mind his small stature and inexperience in archery. Drona was amused by the boy's confidence. The lad stood legs apart, shoulders back, battle-ready. He had a determined look on his face, his eyes steady on his target. Drona glanced at the arrows that lay scattered on the ground in all directions, within a few feet from the boy. He guessed the next one would be the boy's fifteenth shot. A boy of that age would usually have given up after a few initial shots, but this one seemed passionate about getting the shot right.

Drona also noticed the boy held the bow in the right hand and the arrow in the left. His right eye was closed while his left seemed to bore into his target. Drona had never seen an archer with a dominant left eye before. He noticed the boy was untrained. This was evident from his position with respect to the target and the way his dominant hand was angled.

Drona watched with rapt attention as the boy pulled the arrow backwards with his left hand, adjusted the bow vertically, and released the arrow with a twang. Drona winced. As expected, the arrow's acute trajectory just missed the centre of the target. What surprised Drona was the arrow did not miss the target completely, but struck the mango to one side before faling to the ground. The boy was gifted. With training, he could become one of the best archers in Aryavrath.

"Good try, my boy!" said Drona, moving closer.

"Pranam," the boy replied, his face serious. "I am aware it was not a good shot. I have to practice more."

Drona laughed softly. "Yes, if you keep practising, someday you will be able to get the mango in one piece, shearing it at the stem.

The boy turned back towards the mango tree. He pulled out another arrow from his quiver and positioned himself to shoot a second mango that hung next to the first. Drona smiled. The lad was not only passionate but also feisty, a good combination for a warrior. Moving closer to the boy, he crouched down next to him. Picking up a twig from the ground, he drew a line between the boy's feet, and then another ahead of the boy, in the direction of the target. The boy looked at Drona sceptically, without lowering his bow.

"Your position should always be perpendicular to the target, my son. Only then can you be sure of the arrow hitting something within the range of the target." The boy gave him a small smile and adjusted his stance.

"And to finish off the shot perfectly, you have to remember one important thing." The boy looked at him, his eyes direct and questioning.

"The dominant arm, in your case the left arm, should always be parallel to the ground, while your bow hand should hold the bow vertically, perpendicular to the ground." Drona adjusted the boy's left arm to the correct angle.

"Now shoot!" Drona ordered.

Without a second's thought the boy released the arrow. It whooshed through the air, cutting through the tender leaves and hitting the target exactly. The stem holding the fruit snapped and the mango fell with a satisfying thud onto the ground. The boy's eyes shone with happiness as a huge grin stretched from cheek to cheek, bringing his dimples to sudden life. He bowed low in acknowledgement, his hands folded.

"Are you an archer too?" he asked, his eyes alight with admiration for the stranger.

"Indeed I am," Drona replied.

"Will you teach me more about archery?" asked the boy passionately. "I want to learn everything!"

"Let time decide that, my boy. For now, just keep practising." Drona smiled as he walked away towards the palace. The boy watched his retreating figure, his heart and mind filled with new fire.

6
Decisions

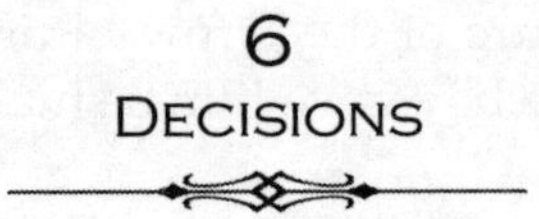

"Pranam, Dronacharya-Ji," greeted Bheeshm, his hooded eyes glittering with rare emotion.

"Pranam, Maharathi Bheeshm."

Drona stood in the private chambers of Maharathi Bheeshm. Kripacharya had returned to his own quarters after performing the formal introductions.

"I hope the journey was not too fatiguing?" enquired Bheeshm.

"I have been through worse," replied Drona, recalling his journeys in the northern mountains.

Bheeshm nodded empathetically. Both men were Lord Parashuram's pupils, but given the years between them, this was their first meeting.

"Would you like to rest first? We can reschedule our session for some time later today," offered Bheeshm.

"I must return to my wife and son as soon as possible. They have waited for me far too long. I cannot linger."

"In that case, let us get this done quickly. I do not wish to delay you. So I was informed you planned to reopen Maharishi Bhardwaj's gurukul now that you have the blessings and the knowledge from Lord Parashuram himself."

Drona smiled. "You have heard right, Maharathi. Long live Lord Parashuram!"

"Long live Lord Parashuram!" repeated Bheeshm.

"I have also heard that you have yet to find deserving students for your first batch."

"Yes, that is true. But I believe destiny alone will decide if the students I choose are, in fact, deserving, for there is no way to know their true potential before training them," Drona replied.

"That is true, Dronacharya Ji, but what about lineage? Is that not an indication of strength and potential?" asked the Maharathi.

"Yes, I do believe his bloodline says a lot about the character and strength of the student. That is why I have decided to teach only Kshatriyas from renowned royal families of Aryavrath," Drona replied, recalling the incident that had occurred a few days after he had returned from Parashuram's abode. A *suthaputhra*, son of a charioteer, a low born, had visited him with the request to accept him as a student. Drona had rejected his appeal, making him suddenly aware of his misfortune in being low born.

"How do you feel about having the Princes of Hastinapur as your first set of students?" questioned Bheeshm without missing a beat.

"You mean the sons of King Dhritarashtra?"

"And the sons of the Late King Pandeshwar," added Bheeshm.

"I was not aware of their return."

"Yes, they have returned, Dronacharya Ji. Following Pandeshwar's death, they had no reason to live in the forest. Also, I believe they should have an equal chance to compete for the throne when the time comes. And that is only possible if all hundred and five Princes are given an equal opportunity to discover and enhance their true skills and potential."

Drona nodded in agreement. "Yes, without the right opportunity to learn and enhance their skills, it would be impossible to discover their true potential."

"Which is why I request you to accept them as your students."

Drona smiled. His prayers had finally been answered. Apart from being the richest and most efficient kingdom in all Bharatavarsha, Hastinapur was also the most powerful. It was both feared and admired for its valiant army led by Maharathi Bheeshm, its well-designed security system put in place by the Late King Pandeshwar, and the cruel sentences delivered to the guilty by its blind King Dhritarashtra. Every kingdom around was therefore, directly or indirectly, ruled by Hastinapur. An alliance with this powerful kingdom would establish Drona and make possible his purpose in life – vengeance on Panchala.

"It would be an honour to shape the future of the Kuru dynasty," replied Drona.

"It will also help you achieve what you have been striving for the last five years, Guru Dronacharya." Bheeshm smiled knowingly. Nothing escaped the Maharathi's knowledge.

***

"Son, it is no longer safe to keep our Shikhandini in Panchala. No matter how much we try, the news of her donning the garland of blue lotuses will reach Hastinapur. And when that happens, God only knows what Bheeshm will do," said Prishatha.

"Father, worry clouds your mind. I do not believe in the prophecy." Prishata was about to retort but Drupada lifted a hand to silence him. "Even if it be true, it will be many years before Shikhandini realises the so-called purpose of her life. She is just a child."

"But what if Hastinapur actually believes Princess Amba has been reborn as Shikhandini? Can you ensure her safety here?" challenged Prishata.

Drupada considered the matter. Panchala, though more powerful than it had ever been in the past, was still no match for Hastinapur. If Bheeshm decided to attack because of the prophecy, it would be impossible to save Panchala. Drupada was aware of the twisted games being played in the Hastinapur court, for the throne. He knew that once the young Princes grew to adulthood, the question of who the throne rightfully belonged to would raise its many sceptered head. There would be in-fighting within the kingdom, which would affect its overall strength. Drupada hoped that in a few years Hastinapur would crumble and lose its power over Aryavrath, something it had prided itself on for centuries. That would then be the right moment to attack and defeat Hastinapur and gain control over the kingdoms allied to it. Till then, he had to keep Panchala safe.

"Son, it is better to be prepared than to be sorry afterwards. Think about it," Prishata advised, walking out of the chamber. He had carefully connected the two incidents – Drona's visit to Hastinapur and Shikhandini finding the garland of blue lotuses. Now, if he could persuade Drupada to send Shikhandini away from Panchala, he could start training her to accomplish the task he had dreamt of for so many years.

Kokila, a silent witness to this meeting between father and son, King and King, glared at her father-in-law's retreating form. "You are not sending her anywhere! I will not permit it!" she hissed, the moment Prishata was out of the chamber.

"Kokila, father is not wholly wrong. He only wishes to keep her safe" replied Drupada, his usually cold eyes alive with concern.

"I do not care what he thinks. I am not letting her go. I cannot live without her!"

"You know how much I too, love her, Kokila. She is as much my daughter as yours," said Drupada softly. In his mind he had already made the decision. Sending Shikhandini away would protect both his daughter and Panchala from the wrath of Hastinapur. With Shikhandini gone, the prophecy and the stories would die.

Kokila saw the answer in her husband's eyes and slumped to the floor crying out, "Why are you doing this to her…to us?"

Drupada kneeled down to embrace her comfortingly, his own eyes moist with tears. "I promise you Kokila, when Panchala is strong enough and Shikhandini has decided what she wants to do, I will get her back. If she decides the purpose of her life is to seek vengeance on Hastinapur, then so be it. I will make sure Panchala is strong enough to support her. My father will guard her, never fear. He will ensure Shikhandini makes the right decision."

Kokila sobbed helplessly. She knew that her opinion did not matter, even though it was about her daughter's life.

Though Prishata sought revenge on Hastinapur more than anything else, Drupada did not favour it. To him, war was a last resort. He believed that if there was any way to form a friendly alliance with Hastinapur, it would be an easier way to strengthen his own power without sacrificing the lives of countless soldiers from both kingdoms.

Drupada had always been sceptical about the prophecy of Amba's rebirth as his daughter, to wreck vengeance on the Maharathi of Hastinapur. He had dismissed the incident of blue lotuses as an innocent act by a naïve child. But Drona's return and his visit to Hastinapur were portentous. A friendly alliance with Hastinapur seemed a fading dream. He realised Panchala had to prepare for war, sooner or later. With so much going on, it would be best for Shikhandini to live away from the kingdom for a few years.

7
Shikhandini Leaves Panchala

Once the decision to send Shikhandini away had been made, Prishata too, began making arrangements to begin her formal education. A palace, many yojanas from Panchala, was renovated and a staff of maids and guards appointed to the household of the young Princess. Dai Ma would go with her to run the establishment and look after her. Teachers specialised in different subjects like statecraft, warfare, the Vedas and Upanishads, were contacted. They were to visit Shikhandini in her new palace outside Panchala to tutor her. This was then Shikhandini's new home.

"Pitamaha, I am sorry. I will not break any rules again, I promise. Please do not send me away! I do not want to go," sobbed Shikhandini, standing beside her grandfather. She knew only he could stop the plan.

Prishata put her on his lap and wiped her tears. "It is for your own good, my child. Vidyakuteera will prepare you for life."

"But I don't want to go," Shikhandini protested.

"Everyone has to leave at some time, my child. Do you not want to become a great warrior like your father? Do you not want to lead the Panchala army someday and make us proud?" asked Prishata, who knew that Shikhandini, unlike other girls, was fascinated by weaponry and warfare.

"I do, Pitamaha," Shikhandini replied with a small smile. "But I can learn all that here at home. You and father can teach me."

"No, my child, you must learn these things from a teacher. It is why young Princes are sent to gurukuls. You will understand the importance of this when you are older," replied Prishata.

Shikhandini considered this and then asked, "Will you visit me?"

"Of course, my child! I will come often," replied Prishata.

"Will Ma and Pitashri come too?"

"Yes, they will come too," he replied, running a hand over her head.

***

When the day arrived, Shikhandini, bid farewell to the only home she had ever known. As she had been taught to do, Shikhandini touched her parents' feet and smiled bravely, assuring her mother she would return soon. As they stood watching their little girl depart, Kokila held back her tears so her daughter would not see them, but her heart felt like it was breaking.

As she crossed the palace threshold, Shikhandini looked back one last time at her parents. Then, accompanied by Dai Ma, a retinue of maids and a phalanx of bodyguards, Shikhnadini left Panchala.

***

Shikhandini's new home was on the banks of river Gomati, in the noman's land between Panchala and the kingdom of Kosala. It was bounded by the Naimisharanya forest on three sides, adding to its scenic beauty. It was in this forest that Maharishika Brahmaramba had her gurukul for girls, *Vidyakuteera*.

In the balcony of her newly decorated chambers in the palace, Shikhandini sat gazing at the setting sun. It was her first time outside Panchala. Everything around her was new and unknown. She liked to watch the sunset. Kokila had told her the setting sun brought with it the promise of a new dawn. Today, however, it did not make her smile. She knew that for many sunsets and sunrises to come, she would not have her mother by her side.

"Don't be sad, Shikha. We will return soon," consoled Dai Ma, gently patting Shikhandini's head. Though Dai Ma was her personal maid, she was like a second mother. Unlike Kokila, who had the palace household to supervise, as well as her duties as Queen, Dai Ma always gave Shikhandidni her undivided attention. When the King had decided to send the Princess away, Dai Ma had chosen to go with her.

Shikhandini looked at Dai Ma now, tears pooling in her eyes. She was grateful to have at least one loved and familiar face from home. She hugged Dai Ma and cried her heart out. From here on, her only family would be Dai Ma.

TWO MONTHS LATER

As the days passed, Shikhandini grew accustomed to her new life. She spent her mornings practising weaponry with the trainers her grandfather had appointed. They were each the best in the weapon of their forte. Every alternate day, a teacher would visit the palace and tutor her in subjects like math, science and sociology, along with the Vedas and Upanishads.

It was one such day.

" Naivastamanamarkasya nodayah sarvada satah I
Udayastamanakhyarn hi darsanadarsanarn raveh II

The *Vishnu Purana* says the rising and setting of the sun is an illusion. In reality, the sun is always there. *Suryayodhaya* and *suryastha* merely imply appearance and disappearance," explained the Guru.

Dadhartha prthivimabhito mayukhaih I
Mitro dadhara prthivimutadyam I Mitrah krstlh II.

"The sun holds the earth in position with its force. He is the power which binds all the celestial bodies together," she added.

Guru Maharishika Brahmaramba was a renowned scholar across Aryavrath, and the only female teacher to start her own gurukul for girls, naming it Vidyakuteera. Though she preferred the students to reside in the premises during the period of their education, she had agreed to tutor Shikhandini at her home. She owed this to Prishata, for he had helped her, providing the resources to set up Vidyakuteera, several decades ago.

"How is that possible Guruji? We always see the sun rise in the east and set in the west," asked Shikhandini.

Brahmaramba smiled at Shikhandini's confusion. "No, Shikhandini, the earth rotates on itself while also revolving around the sun. So during the first four prahars of the day, when we have sunlight, some other part of the earth experiences night. So when we say sunset, the earth is simply changing its position so the other side sees sunrise," the Guru explained.

Shikhandini smiled in amusement. She had never thought about it in that way. "Guruji, are there any other planets like earth?" asked Shikhandini, having recited the *shloka* in her mind.

"Yes, there are many, and an uncountable number of stars."

"But how did they find out about all this?" she asked sceptically.

"The ancients were great men and women, who excelled in many fields. One such field is what we know today as *Khagolashatra*, or the study of the universe. Some of these scholars dedicated their lives to observing and understanding the planets and their positions in various months of the year. They documented their observations for the next generation to continue. Eventually, the documents became textbooks that were studied and referred to by the students in different gurukuls. The *Vishnu Purana* is one such document."

"Guruji, is it possible that they had some kind of *yantra* to help them look more closely at the sky?" asked Shikhandini. It was almost the end of the second prahar and the sun was bright in the sky. She made a mental note to look at the sky at night and try to find other planets.

"That is a possibility. The ancients built many marvellous yantras that people find hard to believe today. One such instrument, or rather a vehicle, is said to have existed thousand years ago in the land of Lanka. Do you know its name, Shikhandini?"

"The *Pushpakavimana*? The flying chariot of King Ravana," replied Shikhandini, recalling the ancient epic *Ramayana* that she had grown up listening to.

Her teacher smiled. The child had been gifted with a quick mind as well as a lithe body."In the next class, we will learn about the force that binds the earth and other planets to the sun," the Guru said as she prepared to leave.

Shikhandini touched the Guru's feet in agesture of respect and gratitude before she left the palace for the day.

Once a fortnight, Shikhandini would have a day to herself, which she could spend as she wished. Usually, she spent it listening to stories from Dai Ma, and strolling about the palace gardens, nurturing the plants that she and Dai Ma had planted together. Sometimes, she would spend the entire day writing to her mother, reminiscing about her days in Panchala.

Sitting on a bench in the palace garden, Shikhandini wondered why her parents had not come to visit her in the last year. Nor had she been permitted to visit them in Panchala. Had they forgotten her? Pitamaha visited often, but this was to make sure her training was being conducted as per his orders. He hardly spoke to Shikhandini about anything other than what she had learnt. A single tear rolled down her cheek as she remembered her carefree days at home in Panchala. Quickly wiping away the tear, she reminded herself to be strong. She was a warrior.

Just then she heard the chime of the gate bell. Walking up to the small door beside the main gate, she saw a cow and calf, followed by a boy who was a little shorter than herself but near her own age. He was dressed in a yellow dhoti and angavastram, with an oversized turban on his head.

"Pranam," she greeted him hesitantly with a small smile when he caught her looking at him.

"Pranam," he replied in turn, showing pearly teeth that stood out against his dark skin.

"Are you a *gwala*?" asked Shikhandini, using the Sanskrit word for cowherd.

The boy nodded his head vigorously until his turban was in danger of falling off.

"What is your name?"

"Govind. And what is yours?"

"I am Shikhandini," she replied moving a little closer. She noticed the pot of creamy butter he carried with him.

"Do you want to try it?" asked Govind, seeing her eyeing the butter.

"Did your mother make it?"

"Yes, she makes the best butter in the village," Govind said proudly. He moved the pot towards Shikhandini, offering her the butter.

Shikhandini dipped her little fingers into the pot and then put them into her mouth. As the butter melted, she closed her eyes blissfully.

Govind chuckled. "Did I not tell you? *Mayya* prepares the best butter." But his words fell on deaf ears as Shikhandini continued devouring the butter.

"You can have this pot," he offered.

"But I have nothing to give you in return," she replied sadly.

Govind thought for a moment, looking around. "There is something you can give me," he said with a mischievous grin.

"What do you want, Govind?"

"Will you let me inside your palace? I have never visited one before," he replied excitedly, his eyes wide.

Shikhandini thought for a while, looking at the gatekeepers on either side of the gate. She knew they would not let Govind in.

"Wait here for a few minutes. I will be back."

Some time later, Govind saw Shikhandini emerge from the palace main entrance, dragging a middle-aged woman behind her.

"What is it child that cannot wait till I have finished cooking your lunch?" asked Dai Ma, trying not to trip as she hurried to keep up with Shikhandini.

"Dai Ma, this is Govind," Shikhandini said, introducing her new friend as they reached the palace gates. The young boy still stood patiently waiting.

"Pranam, Kaki ji," said Govind using 'aunt' as the universal form of greeting a lady.

"Pranam, Govind," Dai Ma replied, smiling. "Where are you from?"

"Gokul, Kaki ji. I belong to the community of gwalas there," he replied proudly.

"Oh, I see." Dai Ma had heard of the gwalas of Gokul and their peaceful way of living. "So you have found a new friend, Shikha."

Shikhandini smiled gleefully. "Dai Ma, can Govind come inside?" she asked, looking at the guards.

"Yes, he can. In fact, come and have lunch with Shikha, Govind. Usually the poor child has only me for company. It will be nice to have a new face," replied Dai Ma, signalling to the guards to let the boy in.

Govind tied the cow and the calf to a tree outside and walked in, looking around in wide-eyed wonder.

"Your cows will be safe, Govind. The gatekeepers will keep an eye on them," assured Dai Ma.

Govind smiled at her and nodded happily, free of care.

***

Four years later

Shikhandini was now eleven years old; a bold and a wise young girl. It had been several years since she had left Panchala, and it had become a faded memory. Except for the letters from her mother and occasional visits by her grandfather, she had no connection with Panchala. But she had learnt to adapt to her new life. Dai Ma's love and Govind's friendship made it easier for her.

"Shikhandini, my child, how have you been?" asked Prishata, entering her chambers. He was on one of his visits.

"I am well, Pitamaha," replied Shikhandini, bowing low to touch her grandfather's feet.

"Happy Birthday, my dear! Your parents have sent their blessings and will write soon," he said, holding his granddaughter by the shoulders. "Can you guess what I have bought you?" he asked, pulling out a bundle from his pocket.

The long and slim gift was wrapped in silk cloth. Shikhandini narrowed her eyes. Knowing her grandfather, she could easily guess it was a weapon of some sort. "Is it a knife?" she asked, not at all excited. The only gift she wanted was for her parents to visit her. She wished for it each year, only to be disappointed.

"I knew you would guess right! You are a smart one!" he said proudly, unwrapping the bundle. "It is a dagger. I got it specially made for you, my dear." Prishata offered the blade to his granddaughter.

Shikhandini accepted the gift and casually shoved it into her waistband, saying desultorily, "Thank you, Pitamaha"

"No, no…open it. It is not an ordinary dagger."

Shikhandini sighed, pulling out the dagger and removing it from its scabbard. Despite her disinterest, Shikhandini found herself taken by the clever piece of weaponry. It was nothing like she had ever seen. In fact, she was not sure if it was indeed a dagger. It was a double-edged knife with a handle of ivory. The handle had intricate carvings and the Panchala logo embedded into it in shining gold. The two blades were long and sharp, curved to form mirror images, like the horns of a bull. They glistened in the light and Shikhandini could see her reflection in them.

"It's called a *Haladie*. It is very rare. There are few like it in our land," Prishata told her. "I believe it is the best gift someone can give you. Do you like it, my dear?"

"I do, Pitamaha," Shikhandini replied, forcing a smile. Only she knew what the best gift would have been.

***

'Govind will be so happy when I show him this,' thought Shikhandini, smiling to herself. It had been four years since they had first met at the palace gate and he had offered her his butter. Govind visited her on her off days and they spent the entire day talking and playing together, sharing experiences and stories. Govind had become the older brother Shikhandini never had.

She waited near the palace gates for Govind to appear from the forest, having carefully tucked the present into her pouch.

"Shikha!" he called, coming into view. The guards payed no heed as he walked in through the side gate, long used to his comings and goings.

"How was your journey, Govind? Have some coconut water." Shikhandini signalled to one of the maids.

She sensed something was wrong. Govind, who usually began telling stories the moment he saw her, was unusually quiet. His sparkling eyes had a hint of sadness and his face looked smaller than usual.

"What is the matter, Govind? Why are you so quiet?" she asked as they sat on one of the benches in the garden.

"We are moving to another place, Shikha. Gokul will no longer be our home."

"But why? What happened?" Shikhandini's her eyes were wide with surprise. She knew how much he loved Gokul and how sad it would make him to leave.

"Gokul is no longer safe. There have been incidents in the past few months. Demonic attacks on my people and our cattle. Untimely rains have led to so much destruction. The people of my village live each minute in fear of what might happen next. That is why the village Panchayat has decided to leave Gokul and move elsewhere," Govind explained.

"I thought Gokul was the most peaceful place in Aryavrath!"

"Yes, Shikha, it was. But not anymore," Govind replied meekly.

For the fraction of a second, Shikhandini thought she saw guilt in his eyes. "Will you still visit me like you do now?" she asked, hopefully.

Govind did not reply. His lips were pursed, his gaze downcast.

Shikhandini understood his silence. “I have something for you, Govind,” she said, wiping her tears. She knew Govind could not be around forever; that someday one of them would have to leave. But it was hard to accept it now. She pulled out the gift she had brought, from her pouch. Without knowing it, it had become a parting gift. It was a single peacock tail feather in vibrant blue-green. “This is for you,” she said, offering it to him.

“Where did you find it? It is beautiful!” exclaimed Govind, beaming with delight.

“In the forest near Guruji’s Vidyakuteera. There are many peacocks around the school,” Shikhandini explained.

“It is a very rare feather. Look, it has eyespots on both sides,” he said turning it over.

Shikhandini took it from him and tucked it into his hair that was tied neatly into a bun. She smiled. “It will remind you of me,” she said.

“I never forget my friends, Shikha. I will always be there whenever you need me,” Govind assured her.

“Promise?”

“I promise.”

PART II

8
PRINCESS AMBA

12 YEARS LATER

A familiar flutter of wings made Shikhandini smile with anticipation. The soft sound brought a sense of comfort and hope to her lonely life. It was the bird courier from Panchala. Despite the passage of years, the thought of a letter from home brought a smile to her face and a rush of tears to her eyes. The bird, having travelled back and forth, carrying messages for her ever since she had left Panchala twelve years ago, seemed to understand her feelings better than her own family. Gently running a hand over the bird, Shikandini set a bowl of grain and some water for it. The bird had travelled for more than two prahars without a break. She had seen how hard these valuable birds were trained in her hometown.

"Thank you, Panchi," she whispered to the bird as she unrolled the palm leaf. Her eyes widened in surprise when she saw her father's personal seal at the bottom of the message. He wrote rarely, and even when he did, his missives sounded formal rather than loving. He was not good with words or feelings. Today however, the letter was meant to express anything but emotion. It was an instruction from the King of Panchala, seeking her participation in an impending war.

The time has come, my child, to prove your valour and bravery, to seek the vengeance that has travelled with you from another lifetime. The time has come to make your father proud.

Panchala has received a declaration of war from the Kurus of Hastinapur. This was bound to happen sooner or later. Drona has trained the hundred and five Kuru Princes to wage war against Panchala, but the arrogant Guru does not know that Panchala has a born warrior destined to destroy Hastinapur. He calls this war his Guru Dakshina, but it is your duty, my child, to change it to a curse that will resound in the Kuru Empire for generations to come.

This war means more to Panchala than just victory. The dignity and honour of your family is at stake. Your grandfather has lived in anticipation of this moment for many decades. You have waited even longer. This might be your only chance to fulfill your life's purpose for if we face defeat, we will forever remain slaves to Drona. Such a life will be worse than death.

Panchala's pride and honour is in your hands, Shikhandini. The war begins in fourteen days from this sunrise. We await your arrival. Vijayi bhava!

Shikhandini read the letter again, making sure every word seeped into her mind. She had been waiting for this moment for a long time. She had dreamt of it every night. Her only fear had been that Hastinapur would not attack and the war would not happen. What if all the years of intense practice, dedication and patience were in vain? Her waiting was finally over. As the intensity of her father's words sank into her mind, goosebumps covered her flesh. Vengeance and hatred for Hastinapur began to flow through her veins with renewed force.

It had been Shikhandini's sixteenth birthday when her grandfather, Prishata, had finally decided to tell her about her previous birth... "You are a special girl, my child. In your last life, you were born as Princess Amba, eldest daughter of the King of Kashi. Even then, you were different; strong and determined. You mastered several weapons and were sagacious in statecraft. No decision was made in the court of Kashi without your knowledge. Your father took great pride in you.

Early in life, you chose your groom. He was your one true love – Salva, Prince of Saubala. But destiny had different plans. On the day of your *swayamvara*, you were to garland Salva, while your younger sisters were to choose from the remaining Princes. Everything went smoothly until the arrogant Maharathi entered the court. He had come uninvited, to represent his unworthy brother, Vichithravirya. He asked for the hand of all three Princesses of Kashi, for his brother. He challenged the attending Princes to fight him if anyone had any objections. Your father, the King of Kashi, was helpless. He knew that if he turned down Bheeshm, Kashi would have to face the wrath of Hastinapur.

Only Salva had the courage to challenge Bheeshm to a duel, unaware that the Maharathi had been blessed by Lord Parashuram himself. The Prince was defeated, heartbroken and humiliated. Shamefaced, he left Kashi without a word.

But you would not accept what had happened. You refused to marry Vichithravirya. Bheeshm had no choice but to let you go to the man you loved. But Prince Salva, true Kshatriya that he was, could not accept you since Bheeshm had defeated him in a fair fight at the swayamvara. Though he felt he had been stabbed in the heart, he told you to return to Bheeshm.

With nothing left to fight for, you went back to Hastinapur, hoping Bheeshm would understand your plight and take you as his own bride. But Bheeshm, who had sworn to remain celibate all his life, rejected your plea. His brother Vichithravirya, who had married your two younger sisters, rejected you too, as Salva's rejected woman. Unable to bear the humiliation, you approached Lord Kartikeya, who assured you of victory and gifted you a garland of ever-blooming lotuses. Now your task was to find a warrior who would agree to help you and garland him with the lotuses. But, fearing the wrath of Hastinapur, no King or Prince agreed to fight for you. King Drupada too, was one of those who turned away. Losing all hope, you left Panchala, leaving the garland of lotuses hanging at the palace gates.

As a last resort, you approached Lord Parashuram, Bheeshm's Guru; the only women in the history of Aryavrath to have dared climb the northern mountains to reach his abode. After listening to your plea, he decided to duel Bheeshm himself. The duel is said to have lasted several days before Lord Shiva decided to put an end to it. The Lord blessed you with a powerful boon – that when you returned to *Bhoomata,* Mother Earth, in your next life, you would be the cause of the Maharathi's death. You will have your vengeance.

With nothing left to live for and seething with the desire for revenge, you ended your life by jumping into the holy pyre outside Lord Parashuram's abode. Parshuram and the Maharathi both witnessed your painful death and heard your last words of vengeance echo in the mountains."

After her grandfather's disclosure, Amba's story began to seem more real to Shikhandini with every passing day. She was able to relate to Amba's sorrow and pain; feel her rejection at the hands of loved ones. The feeling of loss and helplessness was familiar to Shikhandini.

As her eyes skimmed the chamber now, the colourless brick walls that had mocked her loneliness for years on end, now seemed pale with fear. The stack of swords that stood beside her bed as a reminder of her ultimate goal, glistened in the sunlight, battle-ready. It was as if the letter had brought everything around her to life, not in the way a weed sprouts from the barren land or a flower blooms in the desert, but like a wildfire that takes birth from a tiny spark.

Her eyes shifted to the metal statue that stood at the far end of her chamber. A gift from her grandfather, it had tormented her every time she had looked at it. It was an effigy of the man she was destined to kill, the man who had mocked and insulted her grandfather years ago; defeating Panchala and then giving it back as a token of his generosity. The same man who had ruined Amba's life. He was the reason Shikhandini could not lead the life she craved, enjoying the simple pleasures of life. She had sacrificed her childhood and her early youth, locked away far from home, away from her family, for the sole reason of slaying the Maharathi when the time came. Every drop of blood in her body now craved vengeance.

Images of Amba and her lover, Prince Salva, appeared in her mind. How different Amba's life would have been if not for the Maharathi's arrogant intervention in her swayamvara. She would have lived the life she had dreamed of, given of her many talents to those around her. She would have one day been Queen of the small but well-administered kingdom of Saubala. Instead, she had faced rejection, sorrow and humiliation before ending her own life.

Tears clouded Shikhandini's eyes as she recalled Amba's fate and her last words – a promise of vengeance – as she entered the pyre, while Lord Parashuram himself stood witness. The flames had engulfed everything but her pain. And she carried her grief, humiliation and loss with her when she was reborn as Princess of Panchala.

As though possessed, Shikhandini charged towards the statue, her smouldering eyes boring into the metal sculpture as if to destroy it by the heat of her hatred. Sword in both hands, she began hammering at the statue, blow after blow. She did not use a shield, ever. In practice sessions with her Guru and the other students, Shikhandini never used a shield for she never gave the opponent a chance to attack. The statue before her was made of the toughest alloy, almost impossible to break. Prishata, having personally fought the Maharathi, was aware that killing Bheeshm would be a thousand times more challenging than breaking open this metal statue.

Finally, the metal began to crack around the arms. Shikhandini dropped to the floor onto her knees. Taking deep breaths, she quietly put the sword down and looked at her bleeding hands. Letting out a weak laugh, she remembered Guru Brahmaramba's words: *Vengeance is a double-edged sword. It affects both the seeker and the sought.*

A WEEK LATER

Soon after the arrival of Drupada's letter, Prishata personally visited Shikhandini to discuss the preparations for war. Together, they planned what to do. Prishata's experience and Shikhandini's energy and sharp intellect made a deadly combination. A week before the commencement of war, they left for Panchala.

The battle was to be fought in a field outside Panchala. Since Panchala did not follow gender discrimination, but Hastinapur did, Drupada had announced the battle between the two kingdoms would be fought in Panchala. In Hastinapur, the participation of a female warrior would never have been permitted. Although Drona had been sceptical, the Kurus had agreed to let Shikhandini fight.

And so the acceptance of battle was sent to Hastinapur. The rules were laid down and agreed to by both parties. The battle would be fought till one side defeated the other. The laws of Kshatriya Dharma were to be preserved at all cost. Duels would be fought between men of same order, and the cavalry were not permitted to duel with foot-soldiers. Attacks on unarmed soldiers were prohibited and no animals were to be harmed intentionally. The battle would begin at sunrise, with the blowing of the conch from both sides, and continue till sunset. No attacks were to be made after sunset.

Due to internal disputes, Guru Drona had divided the battle into two. The first day, the sons of Dhritarashtra would represent him, while the five sons of Pandeshwar would continue the battle the next day if the Kauravas had failed to achieve victory.

"Make sure all hundred and five Kuru Princes are captured. Only then will the Maharathi be forced to come to their rescue. That will be your chance to finish that conceited and egoistic son of Ganga," said Drupada, surveying the battlefield from the roof of his palace.

"Yes, father." Shikhandini's eyes glowed with an inner fire.

"But is it not impossible to kill the Maharathi?" asked Brahmabrata, Senapati of the Panchal army. "Have you not heard of the boon he was given by the Late Kuru King Shantanu – the boon of *ischa-maran*?"

"Ischa-maran?" asked Shikhandini. Though she had learnt many things about the Maharathi's life from her grandfather, she was unaware of any such boon.

"The boon gives him the choice of leaving the mortal body by his own will. It is impossible to kill him," replied the Senapati.

Shikhandini nodded thoughtfully. Pitamaha probably did not believe this mythical tale, or he would have surely mentioned it to her.

"It is just a story made up to glorify the Maharathi." Drupada waved his hand dismissively. "Even if true, defeat at a woman's hands would definitely make him wish for death."

Shikhandini cringed at his words. How did it matter? Victory was victory; defeat was defeat, whatever the warrior's gender. Men were blessed with greater physical strength but battles were fought and won with skill and strategy as much as strength. That was how men like Dronacharya, Bheeshm and her father, Drupada, had defeated kingdoms ruled by younger and physically stronger Kings. Shikhandini's musings were interrupted by the ringing of the prahar bell. It was almost sunset.

"Go to your chamber and get some rest, my child. Tomorrow is a big day," said Drupada. "And Shikhandini, you will lead the Panchal army tomorrow. Senapati Brahmabrata will follow your lead."

"Yes, father." Shikhandini could feel energy radiating through her body like an untamed river.

Har Har Mahadev! Drupada gave the Panchal war cry.

Har Har Mahadev! shouted Shikhandini and Brahmabrata in unison.

9
THE BATTLE

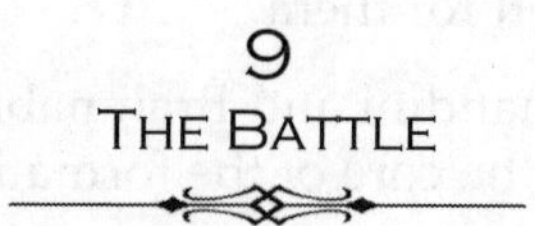

The sound of the conch echoed across the battleground as the sun slowly began to rise above the horizon. The Kaurava army rushed into battle with Dhritarashtra's eldest son, Duryodhan, leading as Senapati. The Panchal Sena stood ready in their well-practiced formations. The foot soldiers were in the vanguard, facing the enemy, their large shields creating the illusion of a wall. Right behind them were the cavalry, with their long spears held in a crossed formation, making the wall impenetrable. Several such formations stood at fixed distances. Between every fifty soldiers, a weak spot was created to deceive the enemy.

"Look Dushasana! See what happens when you let a woman lead the army!" Duryodhan scoffed to his brother. The duo roared with laughter as they viewed the fragile formation.

"You were right, brother. We hundred brothers are enough to defeat the entire Panchal army. It would have been insulting to bring the mighty Hastinapur Sena to fight these wimps," Dushana sniggered.

"Brothers, look out for every opening like this one in their formation. We will each break into their *vyuha* through them," Duryodhan announced. Immediately the Kuru brothers and the Kaurava army scattered across the battlefield.

A high platform had been built at the far end, from where the entire battlefield was visible. King Drupada sat on his throne, watching. Beside him stood Vignajit, his loyal messenger.

"My Lord, how will Princess Shikhandini defeat the Kuru Princes by herself? I have heard that each of the Princes is a *Rathi*, capable of defeating five thousand soldiers single handedly," said Vignajit, his brow furrowed.

"Shikhandini is no ordinary warrior, Vignajit. She has the potential to become an *Athirathi* or even a *Maharathi*. She has been trained by the finest warriors. Above all, she was born to destroy Hastinapur. Nothing, no matter how powerful, can go against destiny," replied Drupada, watching the foolish Kaurava brothers entering the formation in precisely the points left for them.

On the battlefield, Shikhandini and Brahmabrata, Commander of the Panchala Sena, stood at the core of the formation, waiting for the foe.

"I did not expect Guru Dronacharya's students to be so foolish," chuckled Brahmabrata, moving his horse closer to Shikhandini.

"I was taught that underestimating the enemy is the worst mistake one can make in battle, Brahmabrata ji," Shikhandini replied, not taking her eyes off the Kuru Princes, who were now visible. "How many layers have they passed?"

"Seven, Princess. They must cross five more before they realize what they have walked into. The deception has been successful thus far. The Princes think they are breaking into our formation to reach the Senapati."

Shikhandini nodded, satisfied the strategy was working.

It was the beginning of the third prahar when the Kuru Commander, Prince Duryodhan, realized what was happening. The Kuru Princes had almost broken through the Panchal formation and were close to the core where the Senapati and Princess sat on their horses.

"Dushasana, something is not right," stated Duryodhan positively, pulling on the reins of his horse to slow down.

"What has happened?" Dushasana pulled up beside him.

"I do not think we are breaking their formation."

"What do you mean? We are almost through!" Dushasana said, staring at his brother in confusion.

Duryodhan looked back. The weak spots through which they had broken through were now sealed behind them as multiple layers of infantry and cavalry took their positions. A trap! Duryodhana's eyes blazed with anger. "They are creating a formation around us!"

From the high platform, Drupada witnessed the sudden movement of soldiers, layer by layer. He mentally applauded his daughter for having executed the strategy so perfectly.

Duryodhan watched as all his brothers came up to him, each with a proud smile of accomplishment on his face, still unaware what had happened. 'Fools! All of them are bloody fools!' thought Duryodhna. 'And I am the biggest fool of all!'

"We must do something, brother; we cannot lose!" urged Dushasana.

"Too late, my friend," a voice boomed from the core as it parted to reveal Shikhandini and Brahmabrata.

"You have walked into the most deadly of all formations, Prince – the *Panchal Chakravyuha,*" said Shikhandini, a smile playing on her lips.

Suddenly, Duryodhan recalled what Guru Dronacharya had said, that the Panchal Chakravyuha was King Drupada's creation. Unlike other chakravyuhas, this one did not form beforehand. The enemy did not realize he is inside the formation until it was too late. At first it appeared to be a normal formation of infantry and cavalry. But as one penetrated the seemingly weak spot and went forward, that first layer immediately formed a sealed circle. As the enemy crossed each layer, concentric circles formed behind him, strong and hard to break. When the enemy reached the core, they were attacked by the Senapati, leading the the most powerful soldiers. The goal was to ensure the enemy could not escape from the core.

To make the battle fair, Shikhandini had chosen only one hundred soldiers to fight at the core of the chakravyuha. They alone would fight beside her against the hundred Kauravas. These men were the best of the Panchal Sena. Shikhandi considered using the entire Panchal Sena, comprising of two *akshauhinis,* against a hundred Kuru Princes, would be overwhelming and an unequal fight. King Drupada and Brahmabrata had not been happy with Shikhandini's decision. They feared she was being overconfident and heading towards her own doom. But Shikhandini had made her decision.

Soon the on-foot duels between the hundred Panchal soldiers and the Kuru Princes began. A fierce battleground had formed within the *vyuha.* The clink of swords rang in the air. Duryodhan, who had scoffed at an army led by a woman, had agreed to using swords instead of his powerful mace. Both sides fought ferociously, hungry for victory. Shikhandini duelled Duryodhan, while Brahmabrata fought Dushasana. As instructed by Drupada, the Panchal Sena fought only to capture the Princes, not to kill them. The objective was to draw the Maharathi to Panchala to rescue his grand-nephews, and then finish him off.

While some of the Panchal Sena were killed in the fight, the Kaurava Princes were finally captured. Brahmabrata, gifted and experienced warrior that he was, easily defeated and captured Dushasana. He then moved to where the fighting was most fierce. Duryodhana, unrivalled with the mace, regretted his decision to use the sword. He was no match for Shikhandini's exceptional swordsmanship. She fought with a sword in each hand. He concentrated on defending himself rather than attacking her.

"What is the matter Prince Duryodhan; afraid to fight a woman?" Shikhandini mocked, recalling her father telling her that Hastinapur was a male dominated society where women were not allowed to learn warfare or weaponry.

"Shikhandini, this is unfair! The mace is my weapon. You tricked me!" shouted Duryodhana, trying to provoke her into letting down her guard. He raised his sword high above his head, aiming at Shikhandini's neck. She nimbly stepped back, crossing her swords. Duryodhan stumbled as he brought his blade down, meeting nothing but thin air, but quickly steadied himself.

"You had the choice, Prince. But you chose the sword, believing it would be easy to fight a woman. Your arrogance has led you to your doom," Shikhandini replied calmly.

Her words served to ignite Duryodhan's always quick temper. He charged towards her with all his great strength, aiming his sword at her torso like a dagger. Shikhandini stood still, hoping to fool the Prince. She turned sideways at the last moment, using her left sword to meet his thrust. Taking a deep breath, she used all her strength to push him away. Her sword left a deep gash along his arm and the sword fell from Duryodhana's grasp. As he quickly bent down to pick it up, Shikahndini placed her sword on his neck, leaving him no choice but to surrender or die.

Duryodhan knew he had been defeated. It had been a fair fight. With his capture, the other Kaurvas gave up the fight and surrendered. All hundred Kuru Princes were now captives of the Panchal Sena.

***

"Father, all hundred Kuru Princes have been captured," Shikhandini reported to her father.

"Well done, my child. I did not expect anything less from you," Drupad said, swelling with pride. "But the real challenge is tomorrow. The five sons of Pandeshwar are more powerful and clever than these hundred combined. Be careful," he warned.

"Yes, father."

"Vijayi Bhava, my daughter. *Har Har Mahadev!"*

"Har Har Mahadev!"

***

"Brother Yudhistir, this is a golden opportunity. By wining Panchala for Guru Dronacharya, we will not only be able to clear our debt of gratitude but also teach Duryodhana a lesson," said Bheem, grinning.

Yudhistir shook his head in response. He knew that of all his brothers, Bheem disliked Duryodhana the most.

"Brother Bheem, I have heard that Princess Shikhandini herself duelled with Duryodhana and defeated him," added Nakul, one of the twins.

The five brothers were headed towards the battleground, where the Panchal Sena awaited them. The Pandavas, who had been monitoring the previous day's battle, knew about the Panchal Chakravyuha, but were not sure how to break it.

On reaching the battlefield, Arjun announced, "No matter what, do not enter the vyuha through the weak spots. They have been created to deceive us. We will break in from the points they least expect." Among the Pandavas, Arjun was the one who spent the most time learning about different vyuhas and how to break them. But the Panchal Chakravyuha was a mystery even to him.

"What is your strategy, Arjun?" asked Yudhistir.

"We will peel off each layer and clear it out before entering the next."

"So when we reach the core, only Shikhandini will be left, exposed and vulnerable," added Sahadev, the other twin.

"Yes, Sahadev, that is the plan."

"But Arjun, this will lead to many deaths," said Bheem, as he looked at the vast ocean of men in front of them.

"Yes, but we have no choice," replied Arjun.

"Bheem, we do not have to kill them all. Once Shikhandini realizes our plan, she will call off the formation to save the lives of her soldiers," said Yudhistir. Bheem nodded in understanding.

The five brothers moved in different directions, circling the vyuha. They fought every soldier in the outer layer, to the last man. Once they were sure the outer layer could not be reformed, they attacked the next one.

"What are they doing, Princess?" asked Brahmabrata feeling anxious.

"They are peeling off the layers" said Shikhandini calmly, her eyes focused at Arjun, cutting into the layers.

"We will lose all our men like this" said Bramhabrata. The panic in his voice was evident. "When they reach the core, not only will we be as exposed as them, we will be left with no men to fight" said Brahmabrata.

"We must call off the formation and exit the vyuha, Brahmabrata ji," said Shikhandini thoughtful.

"We will save hundreds of lives that way." Shikhandini knew the soldiers used to form the vyuha were the weakest of all and stood no chance against the Pandavas. If she waited for them at the core, she would end up sacrificing all their lives for no good.

Shikhandini asked Brahmabrata to announce their arrival outside the Vyuha. She knew that this decision would cause a huge dent to her image as the Senapathi. Some might even call her a coward for calling off the vyuha. But she knew that her decision would save thousands of lives.

With Brahmabrata's announcement, the Pandava brothers stopped their duels, waiting for Shikhandini to emerge. When she did, the Pandava brothers looked at her with admiration and respect. She was unfaltered in spite of what had happened.

When Shikhandini gave them a choice of choosing a weapon for the duels, the Pandavas decided to stick to their fortes. They knew that underestimating Shikhandini and her sword fighting skills would be a grave mistake. Shikhandini, who should have been worried, was actually happy that the Pandava brothers were ready to duel with her as an equal. Her being a woman did not seem to bother them or make them feel more powerful.

"My brothers, Nakul and Sahadev are swordsman. They are willing to duel with you" said Yudhistir. Shikhandini nodded in response.

"Brahmabhatta, our ex-commander is well versed in the mace" Shikhandini informed Bheem.

Soon the duels began. Both sides fought like true Kshatriya warriors, not breaking any of the war laws. Shikhandini dueled with Sahadev, while Nakul duelled with one of the other warriors in the Panchala Sena.

Two hours later, the Panchal Sena had lost the battle and the Pandavas had captured Drupada, King of Panchala. They invited their Guru to occupy the Panchal throne. They had cleared their Guru's debt by offering Panchala to their teacher as gurudakshina.

***

"Drupada, I have no desire to own your kingdom," said Dronacharya. He looked down at his helpless friend, kneeling in the dust, his hands tied behind his back, a prisoner. "My sole aim behind this battle was to make you realize that even the most powerful King can be defeated, not by a more powerful enemy, but by his own ego."

Behind him stood Shikhandini, tortured by guilt over her father's defeat and humiliation. He had entrusted the Panchala Sena to her, but she had failed him. Yet she had not been taken prisoner; it was against the Hastinapur code to hold a woman as a prisoner-of-war.

Bending down, Drona pulled Drupada to his feet. Holding him at shoulder length he said, "I do not seek to keep all Panchala for myself or my son. I know how much you have striven to make the kingdom what it is today. I do not wish to take it all from you, my friend."

Drupada looked up in surprise.

"My son Ashwathama will rule the northern part of Panchala. I leave the southern part to you. Kampilya will be your new capital. We will live in harmony. It will be a new beginning," Drona smiled.

"Why are you doing this? You won the kingdom in a fair fight."

"Yes, but Ashwathama wishes to return half your kingdom to you as a gesture of honour, good faith and friendship," replied Drona.

Ashwathama forced a smile to his face, wondering if his father would ever stop being emotional. He craved all Panchala and its prosperity for himself. But he did not dare go against his father's wishes.

Drupada, though burning with rage, knew he had no choice but to pretend to accept Drona's friendship. If he was to ever avenge this defeat, he had to remain King, even of a smaller kingdom. The two men, once boys together in the same gurukul, embraced. Behind them, the Pandava brothers stood smiling.

Witnessing the transference of half her homeland, Shikhandini watched dry-eyed, wondering what was really in her father's mind.

"Princess Shikhandini."

Shikhandini looked up to meet Arjun's eyes.

"You are a brave and mighty warrior. You defeated all my Kaurava brothers and skilfully led the Panchal Sena. I salute your courage."

"And I you, Prince," Shikhandini replied, bowing with folded hands.

***

A fortnight had passed since the Panchal defeat. King Drupada and the royal family had moved to Kampilya, the southern capital of Panchala. The defeat had taken a toll on Prishata, who had lived in anticipation of Shikhandini's victory, only to be faced with more humiliation. His health began to deteriorate as he refused to eat, waiting for death to claim him. He refused to look at Shikhandini.

"This would never have happened if you had given birth to a son," Drupada berated Kokila as they sat in her private chambers. Kokila remained silent. She had been relieved to know her daughter had been unharmed in battle. Victory or defeat meant nothing to her.

"My father was a fool to invest all his time and effort in training her. Look what happened!" Drupada said furiously. The news of Prishata's precarious condition had just been brought by the Vyeds, adding to Drupada's anger.

"My Lord, Shikhandini did her best. Do not forget she was the reason Panchala won on the first day," Kokila reminded her husband.

"But her best was not enough to bring us victory," he retorted. "No one cares how many Kuru Princes she defeated or how she did it. All that matters is who finally won the battle!"

Pausing outside Kokila's chambers, Shikhandini listened to her parents argue; her guilt and sadness knew no bounds. Ever since the defeat, no one at court had spoken to her, except her mother. She felt more alone than in all the years she had spent away from Panchala. She knew there was only one way to reduce the pain she had caused her family and Panchala. Now, as she heard her father's words of condemnation, she made up her mind.

***

"Shikha, do not leave! I have waited so long for you to come back. Do not go!" Kokila pleaded.

It was the final prahar when Shikhandini informed her parents of her decision to leave Panchala. Drupada, though surprised at first, seemed relieved by her decision. Her presence in Panchala could only add to her misery. Everyone looked at her with disgust and anger. She was made the sole of Panchala's defeat.

"Stop her, My Lord!" Kokila begged her husband, who seemed unmoved by Shikhandini's decision.

"Let her go, Kokila. It is for the best. The sooner she is out of everyone's sight, the quicker people will forget."

Drupada's words pierced Shikhandini's heart like quivering arrows. "You are right, father. I have caused enough pain to you and Pitamaha. I promise never to return to Panchala," she vowed.

"Shikhandini!" Kokila gasped as she realized what her daughter had said. She would never see her daughter again. Tears filled her eyes.

It pained Shikhandini to see her mother's sorrow, but she knew there was no other path. Folding her hands, she bowed to her parents one last time. For an instant, Shikhandini thought she saw sadness in her father's eyes, but he said nothing.

"Shikhandini, do not go…" Kokila begged.

Unable to look into her mother's pleading face, Shikhandini turned away. Forgetting royal etiquette, Kokila rushed after her daughter, trying to stop her. But Shikhandini had made up her mind. "Ma, please let me go. I cannot stay here any longer. Every minute reminds me of Panchala's defeat. Pitamaha hates me and his health worsens each day. I am the reason. I must leave," she said to her mother.

Kokila realized there was nothing she could do or say to stop her daughter. She stood still, watching Shikhandini mount her horse. Surya had been gifted to Shikhandini by her grandfather when she was just a little girl. The playful pony had become into a strong and beautiful mare. It was spotless white except for the small black patch on its forehead.

Without looking back, Shikhandini galloped away, leaving Panchala as quickly as she could.

10
A New Beginning

It was the beginning of the last prahar. Shikhandini felt exhausted in mind and body. She had been walking for several days now, with no destination in mind; her only thought to leave Panchala behind. Surya plodded beside her, equally exhausted. The horse had travelled hundreds of yojanas without rest. Shikhandini felt as brittle as an empty clay pot left out in the summer heat. Her life seemed to have no purpose. She had no family or friends outside Panchala, to whom she could go. She was helpless, lost and alone.

As she walked on, she found herself at the edge of a cliff, several hundred feet above the ground. Standing at the edge, she looked down. The darkness below looked calm and peaceful, almost welcoming. As she stared into the darkness, memories flashed into her mind – her childhood in Panchala, the fateful day she had laid hands on the garland of lotuses, that changed her life forever, the day she left Panchala for the first time, hoping to return soon, the years she spent with Dai Ma, the battle she had lost, losing everything with it, and finally the day she had left Panchala, vowing never to return.

She inched closer to the edge. Taking a deep breath, she closed her eyes. Tears streamed down her face as she recalled her mother…Dai Ma…Pitamaha…who had lavished their love on her. *A life without purpose is not worth living. A life without honour is worse than death*. She looked at her feet. Cowardice was not a Kshatriya trait but taking one's own life was against the laws of dharma

"Pranam," a voice said behind her, breaking her trance.

Turning around, she saw a young man, perhaps a little older than herself, standing with folded hands, waiting for her to respond to his greeting. Dark-skinned, he had large, deep-set eyes and a charismatic smile. He was lithe and wore a simple cotton dhoti and angavastram.

His dark shoulder length hair was left open to dance in the breeze. At his waist was a *bansuri,* tucked into his cloth belt.

"Pranam," Shikhandini said, her eyebrows scrunched together as she tried to recall if she had ever seen him before. He looked strangely familiar.

"No, you have not," he replied, as though reading her mind, "My name is Shyam. I live in the forest of Mandara, a few yojanas from here. And you are?"

Shikhandini wondered what he wanted from her. "I am Shikhandini," she said simply, giving no further details.

Sensing her discomfort, he changed the subject. "Where are you going to, Shikhandini?"

She found his presence intrusive. She wanted to be alone. She wanted to die, to be free. "Do you want something?" she asked.

"Yes, there is something I want from you," he replied, his eyes boring into hers, as though trying to read her thoughts. "You see, the forest gets darker and denser from here, but I must cross it to reach my relatives. Travelling alone without weapons is not wise. I am sure to be attacked by bandits, or wild animals who will make a feast of me. I could not help but notice how easily you slayed the wild boar a few yojanas behind us," he grinned.

Has he been following her? Shikhandini recalled the incident with wild boar. Having no choice but to protect herself, she had slayed it.

"I wonder if you would be kind enough to accompany me through the forest. I fear I lack your courage. I would be most grateful."

Helping those who sought your aid was an important tenant of dharma, so Shikhandini nodded. She could think of no reason to refuse him.

As they walked on, Shikhandini found herself falling behind. Shyam was a brisk walker. He took long strides, making full use of his tall lithe frame. His movements were casual and effortless. Shikhandini attempted to emulate his fluid movements and after a while, caught up with him. They walked in comfortable silence. Occasionally, Shikhandini stole a glance at Shyam. He was a stranger, yet he looked familiar, like a friend from another lifetime.

"That is the village of the Yakshas over there. They call it Yakshavana." Shyam pointed to a small settlement ahead of them.

"Yakshas?" Shikhandini had heard of them from Dai Ma, in her many stories in which Yaksha miracles had saved lives.

"Yakshas are forest dwellers," replied Shyam, glancing at her. "You must have heard of their magical and supernatural powers."

Many believed the Yakshas, popularly known as nature spirits, to be demi-Gods. Others said they were just mythical beings who did not exist. Yet others worshipped them in many forms, believing them to be gifted with supernatural powers that could both heal and destroy.

"They are nature-spirits," said Shikhandini.

"No, they are not. They are as human as you and I," Shyam said positively.

Characteristically, Shikhandini's eyebrows scrunched together as she waited for an explanation.

"What makes them special is their their lifestyle, vast knowledge, and passion for science, which is beyond the understanding of people in our advanced cities."

"Are you telling me that they perform miracles through science?"

"Could be. After all what is a miracle? Today's miracle is tomorrow's science."

"Hmmmm..."

"The reason something seems unimaginable to us is because the science behind it is still unknown to us. The Yakshas know more and can do marvellous things simply becaue they are better scientists."

"So you believe everything has a scientific explanation; that there is no God?"

Shyam smiled. "Ah...there is the question I had been waiting for. Of course, there is a God...the Divine. There has to be. But why think of God as a magician? Is it not possible that he is perhaps the greatest scientist of all? If God was a magician, why would he have started with a single cell and evolved humans over *yugas*? He could have simply performed a *yagya,* spoken a few mantras, and created a complete human in a day. But it has taken yugas to make this world; to stabilize and maintain the perfect balance in everything; to formulate the ecosystem; to create the food chain; the laws of nature. And we humans reduce it all to magic? God has left evidence of his experiments and inventions everywhere, for us to find, understand and appreciate – in the soil, the air and water – and greatest of all, the *panchabuta* in the human body."

Shikhandini nodded, spellbound by Shyam's wisdom.

"Do you know who the Yaksha tribe worships?" he asked.

Shikhandi shook her head. Dai Ma had never mentioned it.

"*Prakrati*. They are nature worshippers. They believe Mother Nature is the ultimate definition of Divinity."

As Shyam told her more about the Yaksha tribe and their way of life, Shikhandini wondered if this was where her path led. As though in a trance, she walked towards Yakshavana, Shyam's voice fading into the background. As she stood at the threshold of the first house in the village, she knew her life was taking a new turn. Instinctively, she turned towards Shyam, feeling the need for his reassurance. But she stood alone. There was no one no as far as the eyes could reach.

"Pranam *beti*," she heard a voice say from inside the hut.

A FEW MONTHS LATER

"Who is that, Hema?" asked Shikhandini of her friend.

Hema was a simple, good natured girl, the daughter of Sthunakarna, the benevolent leader of the Yaksha tribe, the one who had welcomed Shikhandini not only into his tribe, but his family, when she first entered Yakshavana. Over the past few months, Shikhandini had accepted the Yaksha tribe as her own family. She developed an affection for Hema, who soon became the little sister Shikhandini had always craved.

Hema looked up. "He is Prince Kush of Dasarna. He often visits us, to hunt in the forest. Isn't he handsome?" she giggled into her fist.

Shikhandini rolled her eyes. "Don't you have singing practice in a few minutes? Go, get ready!" She shooed Hema away.

"Yes, Didi!" Hema threw her an impish smile before going back into the house.

Shikhandini observed Kush with keen eyes. His lithe muscular body was clothed in a bright yellow angavastram and red dhoti. The modest turban on his head held his unruly hair in place. His skin was tanned and smooth, lined with battle scars. In his outstretched left hand he held a bow, while his right hand strained to hold the arrow in place against the tension of the string. Behind him stood his horse, watching him as closely as Shikhandini. The Prince looked battle ready, legs planted apart, back upright, and eyes focused. Closing his left eye, he pulled the arrow towards his face. The tautness of the bowstring made his biceps flex. His face was calm and revealing neither fear nor anticipation; his eyes remained fixed ton the target.

Shikhandini smiled appreciatively. Instinctively her eyes followed the direction of his outstretched arm. Oblivious to danger, a fawn stood grazing in the lush green grass beyond. The fawn moved a few steps and immediately the Prince made a slight adjustment to his shot. Taking a deep breath, he released the arrow.

Shikhandini's eyes flitted from the Prince to the hapless fawn. "No!" she yelled, rushing towards Kush.

The sudden distraction caused him to look away from his target. Kush knew without even looking that the arrow had missed. He cursed under his breath. Shikhandini, who had rushed to where he stood, now threw herself towards him. Unprepared, Kush lost his balance and came crashing down with her. Hearing the commotion, the fawn twitched its ears and galloped away.

"*What do you think you are doing*!" Kush yelled, rising to his feet. Looking down at his assailant, he felt his throat go dry. Speech and anger died in silence as he looked at Shikhandini. It was as though the world around him had ceased to exist. The moment he had been waiting for all his life had finally arrived. He stood mesmerized, finding it impossible to tear his gaze from her.

Brushing the dirt off herself, Shikhandini mumbled under her breath in annoyance. The fall had loosened the bun on the top of her head, causing her hair to fall free over her shoulders. Tiny beads of sweat had formed on her wheat coloured skin, like dew drops on a lotus. Her full lips were pulled into a thin line. Her doe-shaped eyes sparkled with anger.

"What do you think you were doing?" scolded Shikhandini, bringing the Prince out of his trance. "What were you thinking, trying to kill that helpless little creature?"

"I…was…" Kush stammered, like a boy on his first day at *gurukul*. The usually intolerant Prince suddenly found her anger amusing and tried hard not to grin.

"What do you have to say for yourself?" Shikhandini asked, her chin pointed at him.

"I…I..." Kush pulled himself together. Clearing his throat, he finally spoke. "I was hunting. It is a common sport. So what is wrong?"

"*What is wrong*!" Shikhandini struggled to control her temper. "Killing an innocent animal, that too a baby! You call that sport? Why not hunt down a lion or wild boar?" spat Shikhandini in disgust.

Before Kush could reply, they heard the sound of drums and conches coming towards them. Turning to look, they saw Sthunakarna and a group of tribal elders, walking towards them.

"Pranam, Prince Kush. It is good to see you back here after a long time," said Sthunakarna in greeting.

"Pranam Guruji." Kush bent to touch the tribal leader's feet.

"Ayushman Bhava, my son," Sthunakarna responded, his hand raised in blessing.

"So are you proposing to disappear once again without bidding us farewell, as you did last time, boy?" Yakshini, Sthunakarna's wife asked in mock anger, pulling his ear.

"Forgive me, Masi," Kush responded, instantly contrite. "I will never do so again, I promise!" From the corner of his eye he saw Shikhandini smirk.

Prince Kush, born in the kingdom of Dasharna, was the son of King Hiranyavarna, a mighty and ambitious King. Hiranyavarna's dream of making his son the greatest King of Aryavrath had led him to befriend Sthunakarna, the Yaksha leader. He, like so many city dwellers, believed the members of the Yaksha tribe were celestial beings in human form; that they possessed special powers and were, in many repects, equal to demi-gods. It was only after an introduction to their lifestyle, that he had realized how scientifically and technically advanced they were.

Hence, apart from his formal gurukul education, Prince Kush had also received lessons in unconventional warfare from the Yakshas. Hiranyavarna wished his son to imbibe the lifestyle, discipline, intellect and fearlessness that made the Yakshas invincible. But he also admired the Yakshas' docile nature; their simple yet intriguing way of life made them extraordinary. They were deadly warriors, passionate artists, charismatic lovers and influential leaders.

"Where is Hema?" asked Kush, looking around.

"At her music class; she will return by the end of the prahar. Meanwhile, Shikhandini, our other daughter, will keep you company. I assume you have already met," said Yakshini, gesturing for Shikhandini to come closer.

"That would be kind of her, Masi." Kush grinned, winking in Shikhandini's direction as the elders moved on.

Shikhandini groaned to herself. Now she would have to spend hours with this arrogant Prince.

"I have no excuse for what I was trying to do, but I promise I will not repeat the offence. No more hunting defenseless animals, I promise!" It was the first time the Prince had felt the need to apologize for his actions. He felt drawn to Shikhandini in a way he could not explain. From the moment she had rushed at him in passionate fury, he had known she was the one.

Shikhandini sighed. Somehow, it was hard to stay angry with him when he looked at her and smiled, his eyes alight with laughter.

"Friends?" Kush asked.

Shikhandini nodded, a furtive smile flickering over her lips. "By the way, you should know that fawn is Hema's favourite. She rescued it from a hunter's trap a couple of weeks ago. If something had happened to it, she would have killed you anyway."

"Oh?" Kush raised his eyebrows in amused hauteur.

"Don't worry, I will not tell her," Shikhandini chuckled.

"So how long have you been with Masi? Where are you from?" asked Kush as they walked towards the Yaksha temple at the far end of the forest. He wished to make his obeisance to the Goddess.

"I have been here for a few months. I come from the north. How about you?" Shikhandini prevaricated, not wanting Kush to know of her past. Only Sthunakarna, Yakshini and Hema knew about Panchala. They had agreed to keep her identity secret.

"I come from Dasarna. My father and Guruji are close friends. During my childhood, I spent all my summer holidays here. They are like a second family to me." Unlike Shikhandini, Kush had no reason to withhold information about who he was. His identity was as natural to him as the air he breathed.

"Now what was Guru Ma talking about? You ran off from here the last time? And why do you call her Masi?"

"Oh it's a long story." Kush scratched the back of his neck in embarrassment, recalling the incident. "It was my last summer here. I had just graduated from the Gurukul and could not wait to join father in running the kingdom. I had come here to seek Guruji and Masi's blessings before being invested as Yuvaraj and heir to the throne of Dasarna."

"What happened then?"

"My father decided it was best I was married before my investiture. Without my knowledge, he came to Yakshavana to ask for Hema's hand in marriage for me."

Shikhandini's brows shot up in surprise. Recalling Hema's excitement at seeing Kush, she wondered if Hema knew about this.

"I was young and naïve. I did not know how to say no to my elders. But I was certain I did not wish to marry so early."

"So you vanished from here?" asked Shikhandini, laughing.

"Yes. I did not know what else to do!" He smiled sheepishly.

As the temple came into view, Shikhandini asked, "And Masi? Why do you call her that?"

"Well, I first met Masi fifteen years ago, on my first summer break from the Gurukul at Dasarna. My mother died giving birth to me and all the mother's love I knew came from my wet nurses. But when I came here, Masi enveloped me in her unconditional love and care. I grew to love her like a mother."

"I do understand that. Guru Ma is the embodiment of motherly love and caring. Not only the Yaksha children, but others who visit us, develop an inseparable bond with her. When I came to Yakshavana, it was she who made me feel that I belonged here. She often says that all the students in the Gurukul are her own children."

Kush smiled at Shikhandini's words. It was the most she had said since they met.

"What?" Shikhandini asked, lifting her chin self-consciously as he continued to smile down at her.

Kush shook his head and looked away. "Tell me, do you believe in Goddess Prakruti? Do you visit the temple?"

"Ummm…no."

"Never?" Kush looked surprised. "You mean you have never been to the temple in all the time you have lived here?"

"No." Shikhandini recalled the day Yakshini had suggested a vist to Goddess Prakruti temple. Shikhandini had turned away saying she had no faith in any God. Since then no one had spoken to her about going to the temple. But today, as Prince Kush was their guest, she could not refuse to accompany him.

"So you have no faith in God?" asked Kush.

Shikhandini did not answer. 'If you were in my place, you would have lost faith in everything too,' she wanted to say.

By now Kush had realized there was far more to Shikhandini than met the eye. She did not wish to speak of her home or her purpose in living with the Yakshas. Her appearance and persona were that of a Princess, yet her physique was neither delicate nor fragile. Her shoulders were broad, her skin tanned; she bore scars on her forearms, and had a noticeable cut on her chin. She had a faraway look on her face, her eyes gazing at something no one else could see. She was a mystery, an enigma that drew him to her. He craved to know everything about her.

"When was the last time you visited the temple? You seem quite excited to be here," Shikhandini remarked after a while.

"Oh, I am, my friend! Soon you will know why."

When they reached the temple, Kush could not help but grin at Shikhandini's expression of wide-eyed surprise. She stood with her mouth slightly ajar, breath held unknowingly. It reminded him of the first time he had visited the temple.

"This place is beautiful!" she whispered, her eyes scanning the place.

The temple was a modest structure built from a single rock. A short flight of steps, carved into the stone, led to the entrance, lined with a row of nine stone pillars on either side. Each pillar had a flowering creeper wound round it, their fragrance spreading through the temple, permeating the senses. Unlike most temples, this one did not have a *gopura* or tower on top. Instead, the entire structure was covered with natural flora that grew within the surface cracks.

"Wait till you get inside," said Kush, leading the way.

The entrance to the inner *garbhagraha* or sanctum sanctorum, was akin to entering a cave. One had to crouch to enter, head lowered per force in humility. Inside, it was cool, the scorching heat outside just a memory. The soothing sound of flowing water was the only sound.

Shikhandini and Kush waited for their eyes to adjust to the dimness. A single lamp stood in the centre of the shrine.

"The Yakshas take turns to ensure the lamp burns continuously, day and night," Kush told her.

Shikhandini nodded. She already knew this since every alternate fortnight it was her family's turn to watch the lamp. She never volunteered, and the Yakshas, as was their way, did not push her. Now, in the light of the lamp, Shikhandini gazed at the idol of Goddess Prakrati, clothed in a simple cotton sari, like the Yaksha women wore. The deity's jewellery was made of fresh flowers and leaves and on her head she wore a crown of forest flowers, beautifully woven together. A gentle smile graced her face and her eyes closed as she sat in *Padmasana*. Just gazing up at the serene figure brought peace to Shikhandi's mind; a sense of calm that she had lost the day her father was taken before Dronacharya, a prisoner of war.

"You know, I am not religious either. I do believe in the existence of God and his powers, but I am not sure of the practices people follow to please him. But this place is different. I find peace here. During my stay with the Yakshas, whenever I felt disturbed or sad, I would visit this temple and sit in silence, watching the flicker of the lamp. After a while I would find my emotions had subsided. It was like meditation," Kush explained.

They too, like the Goddess, sat in *Padmasana* and closed their eyes. They sat in silence. Time ceased to matter.

"Shikhandini, it is getting dark, we better go."

Kush's voice brought Shikhandini back from her trance. Opening her eyes, she felt calm and refreshed, as though she had woken from a deep sleep.

"So…" Kush began, as they walked away from the temple.

"I think I would like to visit her more often," Shikhandini replied quietly, sensing Kush's question.

11
Prince Kush

In the next few weeks, Shikhandini and Kush spent long hours together. They visited Goddess Prakruti every week. On other days, they practised archery and sword-fighting. Shikhandini helped Kush enhance his swordsmanship, and Kush, the science enthusiast that he was, shared his knowledge of the ancient scriptures and the encrypted scientific information they contained. They hotly debated topics of philosophy, theology and medicine. Each day their bond grew a little stronger.

And each day Kush learnt at least one more thing about her. He knew he would soon have to leave the Yaksha village. His father would send for him. But he knew with utter certitude that Shikhandini was his soulmate, and would be the Queen of Dasarna one day. All he had to do was ask Sthunakarna for her hand, but before that he wanted to be sure she shared his feelings.

Shikhandini, on the other hand, did her utmost to suppress the emotions he awoke in her. Having practically lost everyone she had ever loved, she had no faith left in anything. But deep within her, she knew that if she ever decided to accept someone as her life partner, it would be Kush. He made her feel accepted and loved. He respected her for what she was. But she was afraid of her own emotions.

"Didi, is there something you should be sharing with your little sister?" Hema asked, biting back a smile as she watched Shikhandini gazing out of the window, lost in her own thoughts.

"Hmm?" Shikhandini replied absentmindedly, staring at the setting sun. The sky was burnished with gold and the chirping of birds filled the air as they returned to their nests.

"Didi!" Hema poked Shikhandini in the side.

"What is it, Hema?" Shikhandini asked, irritated by her impish sister.

"I asked if there was something you should be telling me?" Hema grinned.

Shikhandini looked at her, puzzled.

"About Prince Kush perhaps?"

"What about him?" A slight flush appeared on Shikhandini's cheeks.

"Oh Didi! Everyone is talking about you two."

"We are good friends, Hema. That is all. There is nothing to tell."

"I have known Kush for as long as I can remember. I can tell what is going on in his head without even looking at him. He likes you. And if I know him, he has already planned on how to ask for your hand," Hema replied, a rather wistful smile on her lips.

"Hema, do not say such things. It is not true!"

"Didi, I know what you are thinking. I will not lie... I like Kush. I have for as long as I can remember. But he does not share the same feelings for me. I have seen the way he looks at you. It is the look I craved from him for so long. Didi, I will learn to overcome it. Do not do this to him because of me," Hema pleaded, her eyes glistening with unshed tears.

Shikhandini rushed to enfold her in an embrace. "Hema, it is not only because of you that I must deny this relationship."

"Then what is it, Didi?" asked Hema, sitting down beside her sister.

"Hema, you know I have lost everyone I have ever loved. Now all I have is this village and its people. I am happy here. I am happy being Kush's friend. I do not want to lose that too. Who knows what might change if he learns about my past?"

"Didi…"

"No, Hema. I do not wish to talk about it anymore." Shikhandini's voice was more stern than she intended.

"I am sorry, Didi. I understand…" Hema replied softly. Rising, she walked out of the room.

As Shikhandini watched the last rays of the sun get engulfed in the darkness of night, she wondered if she was being unfair to Kush, and to herself. 'Maybe I deserve to be happy. Maybe he is the way to joy,' she thought wanly.

***

It was another hot summer's day in Yakshavana. Shikhandini and Kush were walking back from the temple when they heard footsteps behind them. Kush was the first to sense an attack.

"Shikha, move!" he yelled urgently.

They heard the twang of a bow-string followed by the *whoosh* of an arrow. It missed Shikhandini by a hair. Instinctively, her hand moved to the sword at her waist. Lightening fast, Kush strung his bow, ready to rain arrows on the attacker. He scanned the forest for any unusual movement but there was only silence.

Then Shikhandini pointed to a flitting shadow among the trees. "There!"

Twang! Another arrow was shot in their direction but it did not come from the direction they were looking.

"There are many of them," Kush said softly.

Before Shikhandini could reply, four men rushed into the clearing. They were dressed in white dhotis, now brown with mud, and red angavasthrams. Their upper bodies were shielded with animal skin. They looked identical with red turbans, tilaks on their foreheads, thick bands on their right wrists, and waistbands with weapons tucked into them. The four men began to move in different directions, forming a trap around Shikhandini and Kush.

"Who are you?" Kush demanded, stepping in front of Shikhandini.

The men did not answer. Instead, they charged towards Shikhandini from all directions, their swords drawn. Shikhandini and Kush instinctively drew their own swords and stood with their backs to each other, in a defensive position.

Shikhandini dodged the first blow from one of the two shorter men before viciously cutting through the man's biceps. The man yelped in pain but recovered. Powered by rage he began slashing at Shikhandini. She was a far superior fighter with swords than he, and used her skill to make smooth calculated attacks. The man, twice her size and much stronger, soon had two deep cuts across his torso.

Meanwhile, Kush duelled the other shorter man, enthusiastically flaunting his newly acquired techniques.

Somewhere behind them, in the shade of a tree, bloodshot eyes watched. "I want her alive," he had earlier told his men in no uncertain terms. They knew he meant what he said. The girl would have to be taken alive.

Shikhandini finished her opponent with one final blow across his throat. The remaining two men attacked Shikhandini from either side. Picking up the dead man's sword from the ground, Shikhandini began to fight, a sword in each hand, as she had been taught. Her grandfather had told her that she was one of those rare swordsmen who could use two swords simultaneously with equal effect. This surprised her attackers now, who had not expected a woman to be such an exceptional swordsman. Shikhandini pushed on, trying not to inflict any killing blows on her opponents; she had already killed one in the heat of the moment.

Kush, on the other hand, had no such compunctions. He attacked his opponent brutally, finishing him off with a final stab to the stomach. Pulling his gory sword out, he ran to Shikhandini's aid.

The two duels went on for several minutes. Feigning a foolish move, Kush made a low thrust at his opponent. Shikhandini cursed under her breath; she knew what he was doing. The attacker, on the other hand, seized the opportunity to make a killer thrust. With his swordarm outstretched, the attacker leapt towards Kush. At the last moment, Kush spun away. He had spent dogged hours mastering the technique. The sword swished viciously through the air, meeting no flesh. Shifting his weight onto his right foot, Kush swung round in a lightening fast arc and beheaded his opponent.

Shikhandini's opponent had no choice but to surrender, and dropped to his knees.

"Who arc you?" Kush growled, pressing the tip of his sword to the man's neck. The man said nothing.

"Who sent you here?" Shikhandini asked, her face flushed, her breathing ragged.

"Tell me before I decide to behead you!" Kush threatened, pressing the sword till it broke the skin and blood stained the blade.

Before Shikhandini or Kush could question him further, the man pulled a small knife from his waistband and in a split second slit his throat. Blood pooled on the ground as he slowly collapsed.

"No!" Shikhandini shouted, but it was already too late.

Kush drew in a sharp breath. "We have to take him into the village. Maybe someone there will be able to tell us more about this attack."

Shikhandini crouched low to remove the man's wristband. "I think I know who they were," she said, unable to tear her gaze from the man.

Behind them, the dark figure smiled, retreating into the thick forest.

"You know? Who were they?"

"Durmukha's men. They are forest bandits. They moved here a few months ago," she replied, still examining the attacker's corpse.

"But why would they attack us? We had nothing to interest them."

"It was not to rob us. It was to threaten Guruji," she informed Kush.

"Guruji?" Kush was surprised.

"Durmukha and his men moved here in search of something. I only know it has something to do with Guruji and Yakshavana. Initially, they tried befriending the Yakshas. They often visited the village to talk to Guruji. The discussions would go on for a while; then Durmukha would return to the forest, disappointed. The last meeting turned violent. Durmukha threatened to kill Hema if he did not get what he wanted. Guruji, lost his temper and raised his weapon against Durmukha. Needless to say, the whole of Yakshasena was armed and ready for combat within seconds. Durmukha and his men were outnumbered and had to leave."

"Have you spoken to Guruji about it?" Kush asked, his brow furrowed in thought.

"No. He was most upset and did not wish to speak. But the last meeting was more than two months ago. We have not heard from Durmukha since then," Shikhandini replied.

"Well we will have to talk to him now," Kush said grimly.

***

"That scoundrel!" Stunakarna cursed under his breath.

Shikhandini had showed him the wristband she had taken from one of the attackers. It was made of animal skin, embossed with the symbol of an elephant with two crossed swords on its torso – the symbol of strength and valour.

"Are you hurt, my children?" Yakshini asked, her voice heavy with concern.

"No, Guru Ma, we are unharmed," Shikhandini assured her.

"But why would the bandits attack you? What did they want?" asked Hema, confused.

Yakshini looked at her husband and gave a small nod. She knew they had to know the truth.

Sthunakarna sighed, shaking his head before replying. "Remember the *Yaksha Ayuralaya*, Kush?"

"I do, Guruji"

"I think it is time for us to make a visit there."

The Yaksha Ayuralaya, as the name suggested, was a medical facility where groundbreaking medical research took place. It was also the repository of potions and herbal medicines. The Yakshas were known for their ability to cure the deadliest diseases. The Ayuralaya was housed in an underground cave, which helped minimize the influence of environmental changes on the medicines. Only a team of experts, and the leader of the tribe, had access to the cave.

Shikhandini, Kush and Hema followed Sthunakarna out of the village. Behind them, two guards walked in silence. The group walked for an hour and a half before they finally reached the spot.

"I am exhausted!" complained Hema, sitting down heavily on a rock. How far do we have to walk?"

"We are here child," Sthunakarna replied quietly.

Shikhandini and Kush looked around confused. There was nothing there. The place looked just like the rest of the forest; tall trees forming a canopy, the sun rays filtering through them to form patterns on the ground covered with weeds, and some large rocks.

Sthunakarna chuckled, amused by their bewilderment. "Here," he said, pointing to the ground. He signalled to the guards to move the carpet of moss and grass weeds. Hidden below, was a small wooden door, similar to the trap doors used to catch wild animals without killing them. Sthunakarna crouched down and lifted the door; inside, it was pitch dark.

Hema came forward to take a peek. She looked at Shikhandini, her brows raised in enquiry. Kush merely shrugged in response. He had no explanation.

"Do not worry, it is safe. I will go first, then you children can follow."

Sthunakarna descended slowly through the door. Having done it many times before, he seemed to know his way in the dark. Once inside, he lit a small oil lamp.

As Shikhandini, Hema and Kush cautiously followed him into the cave, they realized that the steps they went down were solid, and not the rope ladder they had been expecting.

"Well, your suspicion is justified," Sthunakarna said, "we *do* have something Durmukha is desperate for. It is a potion, a herbal tonic that can change his life,"

"You mean a medicine?" Shikhandini asked.

"Yes and no. Yes, because when administered in the right quantity in the right situation, it can save a person's life. It has the power to rebuild a person's immune system and give him a second life in fatal situations. If taken in large quantities, it can increase one's strength a hundred fold."

"So that is why Durmukha wants it so desperately! For himself and his men, so they can rule the forest and torment nearby villagers," Hema said in disgust.

"Yes, but it is not the only reason we are reluctant to give it to him."

"Then why?" Shikhandini wanted to know.

"The tonic is very unstable. It works differently in different cases. We have not yet begun using it on humans. We recently administered a small dosage to an ox with a fatal infection, in an attempt to save it. A few days later, we found it dead near the lake outside the village. From the postmortem study, we realized the medicine had many after-effects. The tonic has to be administered periodically, reducing the dosage each time, before finally discontinuing it. Once stopped, strength and immunity return back to the original level."

"But how did the ox die?" Kush asked.

"After we administered the first dose, it broke free from its shackles, having gained renewed vigour. It began to destroy everything around it. It even killed some of its predators, which in normal circumstances would have been impossible."

"It must have been the same ox that killed an entire pride of lions a few days ago!" Shikhandini gasped.

Sthunakarna nodded. "Once the effect of the tonic dissipates, a second dose has to be administered. When the immune system is undergoing such abrupt uncalled-for changes, the body becomes weak and prone to infections. Even something as trivial as a cold can be fatal."

"Can we not explain this to Durmukha?" Kush suggested.

Sthunakarna shook his head. "Some people do not have the ears to listen. I have tried to tell him but he does not believe us. He thinks we merely wish to withhold the potion from him."

"This potion, how is it prepared, Guruji? What is it made of?" asked Shikhandini curiously. It was a thing beyond her imagination.

"As you know, every year a group of Yakshas go on an expedition to the Himalayas. They gather rare herbs and flowering plants from the snowy mountains and study their behaviour and characteristics. Once they return, we perform experiments on these plants to understand their medicinal values. Most of these plants have remained a mystery to us over the years. A few herbs which seemed to have almost magical powers of healing wounds or curing diseases in the mountains, have proved useless here. Their nature and characteristics undergo changes when they are separated from their natural environment, which is to be expected."

"We have been working on simulating the environmental conditions needed for the growth of these plants here, but have been mostly unsuccessful. But last year the men returned with a rare plant which had not died or dried out despite the drastic change in surroundings. After a thorough examination of the plant and hundreds of experiments, we finally realized this plant was, in fact, not unknown. It had been discovered yugas ago, and had saved the life of an important warrior of the time," Sthunakarna explained as he walked into the laboratory of the Ayuralaya, Shikhandini, Hema and Kush behind him.

"Who found it?" asked Kush, his curiosity aroused.

The laboratory was a well-lit place. The walls were painted with white chalk pigment and had detailed paintings of rare flowering plants and trees. On a raised platform stood clay pots of unusual shapes and sizes, carrying fuming liquids. Wooden shelves covered one side of the laboratory, filled with hundreds of palm leaf manuscripts. There were also a few men in the cave, engrossed in their work. They stopped momentarily to acknowledge their leader's presence before returning to their tasks.

Shuthankarna turned to answer Kush's question. "The one who found it was Maruti," he said, a small smile playing on his lips at the amazed expressions on their faces.

"Lord Hanuman?" asked Shikhandini, eyes wide.

"The *Sanjeevni*!" Kush gasped.

"You found the Sanjeevni?" asked Hema, excitement and disbelief chasing each other over her expressive face.

"Well, technically he did." Sthunakarna pointed to a young man engaged in his palm leaf book at the far end of the laboratory.

Upon hearing his Guru call, the youth looked up rather reluctantly and came towards them. He was only a little older than Shikhandini, and wore a simple sky-coloured dhoti and white angavastram, as the others in the Ayuralaya did. A long tilak of sandalwood paste extended from between his eyebrows to his clean shaven scalp.

"Pranam," he said, bowing with folded hands.

"Pashupati!" Shikhandini whispered in astonishment. "But you..."

"I am not a ghost, Shikhandini. I am very much alive!" Pashupati's eyes sparkled with amusement.

Pashupati was a student at the Yaksha Gurukul. Shikhandini had spoken to him a few times when she had visited the gurukul.

"But you died in the pilgrimage tour! You were killed by a mountain lion," Hema said, as astonished as her sister.

"That is quite true," Sthunakarna responded.

"Guruji, if not for you, I would have been dead by now."

"It was not I, my son, but the Sanjeevni that saved your life."

Shikhandini noticed that Sthunakarna spoke of the Sanjeevni as if it was a living Divinity; a goddess who had the power to save lives, like the holy river Ganga.

"Pashupati, by circumstance, became our first human experimental subject. When he was attacked by a mountain lion on the expedition to find medicinal herbs, he lost a lot of blood and was near death. It was near the end of the expedition when most of the study on the Sanjeevni had been done. It was immediately crushed and administered to Pashupathi, and miraculously, his life was saved."

“So you are a hundred times stronger than before?” Hema asked.

Pashupathi grinned. “Certainly not! In fact, my regular dosage of the tonic was stopped a few days ago. We now know how to use the tonic to cure the body by restoring the immune system. But we are still suspicious about its ability to boost a person’s strength.”

“Father, do you think Durmukha will attack us again?” asked Hema apprehensively. If the potion was indeed so powerful, who could resist it?

“I will be surprised if he does not,” Sthunakarna said honestly.

“But how does he know about the Sanjeevni?” Shikhandini enquired.

“That, my child, is a mystery to all of us,” Sthunakarna replied.

12
THE BANDIT

HASTINAPUR

A week after Yudhistir's *Rajyabhishek*, the investiture of the eldest Kuru Prince as the future King, Purochan, a well-known architect, visited Hastinapur.

"Pranam, Maharani. Pranam, Yuvraj," he said in greeting, bowing before Kunti and Yudhistir with hands folded.

The news of Yudhistir's investiture as Heir Apparent had travelled the length and breadth of Aryavrath. Every day, well-wishers from near and far visited the royal family.

"Pranam, Purochan Ji," replied Kunti, while Yudhistir merely smiled with folded hands. They were seated in a verandah abutting Kunti's chambers in the palace.

"What brings you here, Purochan Ji?" asked Kunti, signalling her maids to bring in some tender coconut and sweets for the guests.

"I have a request, Maharani," he told her. When she nodded, he proceeded, saying, "Every year, Maharaja Pandeshwar used to spend a few days in Varnavrata. He loved to hunt in the forests there, which are richly blessed with greenery and wildlife. I personally looked after his needs and he was always welcomed with great joy and pomp by my people. His untimely death has left a gaping hole in their hearts. In his memory, I have personally designed a palace, keeping in mind his exquisite taste. It makes me sad to think he will never see it."

A tear escaped Kunti's eyes as memories of her husband's death came rushing back to fill her mind. Seeing this, Yudhistir placed a hand on her shoulder in a comforting gesture.

"If it is not too much to ask, I humbly request that you and your sons visit the palace and spend a few days there. It would perhaps bring you peace, as well as joy to the local people," Purochan said.

Kunti, despite Purochana's emotional words, was a rational thinker. She considered his request for a while and then replied, "I am most touched by your devotion to my husband, Purochan ji. It would have been a great pleasure to visit the palace with my sons."

Purochan smiled in anticipation.

"However, it is perhaps not the right time. Following Yudhistir's Rajyabhishek, much responsibility has been placed on his young shoulders. My other sons too, are busy helping their elder brother in his tasks. Being away from Hastinapur at this juncture would not be a wise choice. I will, however, discuss this with everyone before I give you my decision, Purochan Ji,"

Purochan looked at Kunti, and then at Yudhistir, in disappointment.

"Consider the decision made, Mata," said Yudhistir, smiling reassuringly at Purochan. "What can be more important than bringing peace and happiness to my father's spirit? We shall leave for Varnavrata a fortnight from today."

Kunti smiled at Yudhistir's decision but her eyes betrayed the scepticism that had taken birth in her mind.

"I will make arrangements so everything goes smoothly in our absence. We can resume the affairs of State once we return from Varnavrata," Yudhistir assured her.

But they would not return to Hastinapur for a very long time.

***

Shikhandini woke with a start as she sensed danger. As though on cue, the sound of footsteps came in her ears. She looked around to find Hema sleeping peacefully. Quietly, she tiptoed out of the house, tucking her swords into her waistband. To her surprise, she found Sthunakarna and Yakshini already outside. A few of the Yaksha soldiers were also there, with weapons drawn. Kush rushed onto the scene, his bow upraised.

"We heard it too..." whispered Yakshini.

Before she could finish her words, a rain of arrows poured down on them from all sides. Instinctively, Yakshini blew the conch, alerting the entire village. Within minutes, the efficient and fierce Yakshasena were battle ready.

"Father, waging war after sunset is against the laws," declared Shikhandini, annoyed by this blatant breach of the warrior code.

"It is Durmukha. He and his men are bandits. They follow no rules," replied Sthunakarna, turning to give orders to his men.

The Yakshas always fought battles based on the opponent's nature. They followed no hard and fast rules. This made them fierce and brutal warriors. They followed the codes of war only when their opponent too, was ready to abide by them. Today, they were fighting bandits, who did not follow any laws, social or military. The Yakshas knew that following the rules would only lead to their own doom.

"We need to divide our men to cover all directions. Any idea how many they could be?" asked Kush.

"Durmukha's force is less than half the Yakshasena. But only a fool would underestimate them. They fight like animals; they attack to kill; they follow no laws of warfare; and their only principle is to stay alive," Sthunakarna replied sharply.

Meanwhile, Yakshini had taken charge of safeguarding the women and children of the village. Hema helped her gather the children and usher them into the leader's house. A few women, who were a part of the Yakshasena, stood with the men. While they waited, a fresh downpour of arrows showered down on the Yakshasena.

"Shields up!" Shikhandini yelled.

The Yakshasena, which had engaged with Shikhandini in the last few months during mock battles and practice sessions, trusted her.

"It is impossible to fight them in the dark," observed Kush.

"Use your ears. Listen for the direction of the arrows. We need complete silence for that," said Shikhandini.

Everyone waited in silence for the next attack. Another hail of arrows came down on them.

"This way!" Shikhandini yelled, rushing in the direction of the attack. One third of the Yakshasena disappeared behind her into the dark.

Hearing the rustling of dried leaves on the forest floor, Kush, with another third of the Yakshasena, disappeared into the forest.

The remaining Yakshasena, under Sthunakarna, remained in the village, to ward off attack. Time passed in tense silence.

"For the most intelligent humans in Aryavrath, you are not that smart, are you?" a familiar voice echoed through the village as Durmukha and his men finally made an appearance.

Sthunakarna stood stunned. Durmukha's force had tripled in size to match the Yakshasena. He had gathered bandits from the nearby forests and built an army of his own. But, at that moment, just one-third of the Yakshasena was available to counter the bandit's attack. Durmukha had cunningly laid a trap.

Sthunakarna signalled for the conch to be blown, this time in short bursts, with pauses between. It was the call for help. The sound resonated for several yojanas, reaching deep into the forest.

"What do you want, you coward?" spat Sthunakarna. He hoped to buy time by engaging Durmukha in conversation until Shikhandini and Kush returned with the rest of the Sena.

"You know what I want, O Yaksha! Give me the Sanjeevni."

"I have told you before. It will not help you as much as the damage it will cause."

"Liar! Give your made up tales to the bards to sing! Do not tell me fictitious stories about the Sanjeevni. I know its powers. Give it to me now, or watch your village burn to ashes," Durmukha replied, signalling to his men.

Four men rolled barrels containing an oily solution towards the village, one in each direction. The plan was to trace the perimeter of Yakshavana with this highly inflammable liquid and set it on fire. Within minutes, everything and everyone within the village would be burnt. This was Durmukha's last resort in case Sthunakarna refused to budge.

"If you burn down the village, the Sanjeevni will also perish with us." It was Kush. Stunakarna sighed with relief.

Durmukha and his men turned to face Kush and his section of the Yakshasena. "The Yakshas are not so foolish, boy! They would never hide the Sanjeevni where it can be easily found by anyone," Durmukha retorted.

"That may be true, but if you kill us all, you will never know where it is." Shikhandini had returned with the last of the Yakshasena.

"That is why, my dear, we plan on saving you for last. It will be quite entertaining to get the secret out of you." Durmukha eyeing Shikhandini from head to toe while his men roared with laughter.

"Mind your tongue, you bastard!" roared Kush, pulling out his sword like a flash of lightening.

"Kush, stop!" yelled Shikhandini.

But it was too late. Sthunakarna and his men charged towards Durmukha's army. The atmosphere became charged with violence as men on both sides fought like savages. Durmukha's bandits attacked the Yakshasena. As a counter, the Yakshas attacked in groups. All rules of warfare were forgotten. Both sides fought like mad animals, thirsty for blood.

Some of Durmukha's men escaped the Yakshasena to get to the women and children. To their dismay, the women were armed with knives and sickles, waiting for them. None of Durmukha's men returned alive.

When Durmukha realized he was going to be defeated and killed, he gave the signal. A ring of fire sprang up around the village, trapping men, women and children, as Durmukha stared at Sthunakarna, mockingly. Fire broke out like a bird escaping its cage for the first time. The flames rose high above the ground, tearing apart the dark curtain of night. The entire village now stood within the ring of fire, which kept closing in on them. Durmukha and his remaining men watched gleefully as the village slowly burned.

'I cannot let them get away!' Shikhandini told herself. 'This village is all I have left to call my own. I cannot let it die!' She gave one sharp whistle, and Surya, her horse, galloped through the chaos, towards her neighing. She knew the commotion and fire must have frightened the poor beast. She spoke soothingly into its ear. Hopping onto its back, she directed it towards a narrow path, where the flames were closer to the ground. In one long leap, Shikhandini and her horse were out of the ring of fire. Durmukha and his men watched in awe.

Climbing down from the horse, she walked towards the enemy. Drawing both her swords, she moved towards Durmukha. In that moment Durmukha could see death approaching. Swords in hand, Shikhandi swung the blades in deadly circles. It was enough to chill the enemy. Her eyes glistened with fury. Durmukha had tried to burn down her village and he would now face her warth.

Two of Durmukha's men charged towards her, their swords held high. But they never got a chance to strike. Shikhandini crossed her swords and in one smooth motion, finished them both. It was now a duel between the uncouth bandit and the Warrior Princess.

Durmukha had heard of Shikhandini's mastery with weapons and her fighting skill. He knew his only advantage was physical strength. He was twice her size but no match for her with weapons. He was not a trained warrior; he had only learnt enough to kill unarmed travellers in the forest. Shikhandini, on the other hand, had trained for years under masters, and fought real battles. She was second to none when it came to sword fighting. Durmukha had invited his own death by setting Yakshavana ablaze.

Durmukha successfully countered Shikhandini's first blow. The two swords clinked together, glistening in the reflected brightness of the flames. Shikhandini held her left arm low, waiting for the right moment. While Durmukha concentrated on countering the blows on his left, Shikhandini used her left arm to tear a deep gash in his armour. Durmukha moved back a few steps, stumbling. He rushed in, aiming for her thighs. Shikhandini countered his blade, making sure she did not strike him below the waist. She was a Kshatriya and under no circumstances would she disregard the laws of warfare. Durmukha saw this and swung lower, seeing it as her weakness.

Shihkandini observed that Durmukha, though powerful, was not trained. He had spent all his energy in the first few blows and was now gasping for breath. It was her chance to attack. She lifted her right arm, aiming at his left. Durmukha immediately shifted his shield to his left to counter the attack, leaving the right side of his torso unprotected. He saw Shikhandini, lift her left arm and yelled. But it was already too late.

Shikhandini's sword sliced through his right arm, separating it cleanly from his body. Durmukha roared in pain as blood stained the ground at his feet. Dropping to his knees, he growled in pain and agony. Shikhandini watched in silence. She did not want to attack him. He had learnt his lesson. She turned back towards the village.

Suddenly a sharp pain shot up her spine like a jolt of lightening. Reaching round, she found a knife had pierced her armour. Turning, she saw Durmukha back on his feet, eyes ablaze, his face a macabre mask. Once again he had violated the rules of battle by attacking the enemy from the back.

Shikhandini walked back towards him, trying not to give in to the pain racing up and down her spine. Her blood boiled with rage as she saw his mocking grin. She showed no mercy this time. She leapt towards Durmukha and in a single blow, separated his head from his shoulders. His body collapsed to the ground, forming a pool of blood while his head rolled away. Shikhandini closed her eyes and silently prayed for the departed soul of her opponent.

Meanwhile, Kush and Sthunakarna, with the Yakshasena, had finished the bandits within the village.

"We must put out the fire as quickly as we can," said Kush, looking around.

Men, women and children began drawing water from the wells and ponds. Clay pots filled with water were passed from person to person. Every last person capable of doing so, fought the flames. At last the fire began to slowly hiss and die. But the damage had been done. More than half the village was the smell of burned bodies of the men who had died fighting on both sides, filled the air. Smoke lay like a hazy miasma over the village. The trees had been charred to death and the land looked like it would never bear anything again.

Yakshavana was irreversibly destroyed.

A FEW MONTHS AFTER THE BATTLE

Yakshavana rose like a phoenix from the ashes. Every person in the village toiled day and night to rebuild the settlement. New houses were built, new clearings made in the forest as fields for crops, and the gravely injured were moved to the Ayuralaya. Slowly, life returned to normal.

Kush had been sent for by his father, but had postponed his return due to the destruction of Yakshavana. He worked alongside the Yakshas to rebuild their homes. Finally, he decided it was time to ask for Shikhandini's hand, confident the feelings were mutual. He went to see Sthunakarna.

"The decision is her's alone, Kush. As you know, we Yakshas believe in free will. You are a royal, but you have always been there with us in our hard times. Any girl would be fortunate to have you as her husband. But the decision is not ours to make," Sthunakarna said.

Kush nodded. He had come to inform Sthunakarna and Yakshini that he would be leaving for Dasarna the next day, and to ask for Shikhandini's hand.

"I think you should be sure of what she wants before taking the next step," suggested Yakshini, secretly sceptical that Shikhandini would agree to marry. She wondered if Shikhandini knew about Hema's feelings for Kush.

"I will, Masi, even though I am sure her answer will be yes," Kush replied confidently.

A shadow crossed Yaskshini's face as she looked at him lovingly. No mother could protect her young forever. It was the law of life.

***

"Shikha, I must return home soon," Kush said as they walked in the forests outside Yakshavana, heading towards the lake where they usually discussed different subjects and shared knowledge. Today, however, the reason for asking Shikhandini to accompany him was different.

Shikhandini looked at him sideways, uncertain what to say. She did not want him to leave but she knew that asking him to stay would not be right. They walked on in silence, each lost in their own thoughts. Once they reached the lake, Shikhandini sank down at their usual spot and waited for Kush to speak. Although she knew what he wanted to say, she prayed he would not.

"Shikha, there is something I must ask you. You probably know already, just as I know what your answer is going to be. But I thought I should ask you anyway," Kush said with a smile.

When Shikhandini did not respond, he continued, "I want you to come to Dasarna with me." His eyes scanned her face. "As my wife."

Shikhandini looked at him, her face stoical. She was not surprised; she knew he loved her. But now that the moment had come, she did not know how to respond. It pained her to hurt him.

"Marry me, Shikha!" Kush said, looking deep into her eyes.

Shikhandini let him hold her hands but the missing sparkle in her eyes did not go unnoticed. Kush searched her face for signs of happiness, but in vain. He slowly withdrew his hands and looked down at her, pleading.

"Kush, please understand, I cannot marry you."

Her words felt like daggers to the heart. Tears sprung to his eyes. He had never considered her answer being anything but yes. He knew without doubt that she loved him.

"But why, Shikha?" His voice was a ragged whisper. "Shikha, tell me. What is it?"

"Kush, you know nothing about me. You know me as Guruji's daughter, a part of Yakshavana. You don't know about my past life or what I have been through before this…"

"Then tell me, Shikha. I want to know."

"No Kush, I cannot. I am cursed! I have lost every person I have ever loved; I cannot face such loss again. Yakshavana is my world now and I am happy here."

"Then I will live in Yakshavana. We will live here together, happily."

"No, Kush. You are royalty and that means you are bound by duty. Your father dreams of seeing you on the throne of Dasarna. I could never let you crush his dreams. You are meant for great things, Kush. Do not give it all away for me."

"But Shikha…"

"Even if you chose to leave your father and Dasarna, my answer would still be the same. I cannot marry you, Kush." With that, Shikhandini got up and began walking towards the village.

Kush stood rooted to the spot, as Shikhandini's words sank like heavy stones to the bottom of his heart.

***

The next morning, Hema rushed up to Shihkandi calling out, "Didi! Kush has left!"

"Left? When did he go?"

"Ma told me that when she visited him this morning, his room was empty. His horse is gone too," Hema informed Shikhandini sadly, her eyes wet with tears.

Shikhandini nodded, apparently unmoved. Hema shook her head and walked out. Once Hema had gone, Shikhandini's shoulders drooped. She was alone with her thoughts. He had gone! Shikhandini found it difficult to absorb the thought. She knew it was inevitable, for Kush had said he would be leaving soon. But she had not thought his going would affect her so deeply. She loved Kush.

Tears began to flow down her cheeks and a lump rose in her throat. She was finally free to express her emotions. She found it easier to accept what she felt, now that she knew it was all over. A part of her felt relieved to be able to acknowledge her feelings for Kush; now, when there was nothing left to lose.

13
VARNAVRATA

THE PALACE IN VARNAVRATA

"That coward Duryodhan! I will behead that rat!" roared Bheem.

"Calm down, brother Bheem. We will teach him a lesson when the time comes. But now we have to find a way to get out of here before we all get roasted alive in this palace!" said Arjun.

"He is right, Bheem. The walls are melting like wax! We do not have much time. The roof will collapse any minute," said Yudhistir.

Shielding their mother, the Pandava brothers scanned the place for a way out. Heat radiated from all sides as the palace began to crumble into lumps of molten wax. Ahead of them, the large chandelier Kunti had adored the first time she had laid her eyes on it, crashed onto the floor, shattering into a thousand sparkling shards. Behind them, molten wax tears crawled down the face of King Pandeshwar's statue, as though grieving his family's plight.

Fire leapt forth like some mythological beast, swallowing everything in its path. As the Pandavas and Kunti moved cautiously towards the palace exit, the flames roared towards them. Surrounded by fire, there was no way out. They were caught in a death-trap.

"Oh Lord Agni, please save my children! Take me if you have to," cried Kunti.

In a flashing moment Vidhura, *Mahamanthri* of Hastinapur and uncle of the Kuru Princes, appeared in Yudhistira's mind. "I think there is a way out," he told the others. "Remember when Kakashri Vidhura visited us a few days ago?" he asked. Everyone nodded. "He did not come for a casual visit. He was here to warn us of danger. He said it had something to do with Duryodhan and his maternal uncle Shakuni's plot to finish us."

"That was to be expected after brother Yudhistira's Rajyabhishek ceremony. Only a fool would think Duryodhan would let go of the throne so easily," added Bheem as he moved a charred beam out of their way. Being the strongest and largest of the five brothers, he led the way, removing obstacles from their path.

"Yes, and that is why Kaka-shri was here to tell us about the secret exit from this palace," said Yudhistir.

At these words, everyone stopped.

"There is a secret exit?" asked Sahadev, one of the twins.

"Yes, but first we have to get to the other side of the palace and look for a rat's hole."

Nakul instantly understood the message. "This way!" he said, pointing towards the hallway that led to the entrance.

The brothers and Kunti trusted Nakul's instinct over everything else. He was gifted in that way. Over the years, through sheer devotion and intense practice, he had learnt the art of communicating with other living beings. He could not only understand and speak to animals, but could foresee changes in the environment by listening to the trees and plants. Today, however, he prayed to Lord Agni to help him understand the ways of the fire that was about to engulf them.

Hastinapur

The news of the death of the Pandava brothers and their mother travelled across the length and breadth of Aryavrath. Dark clouds of grief shrouded Hastinapur.

"Arjun's *gandiva,* Bheem's *gada,* Yudhistir's spear, and Nakul and Sahadev's swords, were found in the charred remains of the palace. The messenger from Varnavrata brought them, with the tragic news," said Kripacharya, placing the weapons on the platform, at Bheeshm and Dhritarashtra's feet.

"Oh Lord Parashurama, have mercy! What does destiny have in store for this cursed family? What sin am I repaying that I must live long enough to see my grand-nephews die before my eyes?" cried Bheeshm, losing his stoical calm.

Dhritarashtra wept in silence. A part of him knew his son had played a role in, if not designed, the tragic incident. He knew his son well;

Duryodhan was never one to admit defeat. But Dhritarashtra's phantasmal love for his son made him incapable of judging him.

Outside, Mahamantri Vidhura, Guru Dronacharya, his son Ashwathama, Karna, King of Anga, the hundred Kauravas, with their mother Gandhari, uncle Shakuni, and sister Dushala, gathered in mourning. Bheeshm and Kripacharya joined them. All Hastinapur stood outside the palace gates, mourning the loss of the Pandavas. The Kuru flag descended from the palace tower as a mark of respect to the dead Princes

Gandhari wept like a child. She cried for the loss of a sister whom she had loved more than her own. Duryodhan and his brothers stood in silence, waiting for Bheeshm to make the announcement of the Rajyabhishek ceremony. Now that Yudhistir was gone, Duryodhan, being the eldest living Prince, would be instituted as Yuvraj and future King of Hastinapur. Shakuni, as always, wore a half smile.

Only the Mahamantri seemed unfazed. His nonchalant behaviour did not go unnoticed to the experienced eyes of Maharathi Bheeshm. He looked at Vidhura, his chin lifting in enquiry. Vidhura nodded in silence. Bheeshm closed his eyes for a moment, relieved to know the Pandavas had somehow escaped the fire.

***

It had been a year since Kush's departure from the Yaksha village. To everyone, Shikhandini seemed her old self, but privately she longed for him to return. It was only after his departure that she realized how much she loved him. She missed his presence in all the little things she did – visits to the temple, mock battles with the Yakshasena, discussions on science and philosophy with Pashupati and the others in the Ayuralaya.... Without Kush, it all felt incomplete and uninteresting.

She finally decided to write to him and tell him everything about her past. She was sure he would understand her plight. With ill concealed anticipation, she waited for his response. But, after months of waiting, as the season changed, she realized Kush did not wish to reply. Her sadness was replaced by anger. She spent all her time helping to renovate the village. Occasionally, she visited the Ayuralaya to learn about the Sanjeevni and other herbs. She kept busy so she would not think about Kush.

***

"It is surprising how you find me wherever I go," complained Shikhandini, annoyed the carrier pigeon had found her yet again. In the last few months she had tried to escape Panchi. The poor bird would look for her for several hours and then quietly return to its sender. But this time, Panchi had caught Shikhandini unprepared.

"What is it you have for me this time?" Carefully, Shikhandi pulled the message from the pouch tied to the bird's foot. She smiled at the familiar fragrance of rose and jasmine. It brought back bitter-sweet memories of her childhood. Only one person ever rubbed the flowery fragrance onto her scrolls. Dai Ma…

Shikhandini, my child, you must return! I do not know if this message will reach you or if Panchi will bring it back to me like all the others I have sent you. It has been a long time since I saw you...too long, my child. I know how difficult it is for you to come back, but know this, that there are still some people here who care about you. Your mother spends every morning at the palace gates, hoping that some day you will return. Not a day passes without Sarala and me recalling your childhood together.

And now you have another reason to come back home. The royal family has been blessed with two beautiful children – a son and a daughter. I thought it only right that you should know. You are the eldest, my child, and the little ones should get to know their sister. I know you too, will want to meet them. I well remember how much you craved for a little sister during your childhood. Your prayers have finally been answered. With everything that is happening around us, we cannot know how long peace will last or things remain the same. Come back, my child, and look upon the faces of your loved ones before it is too late. Ayushmaan Bhava. Dai Ma.

Shikhandini's heart filled with joy on learning she now had a baby brother and sister, something she had always longed for. The thought of her young siblings made her want to hurry back to Panchala, forgetting everything that had happened in the past. But her father's last bitter words and the memories of the battle she had lost against the Kuru Princes, held her imprisoned. The very thought of returning to Panchala made her shudder. The humiliation she had faced at the hands of her own people after the battle, the disappointment in her grandfather's eyes as he lay helpless on his deathbed, her father's regret at having made her Senapathi of his army, were bitter memories that flashed into her mind, reminding her of her resolution to never return to Panchala.

But the thought of holding her baby sister in her arms and ruffling her brother's hair made her heart melt a little. She longed to see her mother, the only one in her family who truly cared for her when everyone else had used her as a pawn in their own games. The last time she had seen her mother was at the palace gates, when she had left Panchala, vowing never to return. The agony on her mother's face had made a permanent mark on Shikhandini's mind. She missed Dai Ma, next only to her birth mother. Dai Ma had left her own family in Panchala to take care of Shikhandini; she had been there when Shikhandini's family had exiled her.

With everything that is happening around us, we cannot know how long peace will last or things remain the same. Please come back and meet your loved ones before it is too late.

What did she mean, Shikhandi wondered, her brow furrowed. Was something wrong in Panchala...an impending war? Questions to which there were no answers filled Shikhandini's mind.

A WEEK LATER

Though Shikhandini had been irresistibly drawn to the gates of Panchala, she felt intimidated by the place. She felt all her dark emotions taking hold of her soul as tears filled her eyes. She remembered how she had left this place several times, each time more humiliated and hurt. First as a child, when she had unknowingly violated the unspoken rule by donning the garland of blue lotuses. For this transgression she had been sent far away from her family and friends. She had known nothing of the story of the garland, or her previous birth. She had been just a child, hurt and confused by her parents' suddenly changed behaviour. The second time had been when she had been insulted by her own father for losing the battle against the Kuru Princes, and blamed for her grandfather's death. All her efforts, the sacrifices she had made during all those long lonely years to fulfil a goal that was not her own, were forgotten.

Taking one deep breath after another, Shikhandini tried to compose herself and still her mind. It was just for a few hours, she told herself. She would see Dai Ma, and her childhood friend, Sarala. With Dai Ma's help, she would quietly visit her mother and new siblings, and then return to Yakshavana.

By mid-morning, Shikhandini had reached the village square, where she decided to take a break and ponder on the best way to enter the palace and find Dai Ma. A small group of women stood behind her, involved in a serious conversation.

"Have you seen the boy? Strong and handsome. And the girl? She looks like an *apsara*!" said one, quickly making a gesture to ward off the evil eye.

"It is said that the royal astrologer has prophesied that it will be the Princess, not the Prince, who will make Panchala known in all of Aryavrath. The King has begun preparations for her *swayamvara*."

Swayamvara? Shikhandini brow furrowed in confusion.

Another of the women said, "Yes, yes, we have all heard the prophecy. It is why she is called Panchali, Daughter of Panchala."

"Our King wants to be remembered as the father of one destined to change history, so he named her Draupadi, Daughter of Drupada."

"God willing, this Princess will wipe away the shameful mark on Panchala, due to that cranky old King Prishata, and his undeserving grand-daughter."

Shikhandini closed her eyes, struck to the heart by the woman's words. So this is how how they talk of me, she thought sadly.

A few minutes later the woman hurried off in different directions as the prahar bell reminded them of their pending chores. Their daily chat was done. A young girl with a protruding belly walked past Shikhandini, carefully weighing her steps. Dressed in the white robes of widowhood, her hands bare of bangles, she looked weary, tired of walking in the sun.

"Sarala!" whispered Shikhandini, standing up and walking closer.

"Shikhandini, is it you!" squealed Sarala, her exhaustion forgotten in sudden delight.

"Shhhh…be quiet," Shikhandini warned, finger on lips.

Sarala nodded, looking around quickly to make sure no one had heard her. "But…why…are you…" she murmured, unable to conceal her happiness at seeing her childhood friend again.

"I will explain everything. Can we go to your place? There is much to talk about," Shikhandini replied.

***

"So what do you want to know?" asked Sarala as she offered her friend a cup of buttermilk.

Shikhandini gulped it down quickly, savouring the sweet coolness as it spread down her parched throat.

"First, tell me how you are. Hey Ram...you are going to be a mother soon!" Shikhandini exclaimed, hugging her friend.

"Yes, and you are going to be a Masi," Sarala replied, placing a hand on her stomach.

"How much longer?"

"Less than a month," Sarala replied, her eyes twinkling with joy.

"What has been happening here?" Shikhandini enquired, not knowing how to ask the question that had been gnawing at her mind ever since she first saw Sarala.

"Markhand left a few months ago, to go on King Drupada's *Digvijay Yatra*. He did not return," replied Sarala, tears rushing into her eyes.

Shikhandini embraced her friend again in her silent comfort.

"But I am proud of him. He died the death of a true Kshatriya. I will bring up our son to be like him," said Sarala, placing a hand on her distended belly.

Shikhandini smiled, nodding. They understood each other.

"So, what is it you wanted to know?" asked Sarala.

"About my new sister. How old is she?" Shikhandi put down the clay glass, wiping her mouth.

"Not the first question I would have expected from you, Shikha! Well, I have heard the Princess is about sixteen years old, and so is her twin brother," Sarala told her.

"Sixteen! How is that possible?" Shikhandini asked, confused.

"Sarala, where have you been?" a familiar voice called, interrupting their conversation. Sarala and Shikhandini both turned to look towards the door.

"Hey *Prabhu*...Shikha, my child! You came!" said Dai Ma, her voice trembling as she hurried forward to engulf Shikhandini in an embrace. Shikhandini held her tightly, tears falling down her cheeks.

"Your mother will be so happy to see you, child," Dai Ma said, wiping away Shikhandini's tears. "Not a day passes without her remembering your departure from Panchala. She blames herself for your pain. She has been punishing herself every minute since you left. She has not participated in any festivities or celebrations since the day you left. She did not even grace the naming ceremony of your brother and sister. Poor children, they do not know their mother."

Shikhandini cringed at Dai Ma's words. "I am sorry, Dai Ma, but there was no other way. After what happened, living in Panchala was impossible."

"I know, my child. Do not burden your heart with the past. Now that you are back, I am sure the Queen will smile once again."

"But Dai Ma, how is it possible the children are sixteen already?"

"That, my child, is a mystery to everyone in Panchala; everyone except the King and the Raj Guru." Dai Ma sat down beside Sarala and Shikhandini. "As you know, after Panchala lost the battle, Dronacharya decided to return half the kingdom to your father, while the other half was to be ruled by his son, Ashwathama. But the throne is now in southern Panchala, on the other side of the Ganga, in the capital, Kampilya. But, your father realized that Panchala was not a direct ally of Hastinapur; he could still wage war against it."

Shikhandini was surprised by this revelation. "How so?" she asked.

"Apparently, Hastinapur does not wish to fight against Panchala. It was Guru Drona who urged his students to gift him the kingdom as his guru dakshina."

"But why did Guru Dronacharya want to fight my father?"

"Dronacharya and the King were childhood friends, almost inseparable. They were both students at Maharishi Bharadwaja, Dronacharya's father's gurukul. So, after the Kuru Princes won the battle, they gifted the Kingdom of Panchala to Guru Dronacharya. But, in memory of their childhood friendhip, Dronacharya returned half of the kingdom to your father."

As Shikhandini listened to how her father's ego had ruined the friendship between him and Guru Drona, she wondered why no one in her family had ever told her about this. Perhaps she had not been deemed important enough to know.

"You mean Hastinapur is not Overlord of Panchala?"

"Not until Duryodhan sits on the throne of Hastinapur. Since Ashwathama is his close friend, he will no doubt join hands, and Panchala, by default, will become an ally of Hastinapur."

Shikhandini nodded her understanding of the quicksands of political strategem.

"If that happens, your father will have no choice but to agree, leaving Pitamaha's dying wish unfulfilled."

"Yes, but this may take many years."

"Since the day of the defeat your father has planned to get his kingdom back. He never liked the idea of sharing, that old man," observed Sarala dryly, earning a look of reproach from her mother.

"And this led to Prince Dhrishtadhyumna's birth," said Dai Ma.

"Dhrishtadhyumna...what a strange name," observed Shikhandini.

"The King sought the Raj Guru's advice. Male chauvinist that he is, the Raj Guru proposed a yagya that has long been banned in Panchala by your forefathers.

"The *Putrakameshti Yagya*..." whispered Shikhandini as everything began to make sense.

"Yes. No one knows what happened in that year when your father and the Raj Guru, with some chosen Brahmins, disappeared into the forest. When they returned, your father came with a son and daughter in tow. Popular belief has it the children were born of the ceremonial fire. The children are strangely dissimilar, both in appearance and nature. In fact, they are a study in contrasts. She represents the calm, eerie night, while he is like the bright, sunny day. Rumour also says the King did not want a daughter and wished to leave her behind in the forest, but the royal astrologer's prophecy made him change his mind – that it is the Princess who will write forever the King's name in history; that she was born to change the course of history, and would be remembered as one of the most influential women to have ever graced the land of Aryavrath."

"Hence her names, Draupadi...Panchali..." Shikhandini murmured. She wondered if her father would have bestowed upon her the name Draupadi, 'Daughter of Drupada', had she won the battle against the Kuru Princes. She shook the thought from her mind.

"I do not know what the King plans to do with these children, but I hope they are not dragged into the political quagmire that has spread from Hastinapur to all of Aryavrath."

Shikhandini did not need to know any more to guess her father's intention. He had introduced two new pawns into the game.

14
Draupadi's Swayamvara

Two days later

"What was the announcement, Dai Ma?" asked Shikhandini, hearing the commotion in the street outside Dai Ma's house.

It was the start of the second prahar and everyone in the village was getting ready for their daily chores. Street vendors had begun setting up their stalls; women gathered in the village square to exchange gossip or made their way to the temple or public baths; the day guards changed places with the night guards, as the sun rose in the sky. Into this scene had ridden the public announcer on his horse, scroll in hand.

"It was about your sister's swayamvara, Shikha. King Drupada has invited all the Princes from the different kingdoms," Dai Ma replied. She instantly knew what Shikhandini was thinking and said softly, "I know Shikha, this should have been your swayamvara, being the eldest princess."

Shikhandini was taken aback. "What has father planned, Dai Ma?" she enquired after a while, trying to break the awkward silence.

"I heard he has proposed some kind of challenge. The Prince who completes the challenge first, wins Panchali's hand."

"Do you know what the challenge is?"

"Something related to archery. I do not know the details. But I am certain that whatever the King has devised, will put most of the Princes in their place. He wants only the best warrior for his daughter. The more powerful the Prince, the stronger the ally for Panchala," Dai Ma snorted, turning away.

Shikhandini smiled at Dai Ma's words. A part of her rejoiced for her sister. But she also knew that had she won the battle a year ago, this would have been her swayamvara. She would have been the daughter her father proudly presented to the world. She thought how different life would have been then. She would have challenged every Prince to a duel and happily chosen the one who could defeat her. She imagined duelling with Kush. Would he have come? Would she have agreed to marry him if he had won their duel?

"Are the Kurus invited too?" asked Sarala as Dai Ma helped her sit up on the bed and placed a pillow behind her to support her back.

"Of course, they are. The Kuru Princes are among the best in all of Aryavrath. I hope one of the sons of the Late King Pandeshwar, God rest his soul, wins her," replied Dai Ma.

"But are they not dead? They were burnt alive in that tragic fire at Varnavrata," said Sarala.

"No child, the chances of them being alive are as great as their being dead. Their bodies were not found. Many believe they escaped the fire and are waiting for the right time to come out into the open."

Shikhandini looked at Dai Ma, her eyes quizzical. "But you said you did not want Draupadi to be pulled into politics, certainly not Hastinapur politics. That would be like stepping onto dangerously unstable ground. Her marriage to one of the Pandavas will drag Panchala and the royal family into a political swamp."

"No, my child. The sons of Pandeshwar are simple men of character. In fact, they have not lived in Hastinapur for most part of their lives. Their birth and most of their childhood was spent in the forests of Shratashrunga mountain, with their father Pandeshwar, and mothers Kunti and Madri."

"Why would a King choose to live in a forest, Dai Ma?" Shikhandini asked, confused. "Specially one so powerful."

"Pandeshwar was a wise and brave King. He made Hastinapur what it is today. He lived a simple and righteous life. But destiny always tests the wisest and bravest of men with tough challenges. One day, while he was hunting in the forest, he accidentally shot a sage, in a moment of intimacy with his wife. Pandeshwar's arrow pierced the sage's heart, right in front of his wife. It is said that Pandeshwar was cursed by the sage that if he ever tried to be intimate with his wives, death would come for him in that moment. Pandeshwar, who was a strict follower of Kshatriya dharma, knew that killing a Brahmin sage was the ultimate crime, one that would scar him for all his births. He decided to seek repentance before death finally took mercy on him. He stepped down from the throne of Hastinapur, handing it over to his blind brother, Dhritarashtra, father of the hundred Kaurava Princes and Princess Dushala." Dai Ma narrated the popular version of King Pandeshwar's death tale.

"Kauravas… that is strange," mused Shikhandini.

"Why is strange?" asked Sarala.

"Kauravas is the name given to the descendants of the Kuru dynasty..." Shikhandini said, "so are not the sons of King Pandeshwar Kauravas as well?"

"Well…yes," responed Dai Ma, somewhat reluctantly. "But since the sons of Pandeshwar have always been treated like outcasts by their uncle, King Dhritarashtra, and his family, they prefer to be called Pandavas or 'Sons of Pandeshwar', rather than being known as scions of the Kurus dynasty."

"Hmm…" Something about the story niggled at Shikhandini's mind.

"So did the King die while…" asked Sarala, curiosity getting the better of her.

"Yes, it is said King Pandeshwar died when he, disregarding the curse, was overcome by passion for his second wife, Madri." Dai Ma turned away, her lips pused in displeasure. "Honestly, it was the most shameful way anyone could die. Madri died soon after, unable to bear the grief. But Kunti, Pandeshwar's first wife, was the strong one. She took responsibility for the five boys and brought them up as a single mother."

"But, the curse...then how were the Pandavas born?" Shikhandini asked delicately.

"I am not sure, Shikha. Different people say different things. Some say Pandeshwar is not their biological father; that each of them is a boon from the Gods. Kunti was blessed with a boon by the Sage Durvasa, when she was Princess of Mathura, and he was visiting."

Shikhandini absorbed in silence all she had heard.

Dai Ma chuckled. "Leave it to the people to make anything related to the royal family intriguing. I hardly know if the stories even have a tinge of truth to them. But I am happy Draupadi will be away from

Panchala and live a normal and peaceful life. I was worried the King would use her as a pawn to win back Panchala from Drona."

"He already has, Dai Ma," said Shikhandini, smiling wistfully.

"What do you mean, my child?"

"Is it not obvious? The swayamvara is a trap. The Pandavas were the reason for Dronacharya's victory over Panchala. I had defeated the Kauravas on the first day of battle; they were prisoners. Having witnessed the Pandavas valour myself, I am certain one of them can win Draupadi's hand, no matter how difficult the test. If that happens, the Pandavas will have no choice but to fight on father's side, when the time comes to libertate Panchala from Ashwathama's rule. The Pandavas will be compelled to fight their own Guru."

Horrified, Dai Ma's hands flew up to cover her mouth. "Hey Ram! How can he use his own daughter as a ladder to the throne?"

'In the same way he used his other daughter to avenge his father's defeat,' thought Shikhandini. "And if the eldest, Yudhishthira, is crowned King of Hastinapur, it will pit Drona and his son against Panchala and Hastinapur. We all know the outcome of such a war."

"And I thought the King had finally changed his ways for the sake of the Princess," said Dai Ma, shaking her head.

Shikhandini gave a tremulous laugh.

***

Panchala was decked like a newly wed bride for Draupadi's swayamvara. Excitement and anticipation filled the air. The sound of drums could be heard many yojanas away. The swayamvara was the subject of conversation as the local people prepared for the extravagant ceremony and the arrival of the dignitaries.

Princes from all over Aryavrath had been invited to the ceremony. Many of them, though intrigued by the Princess, were more interested in taking part in the challenge to display their skill, outperforming their rivals. The result of this contest would be talked of for months to come.

Among the Princes, Duryodhan, his younger brother Dushasana, and his close friend Karna, King of Anga, took the first row. The ceremony was being held in Panchala's open stadium, reserved for special occasions and public gatherings. A raised platform had been constructed for in the northerly direction for the King's throne. Two semi-circular platforms on either side of the host platform seated the eligible Princes from across Aryavrath. A central, raised podium held the main prop for the challenge, covered in silken cloth. Other than the royal family of Panchala, no one knew the nature of the challenge. A separate section held the commoners. Among them sat Shikhandini, Sarala and Dai Ma.

Shikhandini was dressed in a simple cotton dhoti and angavastram. She had covered her head to avoid being recognized. She sat with her eyes glued to the entrance. It had been a long time since she had seen her family.

The striking of the prahar gong marked the auspicious beginning of the ceremony. King Drupada and Prince Dhrishtadhyumna made their entry, walking towards the central platform. Shikhandini watched Dhristadhyumna in awe. He was indeed everything Dai Ma and Sarala had described.

Chants of *Raja Drupada ki jai*! filled the air as the people of Panchala greeted their King. Everyone in the stadium, contestants and spectators alike, rose to their feet in respect.

On reaching the platform, King Drupada and his son stood facing the people. Raising his hand, Drupada silenced the crowd. "I welcome all the Princes and Kings who have come here to grace the auspicious occasion of my daughter's swayamvara," he began.

Shikhandini looked at her father. He had aged, appearing older than he was. The defeat against Drona had taken its toll. However, he smiled, happy to present his daughter. A pang filled Shikhandini's heart at the thought that she would never be the reason of his happiness. Her eyes scanned the entourage on the platform, looking for her mother, but the Queen was nowhere to be seen.

"Dai Ma, where is Ma?" Shikhanini asked.

"She does not participate in any ceremonies, Shikhandini. She spends all her time in prayer, and in helping the needy. She has renounced all the pleasures of being Queen."

Shikhandini's eyes welled with tears at Dai Ma's words. Her mind filled with images of her beautiful mother, who had always been as quick to laugh and love as to scold. She turned back to the proceedings.

"As you may have heard, my daughter Draupadi's birth is a boon to all of Aryavrath. The prophecy read at the exact moment she stepped out of the holy fire says she is destined to change the course of history. So the Prince who wins her hand today, will also play a vital role and is destined for greatness. For this reason, I wish to choose only the bravest and strongest among you. The challenge that will be laid down in a few minutes, has been designed to test both your strength and skill," Drupada declared. Turning towards his son, he said, "My beloved son, Dhrishtadhyumna, will now explain the rules of the contest. May the best man win. *Vijayi Bhava*!"

Dhrishtadhyumna bowed to the gathering. He had never seen such a huge gathering, and smiled with excitement. "I welcome one and all to this grand ceremony. Today's challenge is not meant for the average warrior. Winning requires strength, valour and self-confidence." With that, he pulled the cloth from the central display, drawings gasps of awe.

It was a fine sight. Revealed was a bow made of the finest and strongest metal alloy. It was thrice the size of a regular bow and was supported between two pillars. The bow resembled the holy *Pinaka* used by Lord Ram in Lady Sita's swayamvara. Exactly a hundred feet above the bow was a rotating plate with a fish carved into it, the eye painted red. On the ground below, was a pool of crystal-clear water, with the reflection of the rotating fish clearly visible. Drops of water fell into the pool at periodic intervals, creating ripples on its surface. This was to make the task even more challenging. The entire scene replicated the challenge at Lady Sita's swayamvara.

"As you can see, the task is to hit the eye of the rotating fish by looking only at its reflection in the water. Only a true warrior, free of self-doubt and fear, can complete this task. The first participant to hit the eye in a single shot will be announced the winner," Drishtadhyumna announced.

While the smile on the faces of most of the participants had vanished, Karna merely smiled, seeing it as another opportunity to prove his talent. Ever since Lady Sita's swayamvara, the challenge of hitting the eye of the fish by looking at its reflection in the water had become a standard test in archery. Although a well-known challenge, there were only a handful of archers capable of accomplishing it. Karna knew of only one, other than himself – Arjun. A pang of guilt filled Karna's mind as he recalled the incident at Varnavrata. Though he had refused to be part of the crime, he had not succeeded in stopping his friend Duryodhan.

"We welcome to this auspicious gathering my beloved sister, Princess of Panchala, Yagyaseni Panchali!" announced Dhristadhyumna, drawing everyone's attention to the entrance. The title *Yagyaseni,* 'Daughter of Yagyasena', derived from another of Drupada's many names, had been bestowed upon her to mark this special occasion.

Draupadi's entry was the most eagerly awaited part of the ceremony apart from the challenge itself. For most of those present, it was the first time they would actually see her. Everyone was keen to know if she was in reality as beautiful and celestial as rumour claimed.

As Draupadi walked along the aisle, Princes from around the country watched her, mesmerized. She walked with elegance and grace, surrounded by a radiant aura that made the story of her birth from the holy fire real. Lithe and tall, her deep-set almond eyes stood out against her smooth, dark skin. She wore a red and gold angavastram, her torso covered with exotic jewellery designed for the ceremony. Her long, thick hair was braided with flowers whose fragrance added to her charisma. With two female companions walking behind her, she made her way to the central platform. She sat down on her father's left, while Dhristhadhyumna's sat on his right.

Shikhandini found it difficult to tear her eyes off her sister. She was beautiful beyond description, just as Shikhandini had imagined. She wondered if she would ever have the chance to meet her in person.

Karna, who had accompanied Duryodhan to the swayamvara solely on his request, stared at Draupadi, his gaze transfixed. Everything he had heard and brushed of as exaggerated, now seemed perfectly true. In that fateful moment, he gave his heart to her. His desire to win the contest increased fourfold even though he knew Draupadi could never be his, even if he won, for he had promised Duryodhan to stand in as his champion and win Draupadi's hand for him.

"Before we begin, there is someone I wish to welcome among us. He has touched the lives of many people, including mine, with his wisdom and generosity. He has been like a brother to my daughter, ever since her birth. This occasion would forever remain incomplete without his presence. Please welcome Vasudeva Krishna, King of Dwaraka," said Drupada.

Everyone's gaze shifted to the entrance. The stadium, which few seconds ago had roared with chants and applause, was now filled with reverential silence. As Krishna appeared, people whispered prayers, thanking the Lords above for giving them the opportunity to witness his presence. He was dressed in a yellow dhoti and matching angavastram, that stood out against his dark skin. A modest crown with a single peacock feather graced his head, and a flute was tucked into his waistband. A smile that seemed to draw in every person there, completed his charismatic persona. He walked with authority and confidence, yet his face radiated humbleness and wisdom.

Shikhandini watched Krishna, trying to recall where she had seen him. Almost in answer to her silent thoughts, he glanced in her direction momentarily, greeting her with folded hands, his smile mischievous and familiar. His deep-set eyes seemed to bore into hers even from a distance. Her gaze fell to the flute. "Shyam!" she gasped.

"The people of Dwarka call him by that name, but how did you know?" asked Dai Ma, turning her head to look at Shikhandini in surprise. Like many others, she too, believed Krishna to be an incarnation of Lord Vishnu.

Shikhandini found it hard to swallow as her eyes filled with tears. He had saved her life. She recalled the incidence in the forest when, in the heat of the moment, she had decided to end her life by jumping off the cliff. He had not only saved her but guided her to a new life in the Yaksha village. Her eyes moved to the peacock feather in his crown. Govind…

"Pranam, Maharaj Drupada," Krishna greeted the King.

Drupada led him to the throne placed on a slightly higher level than his own – an honour given only to Gods and Maharishis. He looked at Draupadi, a broad smile on his face.

But Draupadi seemed to be lost in another world. Just one thought filled in her mind, was Arjun really dead? The news about the death of the Pandavas and their mother Kunti at Varnavrata Lakshagraha, the lac palace, had reached Panchala just a few days before the swayamavara. Draupadi, who had heard of Arjun's valour from her father, had hoped it would be he who would win her hand and forge a strong bond between Panchala and the great Overlord, Hastinapur.

The news had also stunned Drupada, shattering his dreams of marrying his daughter to the Prince of Hastinapur and making Panchala safe. But Krishna had stepped in to assure him the Pandavas would return, and that he should proceed with Draupadi's swayamavara.

So, with the blowing of the conch, the commencement of the challenge was announced. Each participant took his turn to shoot the fish. Most failed to even lift the bow from its position between the pillars. The few who did, missed the target by wide margins. Finally, it was Duryodhan's turn. To everyone's surprise, he nominated his friend Karna, to participate on his behalf. Bowing to the Sun God, Karna made his way to the podium.

"I cannot permit you to participate in this contest, Angaraj Karna!" declared Dhristadhyumna.

Karna halted in his tracks and looked up at his host.

"Anyone who wishes to win my sister's hand must win the contest himself. He cannot nominate another to take his place."

Immediately a hubbub arose in the stadium. Time passed as the Princes and the hosts entered into deep discussion and argument. The example of Maharathi Bheeshm of Hastinapur, who had won the hands of the Princesses of Kashi for his brother Vichithravirya, was placed before the assembly. Duryodhan felt angered and humiliated when the argument was dismissed saying the rules of each swayamvara were set by the hosts. Everyone knew he was an expert with the gada, not the bow. To save face, he announced Karna would contest for himself, as King of Anga. Bowing to his friend, Karna once again moved towards the bow.

Draupadi, who had lost herself in dreams of Prince Arjun, did not wish to marry anyone else. It was she who had chosen the bow as the weapon of the contest, knowing that only Arjun could win such a difficult challenge. She had never imagined that Karna would be a contestant. All of Aryavartha had heard of his fearsome skill as an archer, his armour and earrings of gold. If he hit the target and won the contest, how could she refuse to marry him? Her heart hammering in her chest, Draupadi knew there was only one way to stop him.

She watched as Karna lifted the bow from its stand as if it was a plaything. As he finished stringing the bow, Draupadi spoke in a clear voice that carried to every person in the assembly. "I will not wed a *sutaputra*!" she declared, addressing Karna as 'son of a charioteer', hence of low caste.

Karna looked up in astonishment, trying to control his sudden rage. Tears glistened in his bright eyes as he was once again made aware of his vulnerability. This humiliation was not new to him. It reminded him of the contest in Hastinapur, when he had challenged Prince Arjun to a duel in archery. The Kuru Princes had just returned from their gurukul. Having been rejected by their Guru, Dronacharya, Karna had dared to challenge the Prince and prove himself. But he had been turned down as being low born; unsuitable to duel with a Prince of Hastinapur.

A mute witness to his humiliation, Shikhandini's heart went out to Karna. She was easily able to relate to him. She wondered if their fates had been written by the same hand. Karna's talent was forever overshadowed by his caste; her's by her gender. Had she been a son and had lost the battle against the Kuru Princes, her father would never have questioned his decision to make her Commander. She would have been given another chance. "If I had a son, I would not have had to live to see this day..." She recalled her father's words. Her thoughts were brought back to the drama unfolding before her when she heard Karna's deep voice reverberate across the stadium.

"I understand the Princess does not wish to marry me. But by mocking my caste and humiliating me and my family, she has not only insulted me but shamed Panchala, which once took pride in the observance of gender equality and equal opportunity for all." Putting the bow back as easily as he had lifted it, Karna turned and bowed to the assemblage, his hands folded. Armour glistening in the sun, he strode out, followed by Duryodhan and Dushasana.

Draupadi knew what she had done was wrong. She looked at Krishna for guidance. He nodded, assuring her silently that she had done what she had to.

With Karna's exit and no news of the Pandavas, King Drupada grew restive; he knew none of the other participants had the skill required to win. He looked towards Krishna, whose eyes were fixed on the entrance, a knowing smile on his face. Drupada followed his gaze. Draupadi too, had her eyes glued to the entrance.

At the entrance stood a group of Brahmin mendicants, who had come for a meal after the grand ceremony. Drupada shook his head in despair. But Krishna nodded to Draupadi, letting her know Arjun had indeed come. The five Pandava brothers stood dressed in worn out dhotis and angavasthrams, their faces covered by long unruly beards, their hair tied in a bun behind their heads. No one looked their way a second time.

"Maharaj Drupada, your worries have now come to an end," said Krishna to his host. "The greatest archer of our time is now a part of this ceremony. But for him to come forward, you will have to invite Brahmins to participate in the contest."

"How is that possible, Krishna?" asked Drupada, perplexed by this sudden development. "This contest is only for Kshatriyas. How can a Brahmin compete with warriors?"

"Are Brahmins not considered above Kshatriyas in the social hierarchy, O King? Lord Parashuram, the greatest warrior of all, was a Brahmin. King of Panchala, your daughter's destiny will unfold as it is ordained, whether she marries a Brahmin or a Kshatriya," Krishna said softly.

Drupada considered in silence. He knew he could not go against Krishna's advice and retain the approval of the people. Finally he looked up and nodded. The announcement was made that the contest was now open to Brahmins.

In one corner of the stadium, Yudhistir turned to his brother. "Arjun, you should take part."

"But brother, what if somebody recognizes us? Everyone here thinks we are dead," replied Arjun.

"Destiny has brought us to Kampilya. Perhaps your fate is tied to that of Princess Draupadi. Not using your skill even when the opportunity presents itself, is the trait of a fool," said Yudhistir.

"Arjun, brother Yudhistir is right. You should participate. There is no one else here who can win this contest," added Bheem.

Arjun's gaze shifted to Krishna. In that moment, he could hear Krishna's voice loud and clear in his mind: *Running away from a challenge is not Kshatriya dharma.*

Touching Yudhistir's feet, he asked for his blessings. "*Vijayi Bhava,*" Yudhistir replied, touching Arjun's shoulders.

Rising, Arjun walked towards the central podium, his eyes fixed on Draupadi. Derisive murmurs ran through the stadium like wind through a field of corn, at the sight of the Brahmin approaching the majestic bow. Draupadi's joy knew no bounds. Drupada watched sceptically. There was nothing he could do; he had given his word.

From where she sat watching, Shikhandini wondered why her father would even consider marrying his daughter to a Brahmin who could never give her the comfort-filled life she was used to. It was only when Arjun lifted the bow with his right hand and strung it as easily as a child's toy, that Shikhandini realized the Brahmin was, in fact, Prince Arjun himself. It made her smile. Though he had been the cause of her defeat in the battle against the Kuru Princes, she admired his skill and valour as a fellow warrior. She hoped he would succeed in winning her sister's hand.

With one knee planted on the ground, Arjun positioned his bow horizontally. Eyes fixed on the reflection of the fish, he picked up the single arrow lying beside the bow and placed it on the bowstring. He pointed the bow and arrow towards the rotating plate above, his eyes still transfixed on the image in the water. Whispering a silent prayer, he pulled the arrow back and with a *twang*, released it skyward.

Draupadi held her breath, waiting for the impact. The arrow flew upward, imbedding itself through the sky in the eye of the fish, exactly in the centre. Shouts of jubilation and wild applause filled the stadium. No one had ever seen such a feat. Flowers were showered on the winner.

King Drupada, who had by now realized the Brahmin was none other than the Pandava Prince, rose to announce the garlanding of the winner by the Princess. He had won afterall.

***

After Draupadi's swayamvara had ended, Dai Ma took Shikhandini to the temple where her mother Kokila spent most of her time. The temple was located in the palace gardens but was accessible to commoners as well. Like most temples in Panchala, this one was dedicated to Lord Shiva. Kokila spent most of her waking hours there, praying to the Lord.

When Shikhandini arrived at the temple, Draupadi and Arjun had just left, having come to seek the Queen's blessings. Dai Ma had told Shikhandini that, despite Kokila not being her birth mother, Draupadi had an affectionate bond with her. The Queen would spend long hours with Draupadi in the palace gardens, teaching her the ways of royal society, the history and culture of the land, and other concepts that were new to Draupadi, who had arrived in Panchala as innocent and pure as a newborn child. The Queen was a good tutor to Draupadi, probably the best, but she hesitated to shower her with motherly love. Draupadi, however, found ingenious ways to occupy as much of the Queen's time as possible. Their bond was special.

As Shikhandini and Dai Ma approached the spot where Kokila sat, the Queen looked up, her eyes placid pools, dark with suffering. A trembling hand covered her mouth as she recognised who came.

"Shikhandini, my child, is that you?" whispered Kokila, trembling.

The sound of her mother's voice felt like the first drops of rain on the parched earth. Tears filled Shikhandini's eyes as she was overwhelmed by emotion. "Ma..." she said, her voice breaking.

"Shikha, my child!" Kokila embraced Shikhandini, holding her close to her heart as if she would never let go again. The fear of separation gave her strength.

For several minutes the two stayed that way, wishing the world around them would stop and time cease at this particular moment for the rest of eternity. It did not escape Shikhandini's eyes how gaunt her mother had become. Like Drupada, she too, looked much older than she was. Her eyes which once sparkled with lightness and laughter, were now lifeless. Her skin was wrinkled and her hair had turned grey. Guilt entered Shikhandini's heart like an arrow as the realization dawned that her mother had suffered all this because of her; because she had left Panchala.

"Where had you been all this while, child? How have you been? Look at you...so thin. Are you not eating well?" Kokila had a hundred questions.

Shikhandini chuckled in amusement. She wondered if all mothers were the same. It reminded her of Guru Ma, back in Yakshavana. She made a mental note to write to Guruji regarding her extended stay in Panchala.

Kokila insisted on knowing about Shikhandini's life after she left Panchala. Shikhandini began her story from the time she met the Yakshas first, skipping the part where Krishna, or Shyam as he had introduced himself as, had saved her life and then taken her to the Yakshas, to start a new life.

Meanwhile, two men watched the reunion of mother and daughter from the balcony of the King's chamber. One was the Raj Guru of Panchala, the other King Drupada.

"So the Queen remembers how to smile," said the Raj Guru.

Drupada nodded slowly. His eyes had a faraway look, as though recalling a long lost memory. "I wish I had not been so hard on

Shikhandini," he sighed. "She was, after all, a young girl. I was the fool to think she could replace a man and lead the army." It was the first time Draupada had made such a confession, but chauvinistic pride forbade him from acknowledging Shikhandini's valour and courage in battle.

"My Lord, she is no ordinary girl. She single-handedly defeated the 100 Kuru Princes. No one can take that away from her," the Raj Guru, who had always been very fond of Shikhandini, reminded the King.

"You are right, Raj Guruji. Shikhandini is no ordinary girl. She is a Princess, my firstborn. I cannot let her wander in the forests, homeless; a prey to man and beast alike."

The Raj Guru nodded silently. It was time.

"I must go and speak to her. If she wants me to humble myself, I will," Drupada said though his pride almost choked him. He had never humbled himself before any woman.

"You need not, My Lord. The Queen will convince her."

Drupada nodded, a hint of sadness in his eyes. The Raj Guru was among the few people in Panchala who knew of the Queen's deteriorating health. The Vyeds had said the disease was rare and incurable. Above all, the Queen had lost the will to live. Drupad, witness to his wife's condition, realized he had made an error he would regret all his life. He prayed for forgiveness, for using his children as weapons of revenge, to ruin a friendship with the one who saved his life, and for performing the Puthrikameshti Yagya, which had been banned in Panchala by his forefathers.

Krishna's words resonated in his ears: "Oh Great King! What use is all this fame and power when obtained at the cost of your loved ones? What has your pride brought you but an empty heart?"

***

"Ma, I must go now," said Shikhandini as she heard the prahar bell. She did not wish to encounter her father. Her purpose in returning to Panchala had been fulfilled. She had seen her siblings, and her mother.

"But Shikhandini, this is your home. You cannot leave!" Kokila's eyes glistened with tears.

"No Ma, this *was* my home. Not anymore. I only came to see you and my brother and sister. Now I must return." Shikhandini could not look into her mother's eyes.

"Shikha, do not do this. You are my only child. Do not go! I know what happened was unjust. You did not deserve any of it. But was it my fault? I was as helpless as you," Kokila pleaded.

"Ma, do not weep." Shikhandini wiped the tears from her mother's face. "I know it was not your fault. In fact, I have nothing against anyone. I have forgiven father, a long time ago. But I cannot live here, with all its haunting memories. Let me go, Ma. I will be back whenever you need me the most. I promise."

"What if I tell you there will never be a time I will need you more than I do now?"

Shikhandini looked at her mother in confusion.

"Shikha, the end approaches. I have only a few more moons of this life, and truly, I do not wish to live any longer, grieve any more. It is enough," Kokila confessed.

Shikhandini's eyes filled with tears. A lump formed in her throat as the truth of her mother's illness sank into her mind. The truth behind Dai Ma's message struck her like daggers to the heart. *Come back, my child, and look upon the faces of your loved ones before it is too late.*

"Consider this a last request. Will you not grant your mother her last wish?" Kokila sobbed. "In the years before you were born, my life felt incomplete... meaningless. All I wanted was to be a mother, to enjoy the little pleasures of motherhood. But fate turned its face away from me, for even after your birth, my child, I had to live the life of a childless woman. Destiny always found a way to keep you away from me. Now, when I have only a few days to count, I want to spend them with you and leave this world without any regrets." Kokila held Shikhandini's hands between her own, unable to let go.

Thoughts and memories played *chori-chupi* in Shikhandini's mind. The only person who had ever loved her without measure, was going to leave her; no one could hold back the hand of fate. There was nothing she could do; nothing except ease her passing. Shikhandini knew what dharma dictated. But above all, she knew what she wished to do.

15
ATHIRATHI

A FEW MONTHS LATER

Shikhandini's return was not announced publicly to prevent unnecessary talk and criticism, both in Panchala and in the neighbouring kingdoms. On Kokila's order, a small ceremony was held in the palace to welcome the Princess. In Dai Ma's eyes it was a special day. Panchala had just bid farewell to one Princess and was welcoming home another.

Shikhandini decided to live in her mother's chambers, and Kokila could not have been happier. They spent each day together, catching up on everything they had missed. Kokila cooked Shikhadini's meals herself, washed and braided her hair, and told her stories about lands near and far. It was during these conversations that Shikhandini learnt about the life of the Pandavas and their mother Kunti, the friendship between Karna and Duryodhan, about the Kauravas' cunning maternal uncle, Shakuni, and many others at the court of Hastinapur.

Shikhandini, on her part, told her mother of her experiences during her childhood in the palace outside Panchala, and her days in the Yakshavana. She sometimes spoke about Kush, but did not disclose away her feelings for him.

The mother and daughter duo set a routine for themselves. Their day would begin with Shikhandini going to the banks of the Ganga for her daily prayers, while her mother cooked them a meal. Then they would walk in the gardens, tending to their favourite plants, which they had planted together. It was as though Shikhandini was once again the five-year-old girl who had walked about the palace grounds holding her mother's hand. At noon, Shikhandini would watch over her mother as Kokila took a nap, first making sure she had taken the potions the Vyed had left. In the evenings, Shikhandini would visit the temple with her mother, helping to teach the village urchins to read and write. The little children instantly developed a fondness for Shikhandini.

One day, when Kokila was asleep, Shikhandini decided to visit the field where the Panchalsena trained every day. It was the same battlefield where she had fought the Kuru Princes as Commander of the Panchal Sena; the most powerful person after the King. It was the same field where she had defeated and captured the 100 sons of King Dhritarashtra of Hastinapur. It was also the field where she had lost the battle to the sons of the Late King Pandeshwar; where she had been shamed for bringing defeat to Panchala.

In one of the conversations with the Raj Guru, Shikhandini had learnt that her brother, Dhrishtadhyumna, was now the Senapati of Panchala. Born with the skills of a warrior and destined to kill Guru Dronacharya, Dhrishtadhyumna was second to none when it came to sword fighting. His skills in archery and mace fighting were also exceptional. In the first battle of his life, he had successfully defeated twelve *Rathis*, earned himself the title of *Athirathi*. It was for this reason that Shikhandini had decided to visit the place she dreaded.

"Pranam, Didi," said Dhrishtadhyumna, when he saw her walking towards the ground, a warm smile on his face.

"Pranam, Senapati," Shikhandini replied formally.

"Didi, I am your younger brother," grinned Dhrishtadhyumna. "Call me whatever you wish!"

His face, like Draupadi's, was radiant and flawless. His eyes twinkled with the innocence and purity that only newborns are blessed with. This was their first meeting, except for occasionally crossing paths in silence in the palace.

"So what brings you here, Didi?" he asked, hoping to extend the conversation.

Before Shikhandini could reply, the words of one of the soldiers behind was carried to them with disastrous clarity: "Isn't that Shikhandini? The cowardly Princess who ran away from Panchala?"

Another voice replied, "Oh yes, she is the one. So the rumours are true! She has returned to Panchala."

"She is really good at breaking her vows," the first soldier remarked caustically. "First she broke her vow to defeat the Kuru Princes and avenge her grandfather's humiliation. And now she has broken her vow never to return to Panchala. Shameful!"

Others joined in with insulting remarks, disgruntled by the pariah Princess' return. As one, they blamed her for their defeat.

"Enough!" roared Dhrishtadhyumna, startling everyone. "Do you forget you are speaking of the Princess of Panchala? I will not tolerate such disrespect towards my sister," he growled at his soldiers.

The soldiers immediately bowed their heads, more from fear than apology. Dhrishtadhyumna's reaction took everyone, including Shikhandini, by surprise. A small smile grazed her lips at her brother's words. She wondered why she had not tried to talk to him earlier. She had assumed that he, like everyone in Panchala, he too considered her an embarrassment.

"Didi, heed them not! They always need something to grumble about. Come, let's go!" he said, signalling to Brahmabrata to take over. Brahmabrata nodded in response, immediately taking position.

But before they could move away, a voice came from behind them, addressing the soldiers, "Yes, it is true! Yes, she is the one who ran away from Panchala after its defeat against the Princes of Hastinapur."

It was Drupada. Shikhandini winced at her father's words. Her eyes pricked with unshed tears. She wondered how much more humiliation she would have to bear.

"But she is also the one who brought pride and honour to Panchala!" Drupada looked at Shikhandini, his eyes glazed with rare emotion. Clearing his throat, he continued addressing the men, "She was the one who lead this army to victory on the first day of the battle. We were all witness to her bravery and valour that day. She singlehandedly defeated the hundred sons of King Dhritarashtra of Hastinapur, and brought us glory. Each of those Kaurava Princes had been named Rathi by their Guru, Dronacharya. A warrior who defeats twelve Rathis in a single battle earns the title of *Athirathi*, second only to *Maharathi*, as the most celebrated title for a warrior in all of Aryavrath."

Shikhandini stood speechless. Her father, who had been nothing but resentful towards her ever since the lost battle, was now lauding her before the entire Panchalsena. She looked at her brother. He smiled, giving a small nod of reassurance.

"I come here to complete an unfinished task; one I should have done long ago. Shikhadnini, it was wrong to deny you what is rightfully yours, won by your own valour."

For the first time, Shikhandini sensed remorse in her father's voice.

"I, Drupada, King of Panchala, honour you with the title of *Athirathi*. May your courage and strength increase a hundred fold and your name remain immortal. *Ayushman Bhava*!"

Shikhandini knelt on one knee and touched her father's feet. It was a new beginning in their relationship. Her father's acceptance washed away the bitterness that had filled her heart, like debris before a flash food in summer. She could finally forgive everything that had happened in Panchala, for she now had everything she had wanted – her father's approval, dignity and recognition in the Sena, and the love of her family.

A FEW DAYS LATER

It was the early hours of first prahar and Shikhandini had just returned to her mother's chamber after her morning prayers at the banks of the Ganga. Usually, when Shikhandini returned, Kokila was ready with a hot cup of tea and their morning meal. On rare occasions, her father and brother would join them. Today, however, Shikhandini was surprised to find her mother still in bed.

"Ma?" Shikhandini sat down on her mother's bed and reached out a hand to touch the sleeping form. When she did not receive a reply, she shook her mother's arm. When there was still no response, Shikhandini's mind began to cloud with her deepest fears. The inevitable day had finally come.

"Father! Father!" she called, running towards Drupada's chambers.

Within a short time the Queen's chamber was crowded. At the foot of her bed stood Dhrishtadhyumna, and on either side knelt Drupada, and Shikhandini. Panchala's royal Vyed, Gyandevacharya, who had been caring for Kokila for several months, stood at her head, waiting for her to respond to the drops he had administered to bring her back to consciousness. Gyandevacharya was a seventh generation Vyed, who had never been to a gurukul or had any kind of professional training in medicine. He had been taught by his father and grandfather, studying the medical texts written by six generations of his forefathers.

"Shikha..." Kokila's faint voice broke the silence of the chamber.

Shikhandini squeezed her mother's hand. "Ma, I am here."

"Bless you, child." Kokila's eyes glistened with tears. A tired smile flitted across her pale face. "You granted me my last wish by spending my final days here with me. I can now go in peace, with no sorrow to bind my soul." Kokila's voice was barely audible, issuing through chapped and lifeless lips.

"Ma, do not say that! You will be well again. Look, we are all here with you." Shikhandini looked up at Gyandevacharya. His face showed no emotion. Every person in the chamber knew the end had come, but none were prepared to accept it.

Drupada held his wife's hand between his own. It had been several years since he had last been in the Queen's chamber. Their worlds had separated the day Shikhandini left Panchala. In the battle, Drupada had not only lost half of Panchala, but his family.

"Forgive me, Kokila," he whispered to his dying wife. In that moment, the ambitious and egoistic King looked fragile and vulnerable. Gyandevacharya, Shikhandini and Dhrishtadhyumna respectfully averted their eyes as Drupada wept.

"I regret shutting you out of my life, My Lord. I only felt my own pain and forgot that you also lost your daughter that day."

"No, Kokila. You were right. It was entirely my fault. I was blinded by power and ego. I did not realize it then, that no amount of riches or power can replace those we love. Forgive me, Kokila. I filled our lives with unhappiness and regret. If I could, I would undo what I did and make amends."

Kokila tried to press Drupada's hand in comfort, but it was merely a tremulous movement of her fingers. "My Lord, there is something you can do, that will bring happiness."

Drupada looked up in surprise. What could he possibly do to change the past? "Tell me what it is, Kokila! I promise to fulfil it, even at the cost of my own life!"

"I wish Shikhandini's swayamvara to be held here in Kampilya...for you to find the best groom for her. Ensure our daughter will never have to suffer again in her life." There was a pause as the Queen struggled for breath. Finally, she said in a whisper, "Promise me you will surrender my ashes to the holy Ganga only after you have performed our daughter's *kanyadan*. Promise me..."

Drupada felt tears fill his eyes. How little he had considered her suffering in his own arrogance and vainglory. He had taken her child from her. He had left her bereft. He had broken the vows he had taken before the sacred fire, to protect her.

"I promise, Kokila. I will not rest till I have found the best match for our daughter. I will make sure she never has to face pain again in her life," Drupada said quietly, holding his wife's hand between his own.

Shikhandini wept, kneeling beside her mother's bed.

It was as though Drupada's words had freed the shackles of Kokila's soul. Like a bird long caged, her spirit left her body, leaving behind all those she had loved.

16
SHIKHANDINI'S SWAYAMVARA

Unlike Draupadi's swayamvara, the one for Shikhandini was simple and modest. It was a period of mourning in Panchala, for their beloved Queen. But the swayamvara, having been Kokila's last wish, had to be held as soon as possible so her ashes could be scattered in the waters of the holy Ganges and her spirit set free from the mortal realm.

Kings and Princes from near and far were invited. Most of them declined to attend. The prophecy about Maharathi Bheeshm's death at Shikhandini's hands made her intimidating and undesirable. No one wanted the most powerful kingdom of Hastinapur as an enemy.

Due to the humiliation they had suffered in Panchala at Draupadi's swayamvara, none of the Kuru Princes accepted the invitation. Several allies of Hastinapur also turned away. The handful of Kings and Princes who made an appearance at the swayamvara came from distant, petty kingdoms, who either did not believe in the prophecy or did not wish to miss out on a potential alliance with one of the strongest kingdoms in Aryavrat. Many of the candidates were either too old, or wished to take Shikhandini as their fourth or fifth wife. Drupada, who had promised his wife the best match for their daughter, was disappointed.

"You look so pretty, Didi!" said Draupadi as she braided Shikhandini's hair with strings of jasmine. When Draupadi had learnt of the Queen's death, she had felt bereft. Though Kokila was not her birth mother, Draupadi felt a deep sense of loss. She hurried to Panchala to be with her family in this period of grief. It was then that she had met Shikhandini. The sisters forged an affectionate bond and got on well. Draupadi could easily see in Shikhandini, traits of the Queen she had been so fond of.

Shikhandini smiled now in response to her sister's admiring words, but her face wore a faraway look. In the next few hours her life would change forever. She would go away to a place filled with strangers, where she would spend the rest of her life. Images of her life in the Yaksha village, where she had experienced love for the first time, flitted through her mind. She wondered if she would ever be able to love another the way she had loved Kush.

"Who knew Shikhandini could look like a woman!" teased Sarala, placing a *teeka* behind Shikhandini's ear to protect her from the evil eye. Sarala was now the mother of a baby boy.

"It is time, Rajkumari," said one of the maids who had been sent to inform Shikhandini that the swayamvara was about to commence.

"I will escort my sister," replied Draupadi, rising, her hand outstretched.

As Shikhandini walked along the long aisle of the assembly hall, one man occupied her thoughts – Prince Kush. With her head bowed under her veil, and Draupadi and Sarala behind her, Shikhandini tried to catch a glimpse of each Prince she passed by. She saw that most of them were older men, some even twice her age. Others looked like they belonged to the distant snow-clad regions, dressed in furlined robes and pointed hats. She wondered which man's destiny was tied to her own.

Halfway to the dais, where her father and brother stood awaiting her, she abruptly halted.

"Keep walking, Didi!" whispered Draupadi.

But her words did not reach Shikhandini, whose mind was transfixed on the person sitting to the right of the aisle. Forgetting all the etiquette Dai Ma had drummed into her in the last few days, Shikhandini moved her gaze towards the man. "Kush!" she whispered, her eyes glazed with unshed tears as questions swirled in her mind.

The other Princes looked at her and then at Kush in confusion. Hushed whispers began to circulate round the hall.

Kush nodded in response, his eyes reflecting the same emotion as her's. They stared at each other for several seconds before Draupadi quickly intervened.

"Didi!" urged Draupadi, giving Shikhandini a slight push. She stepped beside her sister and guided her gently towards the platform, holding onto her arm.

Shikhandini's mind felt split in two. One overwhelmed with emotion that Kush had come for her. The other fumed with rage. He had left her without a word. He had not replied to her letter. He had cut her out of his life completely. So why is he here now, she wondered.

"I welcome you all to my daughter, Princess Shikhandini's swayamvara," said Drupada, welcoming the Kings and Princes. "As you know, in Panchala, no swayamvara is complete without a contest. My daughter, the firstborn of my clan, has chosen swords as the weapon to win her hand."

The Princes and Kings whispered enthusiastically among themselves, as sword fighting was a common sport in every kingdom.

"However, this will be no ordinary sword fight. The Princess, an Athirathi herself, wishes to challenge contestants to a duel. The person who can best her in the duel, will win her hand."

"That is ridiculous!" declared one of the Kings who had come from one of the southern kingdoms, in disgust.

"Fighting a woman is against our dharma," added another.

"Attacking a woman who is not part of the fight, is also against our dharma, just as attacking an unarmed man is. Duelling a woman who is as good a warrior as any of you present here, is not against any of Kshatriya law," replied Drupada calmly. He was prepared for the questions he knew would arise when Shikhandini had told him what she wished to do. Drupada had acceded to her request, making sure that only Kings and Princes of Athirathi rank were invited since she could only duel with one of equal rank.

"I will not raise my sword against a woman," said one of the contestants in a loud voice. Many of the others agreed. Soon, a series of arguments and discussions began among the participants.

Those Princes who had learned of Shikhandini's valour and sword-fighting skills, and her battle against the hundred Kauravas, wished to win her hand and take her home as a prize. But none wished to duel with her, for if they lost, they would become the laughing stock of every kingdom. Losing to a man was acceptable; losing to a woman was worse than death. Such were the norms of society.

"I find it amusing that any swayamvara in this powerful kingdom is incomplete without insulting the guests. Is this a ritual begun by the proud King of Panchala?" mocked another King, who appeared to be the same age as Drupada.

Shikhandini's gaze remained fixed on Kush, silently willing him to step forward. Her heart told her to forgive Kush and accept him as her *var* and perfect mate. But her mind, which always dominated her inner voice, urged her to challenge and defeat him in a duel.

"I accept the challenge!" came a voice which silenced all others. It was the voice Shikhandini had longed to hear since the day Kush had left Yakshavana.

King Drupada sighed in relief. Perhaps there was such a man to be found in Aryavartha after all, he thought. Looking at the athletic young man standing among the seated Princes, he said, "The Princess agrees to fight you, Prince Kush of Dasarna! The duel will begin in the third hour of this prahar. All our royal guests are welcome to attend. Anyone who desires to object to the contest, must fight me." Drupada looked at each participant, seated on both sides of the aisle. None dared look him in the eye. In the ensuing silence, he turned to look at Shikhandi, his face breaking into a smile.

***

When Shikhandini entered the ring to fight Prince Kush, she was surprised to find that all the Princes and Kings who had been so vociferous in their disapproval, were all present in the audience. The ringing of the prahar bell announced the commencement of the duel.

Shikhandini was the first to attack. She had decided to use a single sword instead of the two she usually did. She required them in battle, when she needed to fight several warriors at the same time. Now, with a sword in her right hand and a shield in her left, she began her attack. Kush, who had often practiced swordplay with Shikhandini in Yakshavana, was aware of her every move. He was amused to see she was not cutting him any slack in the name of the friendship they had once shared. Her face was fierce, hot with rage, her eyes deep pools of swirling emotion. Kush blocked every parry with his own sword, occasionally using his shield to fend off a heavy blow. He knew Shikhandini would cool down soon; she just needed to vent her anger. He smiled inwardly, knowing her emotional intensity meant only one thing – she shared what he felt.

"Why is he not attacking?" Dhrishtadhyumna asked. When he did not get a response, he looked at Drupada. "What is the reason for your mysterious smile, father?" he asked, perplexed.

"He is not attacking because he knows that my daughter, hot-headed Princess that she is, cannot handle defeat. But he wants to win her hand, so he is only defending himself to stay in the duel."

"He is smart," Dhrishtadhyumna replied, admiringly. "But how does he know this about her?"

"That, my son, you will know soon enough."

The duel progressed as per Drupada's prediction. The impact of Shikhandini's blows eventually reduced in intensity and power, exhausted mentally rather than physically. In that moment, she realized how important focus of mind was. Had it been a fight against an enemy or in battle with an enemy kingdom, she would have felt more energized with each attack. But today, she was fighting someone she knew she could never hurt. She felt dazed and confused. What she was fighting for? What was she trying to prove?

Kush, who had been observing the various emotions flitting across her face, knew the moment had come. When he sensed Shikhandini no longer wanted to fight, he decided to finish the duel. With a single blow to the middle of Shikhandini's sword, he disarmed her. Her sword fell to the ground.

What happened next took everyone by surprise. Instead of picking up her sword and continuing the duel, Shikhandini walked out of the ring, accepting defeat. While all those watching murmured in disappointment, some even urging Shikhandini to return and continue the fight, two people smiled, relieved it was over. One was Prince Kush, the other King Drupada.

"I am proud of you, son. I know what you did. There was no better way to win. You have not only won my daughter, but also made a special place for yourself in our hearts," Drupada said, placing both his hands on Kush's shoulders. "I think it is the right time to announce the marriage."

Kush put his palms together. "King Drupada, with all due respect, I wish to speak to your daughter before you make any announcement. I wish to know for myself that she agrees to this with a free heart."

"Ah, yes. Go...we will await you, my son."

Once Kush was out of sight, Dhrishtadhyumna approached his father. "Do you think Didi will refuse to marry Prince Kush?"

"No, my son, I have no such apprehension. Prince Kush is the ideal match for our Shikhandini. He will surely win her heart. Call the astrologer and let us decide on an auspicious time for the ceremony."

"Yes, father. I will send for him immediately," smiled the Prince.

***

When Kush entered the chamber Shikhandini had once shared with her mother, he found her seated on her bed, looking at her mother's portrait. Her face was free of all emotion, like a calm river after the passing of a catastrophic flood.

Kush knelt before her, his voice gentle with empathy. "I am sorry Shikhandini, that you had to face the pain of losing your mother."

Shikhandini shifted her gaze to her hands, that now lay ensconsced in Kush's. She quickly averted her eyes.

"Listen to me, Shikha," he pleaded.

"Why?" Shikhandini asked, her voice almost inaudible. "Why did you leave?" Her throat felt dry and her breath hitched as she spoke.

Kush closed his eyes shut. It pained him to see her hurting and vulnerable. "What was I supposed to do, Shikhandini? You rejected me. You refused to give me a chance."

Shikhandini had no words. It was true she had decided to turn away from him so her cursed fate would not touch his life. She had lost everyone she had ever loved. Not wanting to bring trouble into Kush's life, she had decided to bury her feelings. But destiny had brought them back together. She thought how far she had come. She now had her family; her father had forgiven her; her brother looked up to her; and her sister viewed her in her mother's place. She had everything she had yearned for. The prophecy relating to her birth seemed as ephemeral as the wind. For a brief moment she remembered Bheeshm and the tale of Amba's life. She wondered if she was indeed the right person to render justice for the Princess of Kashi. Had Amba loved Prince Salva as much as she loved Kush? Would she be forgiven for choosing to marry Kush and live a normal life instead of slaying the man who had ruined Amba's life? Would the Princess, of all people, understand the meaning of true love and the agony of losing it forever?

"Speak, Shikha. What is it?" Kush's voice pulled her from her reverie.

Tears, too long suppressed, rolled down Shikhandini's cheeks. Kush pulled her into a comforting embrace. A wave of relief washed over him as he realized she had forgiven him. Losing all sense of time, they held each other.

"It was not your fault. I should have waited. I should have stayed and tried to understand the reason for your rejection instead of leaving in haste," Kush confessed, knowing he too, had been at fault.

"But why did you not reply to my letter?" Shikhandini asked.

"Letter? What letter?" Kush asked pulling back so he could look into her face.

"I wrote to you, hoping you would reply.When you did not, I felt lost and helpless," Shikhandini replied, wiping her tears.

"Shikha, I swear in the name of Lord Shiva that I did not receive a letter. Had I received any kind of communication from you, I would have come to Yakshavana without a second thought."

"But how is that possible? My letter did not come back, unopened. That was why I assumed you had chosen not to reply." Shikhandini, who had used the bird courier as the only means of communication with her mother since her childhood, knew the bird would have brought the letter back if it did not find the recipient. If the bird returned without the letter, it meant the recipient has not sent a reply.

"If you did not get the letter and I did not get it back, then where did the letter go?" Kush wondered.

A soft knock on the door interrupted their conversation. Hastily, they composed themselves. It was Drupada and the Raj Guru.

"The wedding ceremony will be held four days from now, in the second prahar. Invitations are being sent to everyone without whom this wedding would be incomplete. Kush, I have despatched a rider to your father, King Hiranyavarna," said Drupada., who had lost no time in beginning the preparartions in accordance with his wife's wishes "And Shikhandini…an invitation has been sent to Yakshavana too. Without Sthunakarna, I would never have learned about Kush," said Drupada, a twinkle in his usually sombre eyes.

Shikhandini and Kush looked at each other and smiled. After darkness and sorrow, joy had finally come.

17
Indraprastha

Kush and Shikhandini's wedding was as modest as a nuptial between royals could be. Apart from Drupada, Sthunakarna and the immediate family, Dai Ma and Sarala were present to bless the couple. Kush's father, King Hiranyavarna, graced the occasion with his presence, though he was less than pleased at the union. This did not escape either Kush or Shikhandini's notice.

The ceremony was held in the temple in the palace gardens where Kokila had spent so much of her time. For Shikhandini, there could be no better place to begin her new life. Here, she felt closest to her mother; the place they had been reunited after years of separation. And it was here Shikhandini had spent evenings with her mother, teaching the village children in her last days.

The couple sat before the holy fire, into which the Raj Purohit poured *ghee,* fruits and sandalwood paste, as offerings to the Gods. As Shikhandini closed her eyes in prayer, she sensed someone's gaze upon her. Slowly opening her eyes, she looked around. Everyone seemed to be engrossed in the ceremony. Draupadi and Sarala were whispering to each other, while Dai Ma bent a stern look upon them for not respecting the ritual in silence. Shikhandini shook her head' maybe she was imagining things. She closed her eyes again.

But the feeling of being watched did not go away. In fact, it kept getting stronger. Opening her eyes again, she turned to her left. A smile crept onto her lips. It was Kush. His gaze was fixed on her; his eyes soft with tenderness. It was something she had craved to see. They looked at each other, treasuring this moment that would bind their lives and destinies forever. Time ceased to exist.

It was during these moments, as the ancient chants rang in their ears, that Shikhandini found herself lost in reflection. Along with others, father had contacted Sthunakarna at Yakshavana, to know if he knew of any suitable grooms. On Sthunakarna's advice, Drupada had personally invited Prince Kush to the swayamvara. Everything had then gone as per plan. Shikhandini felt a wave of affection for her father. But one question lingered in her mind, where had her letter to Kush gone?

***

"Father, why did you do that?" Kush was shocked beyond belief.

After the wedding, King Hiranyavarna had accompanied the newly married couple to Dasarna. They arrived home to a rather muted bridal reception. Then, as day followed day, one matter kept niggling in Kush's mind. He finally decided to confront his father about the letter Shikhandini had written him, which he had never received.

Hiranyavarna looked at his son in silence for a few moments before saying, "I had no choice. I was afraid you would want to marry her."

"But why, father? I love her. She is a good woman, a valiant warrior. And is not allying with Panchala a dream you have cherished?" Kush knew that his father's ambition had led him into forging alliances with powerful and prosperous kingdoms, no matter the cost.

"Panchala is a great kingdom, my son, far greater than Dasarna. Under different circumstances, I would be proud. But Shikhandini is not an ordinary girl. Her destiny is as clear as the water from the holy river. She is the chosen one. She will be the cause of Maharathi Bheeshm's death. And when that happens, everyone associated with her will have to face the wrath of Hastinapur."

Kush looked at his father in astonishment. He had never considered that foolish prophecy to be anything but gossip in the wind.

"I know that you do not believe in prophecies, but the truth is the person who read her destiny after her birth, was no ordinary man. The world has yet to see one of his prophecies prove untrue. His knowledge and understanding of the stars is unquestionable," the King said, remembering the Late *Raj Jyothishi* of Panchala.

"But father, Panchala is an ally of Hastinapur. Shikhandini's younger sister, Princess Draupadi, is married to the Pandava Princes. A war between Panchala and Hastinapur seems unlikely." Kush attempted to counter his father's words with logic.

"Destiny will have its way, my son. Nothing, no matter how powerful, can change its course. If Shikhandini is meant to kill Maharathi Bheeshm, it will happen," Hiranyavarna sighed.

Kush did not know how to convince his father and decided to hold his peace. He knew his father would never do anything to hurt him. It would take him some time to accept Shikhandini, but he would eventually come around.

Hiranyavarna too, knew he would have to accept the marriage. He loved his son. But as King of Dasarna, the safety of his kingdom was his fisrt priority. The well-being of his people came before that of even his own family. "I accept your marriage to the Princess of Panchala under one condition. If and when the day arrives when Shikhandini has to fulfill her life's purpose, Dasarna will not be a part of it. She will not receive any help from our Sena. Her battle will be hers alone," he said sternly in a voice from which all emotion had fled.

"I accept, father. I promise Dasarna will never have to face danger because of me or my wife. If the day comes when I have to choose between my love or my people, I will make sure Dasarna remains safe," Kush replied, his eyes staring into those of his father.

Shikhnadini, who had been a silent witness to the exchange between father and son, now spoke. "I too promise that under no circumstances will Dasarna suffer because of me." She knew the King's fear was not unfounded.

Hiranyavarna nodded in response and walked out of the chamber, not completely convinced.

TEN YEARS LATER....

Ten long years passed by. Much had changed in the royal families of Hastinapur and Panchala, but to King Hiranyavarna's relief, Dasarna remained prosperous and safe. Over the years, Draupadi and Shikhandini's bond strengthened. They wrote frequently, filling each other in on their lives.

When Shikhandini had heard of the trick fate had played on her sister, making her the wife of not just Arjun, but all five Pandava brothers, she had been shocked, wondering what destiny had in store for Draupadi. She prayed the brothers would treat her well. From Raj Purohit, the royal priest of Panchala, who had also conducted the Puthrakameshti Yagya, Shikhandini understood how such an incidence in a society where polygamy was accepted but polyandry unheard of, came to be.

"Again and again, there comes a time in history, where all rules and conventions have to be amended or broken for the larger good.

Panchali's marriage to the five Pandavas ensured that the five sons of King Pandeshwar remained united, for there is no greater tie than the marital bond. The five brothers together took the vow to protect Panchali, and to live and strive as one. Panchali is the force that binds them. This will be the most important factor in the restoration of dharma when the time comes," he explained.

It was through her correspondence with her sister that Shikhandini learned of the partition of the Hastinapur kingdom between the Kauravas and Pandavas, and how the Pandavas had been given the wild forest land of Khandavaprastha, as their share. Draupadi wrote how she and her husbands planned to build a magnificent kingdom there with the help of the tribal serpent-people and their leader, Thakshak. It had been almost a year since Shikhandini had last heard from Draupadi. She worried that her sister was enduring difficult times. Finally a letter arrived.

Pranam Didi. I hope this finds you in good health. I apologise for not writing to you more often but I was waiting for something good to write about, and now the time has arrived. Our palace is finally ready. We call it Indraprastha, in honour of Lord Indra, without whom we could not have succeded in this task. To mark this and Yudhistir's coronation, a grand feast has been prepared. My husbands have invited all the Kings and Princes of Aryavrath, including Prince Duryodhan of Hastinapur. They believe it will be a great opportunity to mend broken bonds.

Didi, I know the thoughts that must be in your mind as you read this. I also know that you do not wish to cross paths with anyone from Hastinapur, especially Maharathi Bheeshm. I respect that. So I have arranged for you to visit after the ceremony. It will be just you and me. We can talk to our hearts' content about everything we have missed in the last few years.

There is so much more to tell you. I will count the days to your arrival. I ask you to come on behalf of my entire family. Please do visit us. I will eagerly await your arrival.

***

Indraprastha was the most magical and magnificent capital city in all of Aryavrath. Designed by the best architect of the time, Mayasura, it was next only to the heavenly abode of Lord Indra. It was located in what had once been the Khandavaprastha forest, home of the serpent-people, who worshipped Lord Vasuki, the seven-hooded snake that formed the throne of Lord Vishnu. The leader of the tribe was Takshak, beloved devotee of Lord Indra. When the serpent-people had been banished from the mainland, they had prayed to Lord Indra, who had created Khandavaprastha for them.

When the Pandavas received Khandavaprastha as their share in the division of Kuru land, they too, prayed to Lord Indra to help them build their own capital to be as magnificent as Hastinapur. In return, they promised to look after the serpent-tribe. Pleased with this, Lord Indra granted them their wish and appointed Mayasura as chief architect. The establishment of such a divine city would have been impossible without Lord Indra's blessing, so the new capital was named Indraprastha, in his honour.

It was the second prahar when Shikhandini reached Indraprastha. Several days had passed since Yudhistir's *Rajasuya Yagya,* when he had been crowned King of Indraprastha. The ceremony had taken place in the presence of several Kings, who had all sworn allegiance. Kunti, mother to the Pandavas, Princes Duryodhan and Dushasana, as well as their maternal cousin, Krishna, had also been present to grace the occasion.

The palace at Indraprastha looked no different from other palaces from the outside. It was a vast structure, built at the exact centre of the new city. People from all over Aryavrath, including Hastinapur, had begun moving to this prosperous new place. Many of the larger kingdoms had declared allegiance to the Pandavas.

As Shikhandini arrived at the palace, she looked around in awe. It was nothing like she had ever seen. On either side of the entrance, were high waterfalls, the water from which dropped in a particular cadence onto the metal plates below to form a melodious tune, to welcome the guests. On either side of the walkway that led into the palace, were small flowering plants, brought from near and far, the fragrance of which, along with the sound of the singing waterfall, created a serene ambience.

"Didi, you have come!" squealed Draupadi at the sight of her sister.

Shikhandini embraced Draupadi, who looked much older than Shikhandini remembered. "This place is beautiful, Draupadi!" beamed Shikhandini, looking around.

"Yes, Mayasura has created a msterpiece. Wait till you see the audience chamber. It is truly remarkable. It is called the *Mayasabha.*"

As the name suggested, the Mayasabha was a place of wonder. Everything was a feast for the eyes. At the entrance stood two fountains made of crystal carved in the shape of maidens, their hands cupped to form a bowl, from which poured sparkling water bright enough to blind the beholder for a moment. The floor was made of glass, under which ran a stream. Fish and seaweed of different shapes and colours swam and floated in it. Above the chamber was a magnificent dome, with intricate carvings that symbolized the wonders of nature. The apex of the dome was made of glass, through which entered rays of sunlight, illuminating the entire space. The walls were painted white, symbolizing purity and peace. The pillars were carved with unusual designs and embedded with tiny mirrors that reflected the sunlight, creating mesmerizing illusions.

In the centre of the room, on a raised platform, sat the most beautiful throne Shikhandini had ever seen. It was a throne meant for two – the King and Queen. Shikhandini beamed with pride at the thought of her sister being Queen in such a place.

"Is is not amazing?" asked Draupadi proudly. Unable to contain her excitement, she explained every detail of the palace infrastructure.

Shikhandini nodded in response. "I have no words for it, Draupadi. I am really happy for you," she said, placing her hand on Draupadi's head in an affectionate gesture.

"Let us talk in the garden, Didi. You will love it there," suggested Draupadi, dragging Shikhandini along by the hand.

Behind them, on a balcony on the first storey of the palace, stood Arjun, an amused expression on his face.

"What is so amusing, Arjun?" asked Bheem, who was passing by.

"She reminds me of the time I first met her, carefree and feisty," his brother replied, gazing at Draupadi. Her sister's visit had brought out the delighted child in her. "Our struggles have taken a toll on her. I have not seen her so happy," he said, a sad look in his eyes.

"You are right, Arjun. She has seen nothing but hardship ever since she married us. I hope Indraprastha will put an end to that."

Below, in the garden, Draupadi had found a spot to sit. "Didi, there is so much I have to tell you!" she said, barely able to contain her excitement. "During the Rajasuya Yagya, there was an incident," she began mysteriously.

"What incident?" asked Shikhandini, instantly concerned. She had heard nothing of this.

"Madhav used his *Sudharshana Chakra* on Sisupala," Draupadi whispered, as though saying it aloud would be a bad omen.

"What!" Shikhandini gasped. "But why?" She knew Krishna had many names, Madhav...Shyam....Gopal... but that his main weapon, the Sudharshana Chakra, was one of the deadliest ever known. She also knew that it was unlike Krishna to use it to kill someone.

"Sisupala, that arrogant beast, insulted us with his spiteful words," Draupadi replied, gritting her teeth as she uttered the name. "He humiliated Mother Kunti and Maharathi Bheeshm. He called my husbands cowards, and provoked the other Kings to rise against Madhav, saying he was just a cowherd. Madhav warned him several times to mind his tongue, but he paid no heed."

"Who is this Sisupala, and why does he hate you all so much?"

"Sisupala is cousin to both Madhav and my husbands. His hatred for Madhav goes back to the time of a prophecy that his death would occur at Madhav's hands. Fearing the death of her son, Sisupala's mother, Madhav's aunt, pleaded with him to spare her son's life. Madhav promised to forgive Sisupala one hundred offenses before killing him. Sisupala is an arrogant man who does not respect anyone. He had already squandered ninety-nine of his chances before coming to the yagya," Draupadi explained. "So when he questioned my character and cast doubt on my relationship with Madhav, all hell broke loose. Madhav used his chakra to silence him."

"I am sorry Draupadi, that you had to witness this on such an important day in your life," replied Shikhandini gently.

"I know, Didi. Death in the palace was the last thing I had imagined," said Draupadi, her beautiful face sad.

As the hours flew by, the sisters talked about everything under the sun. For those few hours, they were just two sisters who loved gossiping and joking, not Princesses and Queens. As they strolled about, they came across a small pond in a pavilion, surrounded by white pebbles and colourful flowers." Shikhandini peeked into the pond, looking at her reflection among the fish and admiring the serenity of the place. She wished Kush could see this place. He would have surely have enjoyed it. She wondered what he was doing. Her thoughts were interrupted by the sound of Draupadi giggling.

"What is it, Draupadi? What is so funny?"

"Nothing, Didi. Just a funny incident I happened to remember," Draupadi replied, trying hard not to laugh.

"What incident?" Shikhandini could not help but smile at Draupadi's contagious amusement.

"While Duryodhan was touring the palace, he walked into this pond, assuming it to be a glass floor, like in the Mayasabha," Draupadi giggled.

"Well, who can blame him? The water is so still and clear, it looks like it is covered by glass. An illusion, of course," replied Shikhandini.

"Yes, Didi. But the sight of such a giant of a man, an exceptional warrior and future King of Hastinapur, falling into a tiny pond and scaring the poor fish, was hilarious!" replied Draupadi, giggling.

"Draupadi, it is not right to mock anyone like that. He is a Prince, an arrogant and egoistical one at that. You never know how he may try to avenge his humiliation." Shikhandini, who had heard several stories about Duryodhan and his cunning uncle, Shakuni, knew they could stoop to anything to destroy the Pandavas.

"I am sorry, Didi," replied Draupadi, half-apologetically, her smile not fading one jot.

Little did she know that her girlish laughter would one day cost her everything she had.

18
GAME OF DICE

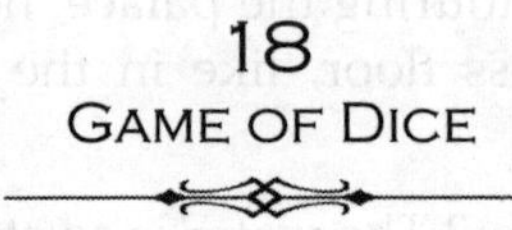

"I will teach that arrogant Panchali a lesson she will never forget! Every time she thinks of me she will shudder in fear!" swore Duryodhan as he paced back and forth in his chamber, burning with anger and humiliation.

"Be calm. Do not make any decisions in haste," cautioned Karna, attempting to cool his friend's wrath but Duryodhan dismissed Karna's words with a wave of his hand.

Karna had just heard of the incident that had occurred in Indraprastha, how Duryodhan, while casually strolling through a garden pavilion had stepped into a pond, assuming the clear surface to be hardened glass. Draupadi's giggles at his predicament had angered the already embarrassed Duryodhan, who had instantly announced his return to Hastinapur. It was given out that state affairs required his presence in the Kuru capital. But Duryodhan was not one to forget his bruised ego, nor forgive.

Karna knew Draupadi had not meant to insult the Prince, though the Queen of Indraprastha was in many ways still naïve and impulsive. She was not one to think of consequences before acting on her thoughts. But Karna also knew this would make no difference to the hot headed Prince of Hastinapur.

"Brother, we will show Panchali and those good-for-nothing husbands of her's, that it is unwise to insult the Prince and future King of Hastinapur," said Dushasana, adding faggots to the already burning fire in Duryodhan's mind.

Duryodhan lit his *chillum*. The others sat in silence as Dushasana walked around, murmuring to himself. Karna was lost in his own thoughts, wondering how many more years this bitter relationship between the cousins would last.

It was Shakuni, who had thus far been silent, finally broke the silence. The sound of his chilling laughter suddenly filled the chamber. "I have the perfect plan to avenge Duryodhan's humiliation without breaking any rules or angering the elders. In fact, Maharathi Bheeshm will himself invite the Pandavas to Hastinapur," said Shakuni, a smirk on his angular face.

"What is this plan, Uncle?" asked Duryodhan skeptically.

"By inviting you, Indraprastha has taken a step towards rebuilding a relationship with Hastinapur and mending the broken bonds between the families. It is now our turn to respond. We shall arrange a grand feast to return their hospitality," said Shakuni dryly.

"Uncle Shakuni, have you forgotten what happened?" growled Dushasana, exasperated.

Duryodhan raised his hand, signalling to his younger brother to let Shakuni finish.

"When the Pandava brothers are in high spirits, we will use their greatest weakness to avenge Duryodhan's humiliation."

"But Uncle, the Pandavas are known to be righteous and wise. I doubt they have any glaring flaws we can make use of," said Dushasana as Shakuni's plan sank into his mind.

"Any man, no matter how wise, always has a weakness, an addiction, a soft spot for someone, a dear possession...something that makes him vulnerable. No man is perfect, my child. No man. Each has some flaw. Some are just good at hiding their flaws," Shakuni told his nephews, knowing more of the world than they did.

"What flaw are the Pandavas hiding, Uncle?" asked Dushasana, still not convinced.

"Even if there is a flaw we can use, how can we discover it?" added Duryodhan, his agile mind more perceptive than his brother's.

"I think we already know," replied Shakuni quietly, pulling something from his waist pouch and unrolling it on the low table in front of him.

Everyone gathered around. As he peered over Shakuni's shoulder, Dushasana beamed with delight. A smile crept across Duryodhan's face for the first time since his return from Indraprastha.

On the table sat two long, perfectly carved dice, made of human bones, showing a perfect six…each.

THE PALACE OF HASTINAPUR, A FORTNIGHT LATER

Draupadi sat in the chamber Gandhari had set aside for her use. Several hours had passed since the game of dice had started. Draupadi was anxious to learn how the game was progressing, wishing her husbands had not chosen to participate at all. She had a premonition the game was a trap. Shakuni was known to be cunning, and a master of the game. She was also aware of Yudhistir's weakness. The eldest of the Pandava brothers, known to be wise and compassionate, had a fatal addiction. He could never refuse a game of dice. It was the weakness Shakuni had spoken of. Yudhistir believed he was the best player in all Aryavarth.

But as the hours passed, a maid brought Draupadi the news that her husband had staked and lost much of his wealth. Prince Duryodhan was playing against him, under the guidance of his uncle, Shakuni. Draupadi's heart sank as dismay filled her mind. But what she still did not know was that Yudhistir had not only lost Indraprastha to Duryodhan, but also his four brothers, who were now slaves of the Prince of Hastinapur.

At the sound of heavy footsteps approaching her chamber, Draupadi stood up in trepidition. Instinct warned her of impending danger. Holding a dagger, she stood alert, ready to attack. But, though bold and agile, she was untrained, and did not stand a chance against a well trained warrior.

Dushasana appeared at her door, a lacivious grin on his face as his eyes roamed over her slim form. "I am here to escort you to the *sabha*, Panchali," he hissed,

"I will not appear in the *sabha* unless the Queen permits me to," she replied, taking a step away from him.

It was an accepted custom that royal women did not appear when men were feasting or gaming. They were protected from such scenes.

"That is not a decision for you to make, you whore! You now belong to Prince Duryodhan. You are no longer a Queen. Your husband has lost everything, including you, in the dice game," he announced, roaring with laughter.

"Mind your tongue Prince, for you speak to the Queen of Indraprastha!" warned Draupadi, seething with anger. She refused to believe him.

"Do not seek to teach me, you arrogant wench!" growled Dushasana, moving towards her. With one hand he grabbed her hair and pulled her out of the chamber.

Draupadi's agonized screams tore through the silence of the night as they approached the sabha. Somewhere outside the palace, a flock of crows cawed, mourning the death of one of their number. Clouds veiled the moon, as if afraid to witness the actions of men.

Dushasana paid no heed to Draupadi's protests and pleas. He dragged her to the centre of the hall, where Duryodhan stood, legs apart, hands on hips, a look of deep pleasure on his handsome face. Draupadi looked towards her husbands, her eyes pleading. But they averted their eyes from her distress, helplessness to aid her. Yudhistir stood as though dazed, while Bheem, the giant warrior, bawled like a child in pain and despair. Never before had he felt so disabled. Nakul and Sahadev, the valiant twins, took a step towards her, but Arjun stopped them, fearing to further anger Duryodhan and thus cause Draupadi more harm. Tears filled their eyes, as they witnessed the humiliation their wife was facing at their cousins' hands.

When she realized her husbands would not come to her rescue, Draupadi turned to Maharathi Bheeshm, whom she adored like a father. But her cries to him fell on deaf ears. Maharathi Bheeshm sat with his head hung in shame. The strongest and most invincible warrior of all time was helpless. In that moment he realized what a worthless life he had led. His immortality was nothing but a curse bestowed upon him for the sins of a previous life.

Prime Minister Vidura and Guru Dronacharya stood on the platform along side Maharathi Bheeshm, watching Draupadi being dragged to the centre of the sabha. They too, were helpless. The fact that Yudhistir had willingly staked his wife in the game prevented anyone from intervening. Prince Duryodha had won and Draupadi was now his chattel.

Draupadi's scalp pricked as Dushasana pulled at her hair, wound round his fist. He showed no mercy as he pushed her forward to where Duryodhan and the Pandavas stood.

"A day shall come when I will pull out the very arms that have dared to touch the Queen of Indraprastha!" Bheem's voice echoed in the vaulted chamber.

A shiver ran up Dushasana's spine at the words, but he did not let go of Draupadi. In a last feeble attempt to save her dignity, Draupadi looked towards Karna, who was known to be a righteous man despite his friendship with Duryodhan. Karna, like the other great men in the court, averted his eyes. He too, was helpless.

"Ah, there she is! I have waited long for this day!" exclaimed Duryodhan, staring at Draupadi in disdain.

Draupadi stared back at the Prince, her eyes filled with pride, despite the hammering of her heart in her chest.

"You do not deserve to sit on a Queen's throne, Panchali! Come, sit on my lap!" Duryodhan said, roaring with laughter as he took a seat on the platform.

Draupadi was shocked by his crude words. The Pandava brothers looked as though their very souls had been torn from their bodies. They knew Draupadi had no choice but to follow Duryodhan's orders; she was his slave.

"Watch your tongue, Duryodhan!" roared Bheem once again. Of the five Pandavas, it was Bheem who loved Draupadi most dearly. He was also the only one of the five to speak, not caring in that moment about dharma or adharma. All he knew was that Draupadi did not deserve to be treated in this manner. But he could not raise his weapon without Yudhistir's permission. "There will come a day when I will flay you alive! I will destroy your thighs; the thighs on which you summoned Draupadi to sit. I will personally escort you to your doom. This I promise you, Prince Duryodhan!"

As Bheem's words echoed in the chamber, King Dhritarashtra moved in his seat. He had been sitting in silence, frozen by the turn of events. Prince Duryodhan was the dearest among his sons. He loved the Prince more than his throne or even his principles. His love drove him to condone all Duryodhan did, blind alike to right and wrong. When he heard Bheem's vow, a cold sweat formed on his brow. He knew the giant warrior had never failed to fulfil his words; he would do exactly as he had vowed.

"Do not waste my time, Draupadi. Obey your master's orders!" shouted Duryodhan, angered by Bheem's words.

"I am no one's slave, Prince! King Yudhistir had no right to stake me in the game without my consent. I will not obey your orders." With that, Draupadi turned to walk out.

"Draupadi, you have dared to disobey me! For this you shall be punished," said Duryodhan, who had never been disobeyed before. "Dushasana, disrobe the arrogant woman. Strip her of her dignity. Show her lowly place!" orederd Duryodhan.

Draupadi stood shocked, her mind spinning in disbelief as Duryodhan's words seeped into it, insidious as poison.

Dushasana approached Draupadi, grinning malevolently. The thought of disrobing his sister-in-law in the presence of the court, filled him with anticipation. Grabbing hold of her angavastram, he pulled her to the centre of the sabha once again. As though protesting such indignity, the last vestiges of the moon disappeared from the sky, leaving darkness.

Draupadi stood with folded hands and closed eyes, chanting the name of Krishna, whom she, like thousands of others, believed to be an incarnation of Lord Vishnu himself. Scenes that seemed to have occurred in another lifetime, flashed in her mind: She and her husbands had been invited by Krishna to Dwarka, for the kite flying contest. They had all gathered on the terrace of the palace, waiting for their kites to pick up speed. Krishna and Arjun were contesting, hoping to cut each other's kite lines. The air was filled with joy and enthusiasm. For the first time Draupadi saw her husbands carefree and happy. She noticed a drop of blood near Krishna's left foot. Oblivious to the cut on his palm, made by the kite string, Krishna kept pulling his kite higher. Instinctively, Draupadi tore a piece off her angavastram and tied it around his hand. Pleased by Draupadi's gesture, Krishna placed his hand on her head affectionately, promising to be by her side in her times of adversity.

When Draupadi opened her eyes, she was surprised to see an exhausted Dushasana kneeling on the floor, surrounded by lengths of sari. Her body was still covered. Krishna had indeed heard her.

There was utter silence in the sabha, every eye on the endless drapes being pulled from the woman who stood as still as a statue, her eyes closed, her lips moving in prayer. Draupadi would later hear from Arjun what had occurred in the time her eyes remained closed. A divine light made its way into the sabha and formed a barrier around her. It was blinding. Dushasana kept dragging at her angavastram, but it seemed endless. It was only when he finally stopped, exhausted, that the light slowly faded away, revealing Draupadi as she had been before the incident.

***

Following her visit to Indraprastha, Shikhandini was relieved of worry regarding her sister. She was proud of how Draupadi had stood by her husbands and built the magnificent Indraprastha. Several weeks after returning to Dasarna, Shikhandini wrote Draupadi, wanting to know how things were in Indraprastha, but her messenger bird brought her letter back. Shikhandini wrote again after a few days, but that letter too, was returned. Shikhandini began to worry about Draupadi's well being.

On the auspicious occasion of *Deepawali,* the festival of lights, Shikhandini decided to visit Panchala, as she did every year. It was a festival that marked the return of Lord Ram to his kingdom, Ayodhya, after his victory over Ravana, King of Lanka. Deepawali was always celebrated with great festivity and joy in Panchala. Shikhandini was sure her father would have news about Draupadi.

Since Dasarna was a small principality with limited resources, it was considered insignificant to the larger ambitions of the more exalted kingdoms. It was usually one of the last to hear of any incidences that occurred in Panchala or Hastinapur. It was nearly three weeks after Shikhandini's visit to Indraprastha, that news of the grand yagya at the new kingdom reached Dasarna's common people.

Shikhandini left Dasarna for Panchala with a small group of maids and bodyguards. She chose to ride her horse Surya, instead of travelling in a palanquin like royal women usually did. Since Dasarna was close to southern Panchala, it was a short journey to her father's kingdom. Kush was also away, on a *Digvijay Yatra.* He was due to return to Dasarna after the festival.

On her arrival in Panchala, Shikhandini was welcomed at the palace gates by her father, the Raj Guru, and Dai Ma. Sarala and her son were also present. In one of her letters, Dai Ma had mentioned Sarala now worked in the palace, while her ten-year-old son, Dhruv, trained with the soldiers of the Panchalsena.

"Pranam Pitashri! Pranam Dai Ma," Shikhandi said in greeting, bowing, having dismounted from her horse.

"Pranam Shikhandini," replied Drupada.

Dai Ma embraced her, murmuring blessings, and Sarala welcomed her friend with a warm hug.

Drupada left for the council chamber while the women walked towards the chamber Shikhandini had once shared with her mother. There, Sarala left them to go to the royal kitchen.

Left alone, Shikhandini decided to ask Dai Ma the question that had been gnawing at her mind. "Dai Ma, I have not heard from Draupadi ever since I returned from Indraprastha. Is there something I should be aware of?"

Dai Ma looked at her with sad eyes as a single drop of tear traced it a path on her wrinkled skin. It was not too long before Dai Ma had a breakdown for the nth time, ever since the incident had occurred.

"Dai Ma..." Shikhandini walked towards her with a look of horror. Dai Ma was not someone who cried easily. Now thinking of it, Shikhandini had seen Dai Ma cry just once before today. It was when the news of Sarala's husband's death in a battle had reached them. Sarala's husband, Markhand, was a soldier in the Panchala Sena.

"Dai Ma, Please tell me what happened"

As Dai Ma narrated the events of the Dhyutsabha, Shikhandini's world seemed to crumble and fall apart. The thought of Draupadi being disrobed in the courtroom of Hastinapur felt surreal. Her sister was the *Samragini,* the Queen of Queens. How did they let this happen to her? Prince Duryodhan was an evil man. This was expected from him and his good-for-nothing brothers. But what shocked Shikhandini was that the incident had occurred in the presence of Guru Dronacharya and Maharathi Bheeshm. The Maharathi's silence against this heinous crime added ammunition to Shikhandini's already blazing hatred towards him.

"Where is Draupadi now?" asked Shikhandini as she looked at the setting sun from her window. Her glassy eyes reflected the red sky as though burning with fire within.

"I do not know, my child. There are rumours they have been sent into exile by the Prince of Hastinapur. The Pandavas lost everything in that insane game," replied Dai Ma, gritting her teeth. Her hatred for the game was evident in her tone.

Emerging from her chamber, Shikhandini walked towards the inner garden. She knew it was where her father would come to feed the birds once his council session was ended.

When Drupada arrived, he was surprised to see a serious faced Shikhandini waiting for him. He realised she had heard the news.

"Father, Dai Ma told me everything."

"It was a most unfortunate incident, my child," replied Drupada trying to hold back his tears.

"Where is she now? Where are the Pandavas? Why did you not go to her rescue?" Shikhandini asked urgently, anger consuming her.

"Panchali is no longer ours to save, my child. Intervening in this matter would be to insult the Pandavas. They have vowed to avenge her humiliation. Bheem has sworn to tear open Prince Dushasana's chest and drink his blood. Panchali herself has vowed not to bind her hair, by which she was dragged by Dushasana into the Hastinapur sabha, till the day she can wash it in Dushasana's blood." Drupada's face was shadowed with foreboding as he uttered the words.

Shikhandini, however, felt a strange relief when she heard the vows. "I must see Draupadi," she told her father.

"That is not possible, my child. Their whereabouts are unknown. They were sent into exile for twelve years, after which they must spend another year in disguise. The Raj Jyothishi has predicted a Great War soon thereafter," Drupada told his daughter sadly.

"A Great War?"

"Yes. It will be fought for the restoration of dharma. What happened to Draupadi was adharma. When a woman's dignity is stripped in a room full of warriors and learned men, one knows that the world order as we knew it, must come to an end. It is a precursor to doomsday. The Great War will mark the end of this *yuga*." So saying, Drupada walked away, leaving Shikhandini perplexed.

As Shikhandini walked back to her chamber, dark thoughts clouded her mind. She wondered how Draupadi was. Her cheerful face in Indraprastha flashed before Shikhandini's eyes. Sadness filled her heart as she realized how fleeting had been her sister's happiness. Everything had been stripped from her – position, palace, power, dignity...everything. Shikhandini felt anger rise as images of the *Dhyutsabha* formed in her mind. She said a silent prayer of gratitude to Krishna for saving her when none other would. She felt infuriated at the thought of the helpless Pandava brothers, who, despite their strength and valour had not come to Draupadi's rescue.

As she hurried along, Shikhandini felt her legs tremble. Her breathing was laboured and she felt lightheaded. Her vision began to blur and beads of sweat formed on her forehead. Her hands and feet felt deathly cold. Before she could call for help, she dropped to the floor and darkness engulfed her.

***

When Shikhandini regained consciousness, she was surprised to find an air of rejoicing around her. She heard her father say, "Let Panchala be decorated like never before! Let there be a grand feast for everyone in the kingdom and beyond! Let it be known that King Drupada will soon bear a new name – Pitamaha!"

Shikhandini could not believe her ears. She looked around to find Dai Ma watching her tenderly. She nodded, assuring Shikhandini that what she had just heard was true. It had been ten years since Shikhandini's marriage to the Prince of Dasarna. Though Kush never mentioned it, he had longed for a child. But King Hiranyavarna often spoke of the royal succession. Shikhandini had felt guilty and helplessness for not being able to give Dasarna an heir.

She now longed to return to Dasarna as soon as possible, to tell Kush the happy news about the impending arrival of a little Prince. It was a ray of sunshine in the dark clouds that had formed over Panchala.

***

Shikhandini returned to Dasarna a week later. She had not written to inform them of the arrival of the little Prince. She longed to tell Kush herself and watch his face transform with happiness. Shikhandini left Panchala in one of the royal Panchal palanquins. Dai Ma accompanied Shikhandini to Dasarna; to remain till the baby arrived.

When Shikhandini reached Dasarna that evening, she had no premonition that fate would once again turn her world upside down. As she stepped into the palace, she wondered if the news had beaten her to Dasarna, for the palace was decorated like a new bride. The courtyard was covered with beautiful *rangolis*, the walls painted with bright colours, and the palace illuminated with thousands of little clay lamps. She had never seen such joyous celebration in Dasarna.

When Shikhandini entered the courtyard within the palace, she halted abruptly. She saw Kush seated with a young woman by his side, both grandly dressed and laden with jewellery, like newlyweds. To one side stood noblemen from the court, while King Hiranyavarna sat beside his son, on a decorated chair fitted with wheels, to allow him mobility. The joyful air suffocated Shikhandini.

Dai Ma, who immediately understood what had happened, quickly ushered Shikhandini towards her chamber. Shikhandini moved away reluctantly, glancing over her shoulder at Kush. He looked at her apologetically, while the young woman beside him, his second wife, kept her eyes fixed to the ground. The prominent mole on the bride's forehead did not escape Shikhandini's searching gaze.

With tears glistening in her eyes, Shikhandini walked away from the ceremony, with Dai Ma beside her. Her world had been shaken to its core. She felt betrayed...by two of the people she had loved the most.

PART III

19
Betrayal

Three prahars had passed since Shikhandini retired to her chamber. She had made arrangements for Dai Ma's stay and then requested to be left alone. She did not wish to talk to anyone. She knew no one would understand what she felt. In a country where polygamy was a matter of pride, where the first wife was expected to welcome her husband and his new bride with a smile, no one would understand why she felt humiliated. Her father-in-law had often dropped subtle hints about Kush remarrying. Dasarna needed an heir. Shikhandini's inability to bear a child had been a sadness she and Kush had shared but he had assured Shikhandini she was the only woman he had ever loved; that he would never take another wife. But it was a promise made to be broken.

Shikhandini knew her father-in-law was capable of manipulating his son. King Hiranyavarna was getting old and his health was deteriorating. Sometimes, she wondered if he had held onto life just to get a glimpse of his grandson. She understood his plight. What stabbed her to the heart was not Hiranyavarna's words and actions, but what Hema, her beloved sister from Varnavrata, had done; the sister she had loved more than even Draupadi. While Shikhandini was aware Hema had a soft spot in her heart for Kush, she had never dreamed it would come to this. She would never have married Kush.

"Didi…" a soft voice broke into Shikhandini's thoughts. She did not have to turn around to know who it was.

"What do you want Hema?" Shikhandini asked without looking up.

"Didi, I know there is nothing I can say that will make you forgive me, but it kills me to see the hatred in your eyes," cried Hema, her voice quivering.

"Hema, I do not hate you," replied Shikhandini. No matter what Hema had done, she was still her little sister. Although their relationship had been broken beyond repair, Shikhandini knew she could never bring herself to hate Hema.

"Didi, perhaps you do not believe me, but I am as hurt as you are. I did not expect the King to play such a disgusting game."

At this, Shikhandini turned around, confusion writ on her face. "What are you trying to say, Hema?"

Hema was still standing at the threshold of Shikhandini's chamber. Shikhandini gestured for her to come in.

"King Hiranyavarna visited Yakshavana with a marriage proposal for his son. He approached my father for my hand. He declined for obvious reasons. The King then came to me. I was surprised to know he had come with your consent."

Shikhandini stared at Hema wide-eyed. She knew Hiranyavarna was a manipulative man, but this was outright deception.

"When I asked for you, he said you had left for Panchala and would return only after the wedding ceremony had been concluded; that it was you who had suggested he seek my hand for Kush. He said…" Hema floundered, at a loss for words.

"What did he say, Hema?"

"That you were doing this because you were unable to…" Hema sobbed, sickened by her own naivete. She had taken Hiranyavarna's bait so easily. How he must have laughed at her silliness. "I have never seen a father bow so low. He wept before me and said he feared leaving this world without seeing his grandson. Emotional fool that I am, I agreed, despite father's disapproval. Didi, I never stopped loving Kush. He was my first and only love. I am sorry you feel betrayed."

Shikhandini sank onto her bed, holding her head in her hands. She knew Hema spoke the truth. She did not doubt Hiranyavarna's role, but what she did not understand was how Kush fit into all this. "Hema, leave me alone for a while," she said quietly.

Hema walked out of the chamber wondering whether Shikhandini would ever find it in her heart to forgive her.

***

An hour later, Shikhandini decided to send for Kush. She knew she had to know the answer to all the questions that had taken birth in her mind after Hema's visit. One part of her reminded her that this was the same Kush who had waited for her till she was ready to be married; the one who had vowed never to take another wife; the one who had stood against his own father in order to marry her. Her heart wanted to believe. But the truth remained that he had gone back on his word. She felt betrayed.

She looked up as Kush hurried into the chamber, hands outstretched. "Shikha! I am so glad you decided to talk to me. I was worried you would not listen to my side of the story."

Shikhandini did not respond to his gesture and remained standing by the window. She watched as his hands dropped to his sides. "I wanted to know the truth, she said, staring into his eyes, searching for the man she loved. "Whatever you say, I will believe it."

"I am as much at fault as my father," Kush confessed with a sigh. "But Hema...she is innocent. She fell into the trap laid for her."

Shikhandini did not respond, her face frozen. "Stop talking in riddles, Kush," she said. Exhausted by the maelstrom of emotions, she walked over to the bed and sat down.

Kush sat down beside her. "Shikha, father's health is fragile; you know that. The Vyed has said he will not live more than a few months; a year if we are lucky. His desire to see his grandson before breathing his last, and our inability to fulfil that desire, has been gnawing at my mind." It was the first time Kush had admitted to it. "The day I returned from my Digvijay Yatra, I was welcomed by sadness and despair instead of pomp and joy. Father had been bedridden for several days. The Vyed said there was nothing to be done. The old man had given up food and water; given up on his life. My refusal to take a second wife had made him stubborn. He did not wish to understand my plight. Shikha, I was torn between being a dutiful son and a loving husband. I am sorry…" Tears filled his eyes.

For a moment Shikhandini wanted to hold him in her arms and tell him he had done the right thing. But that was not the truth. What he had done was unforgivable in her eyes. He had betrayed their union.

"If only we had a child..." Kush whispered disconsolately.

Shikhandini's bitter laughter caused him to look up. "Why are you laughing?" he asked, perplexed.

"Destiny is sometimes sadistically humorous, Kush." She lifted Kush's hand and placed it on her stomach, tears tracing their way down her cheeks.

Kush's eyes widened in shock. Speech deserted him, just as he had betrayed her. Shikhandini rose and walked out of the chamber without another word.

TEN MONTHS LATER

Joy and excitement filled Dasarna as they welcomed their Prince. Hiranyavarna's joy knew no bounds as he held the little boy in his arms. Though not completely recovered, he had miraculously outlived the Vyed's prediction after the news of the Prince's impending arrival had been delivered to him.

Kush and Hema had decided to live as though the wedding had never happened. Hema wished to atone for what she had done to her sister. Kush, unable to forgive himself, busied himself with affairs of state. He was no longer the man Shikhandini had fallen in love with.

Hiranyavarna developed a sudden fondness for his daughter-in-law, now that she had given Dasarna the future heir he had so craved to see. But to Shikhandini, the only person whose love and affection mattered now was Kshatradeva, her forty-five-day-old son.

Hema's pain did not go unnoticed by Shikhandini, who knew she was responsible for Kush and Hema's strained relationship. She was also concerned for her son's future. She did not wish him to be brought up in an unhappy, broken family. She wanted him to have everything she had craved a child.

Dasarna was decked for the viewing ceremony of their Prince. It was an occasion the people had looked forward to. A grand feast had been arranged for everyone following the rituals. Everyone in the kingdom would have the opportunity to view and bless the infant Prince and take away gifts in return.

It was the end of the third prahar when the ceremony concluded and the crowds had finally departed, content, their purses and bellies full.

Shikhandini, with Kshatradeva in her arms, was about to retire to her chamber when she heard a familiar voice say, "Pranam Devi! Am I too late? Is there nothing left for this hungry traveller?"

It was a young man dressed as a hermit, sporting a long beard and a lush dark mane.

"Pranam," replied Shikhandini, welcoming the unexpected guest into the almost deserted hall. "The ceremony has ended but we never let any guests return hungry or empty-handed. Pray be seated while I go and arrange for your meal." The man smiled in response.

Shikhandini soon returned with two maids in tow. One carried a large *thali* filled with delicacies that had been prepared for the occasion. The other carried a bundle of clothing; a traditional gift given to all hermits and travelling sages. They placed both the food and clothing before him.

Shikhandini signalled for the maids to leave. "I hope you still enjoy butter with your food, Govind," she said as she placed her little boy on Krishna's lap.

Krishna smiled, realizing that for once, he had not been able to fool someone with his disguise. Placing a hand on the little boy's head, he blessed him with a long and healthy life. Shikhandini took her son onto her own lap and urged Krishna to begin his meal.

As he ate, he glanced at Shikhandini, lost in her thoughts. "What is the matter, Shikha?" he asked. "Is something worrying you?"

"Gopal, today is one of the most joyous days of my life. My son has been blessed and showered with love by everyone in the kingdom. But my own sister, Draupadi, is not here to do so. It has been so long since I last saw or heard from her. I do not know where she is or how she is." Shikhandini looked sadly at Kshatradeva, asleep in her lap.

"Shikhandini, what happened to Draupadi was adharma. The perpetrators of her humiliation will be punished soon. It is all a matter of time before karma shows everyone their real place."

"Govind, is it true a Great War will be declared?" asked Shikhandini.

"Yes Shikha, the time has come. Once Draupadi and the Pandavas return from exile, preparations for the war will begin. It will be the greatest bloodbath of all times. The war will mark the end of this yuga. But it is necessary. Our land has to be cleansed. People have forgotten what dharma is. The dictates of dharma and the consequences of karma, no longer reside in the hearts of the people."

Shikhandini nodded her understanding. "I wish there was something I could do to help Draupadi," she whispered.

"That is the reason I came here today," replied Krishna unexpectedly. Shikhandini looked at him in surprise.

"It will be impossible for the Pandavas to win the Great War and restore dharma without you," said Krishna, finishing his meal and getting up to wash his hands.

Shikhandini rose and followed him, the sleeping infant on her shoulder. "What are you saying, Govind," she asked.

"Do you know what the biggest hurdle to victory will be?" asked Krishna, wiping his hand on a muslin cloth a maid handed him.

They walked to the neighbouring chamber, prepared with bolsters for guests to rest a while and sat down.

When Shikhandini did not reply, Krishna said quietly, "Maharathi Bheeshm. He has vowed to remain loyal to the Hastinapur throne no matter who is on it. So, when the time comes, he will be on Dhritarashtra's side, the present King, and hence the Kauravas."

"With him as Senapati, it will be impossible for the Pandavas to win," Shikhandini said, completing Krishna's explanation.

"I am sure you understand the role you will play," he said.

Shikhandini looked down at Kshatradeva, her heart and mind torn.

"I know it will be hard to part from your son, Shikha, but we all have to make personal sacrifices for the greater good," said Krishna, looking into her eyes.

Early that morning, a strange thought had occurred to Shikhandini, which she had dismissedas soon as it arose. In that moment she had seen herself leaving Dasarna, her son safely held in Hema's arms, Kush standing beside them, a smile on his face – a perfect family. Shikhandini wondered if the passing thought had, in fact, been a harbinger of the future. Was Govind here to guide her to her destiny?

"Shikha, what happened to Draupadi was cruel. No woman, Queen or handmaid, should ever be subjected to such harassment and humiliation. From birth, women are victimized for no fault of their own, treated as chattels and trophies, possesions one can gamble and trade. It has to stop. Ours is a holy land we regard as *Bhoomi Devi*. To Everything from the rivers that nourish our fields to food and shelter, comes from Goddess Prakruti, our mother. The Great War will serve as a lesson to future generations that righteousness triumphs and adharma will inevitably meet its own end."

"But I am not sure if I *am* the reincarnation of Princess Amba. I have been told I am by my grandfather, and then my father, following that unhappy incident in my childhood, when I wore the garland of lotuses. But I myself have never felt it to be so."

"Shikha, you have heard Princess Amba's story. Do you think what Maharathi Bheeshm did was unjust?"

"I do. What the Maharathi did was unforgivable."

"Then, do you really need to be sure of your relation to Princess Amba to bring her peace and justice?" replied Krishna, a small smile playing on his lips. "The purpose of your life is not just vengeance on those who have wronged you and your loved ones, but to restore dharma in this great land. The decline of adharma will be impossible without your participation in the Great War."

Shikhandini nodded in response. She had always known her fate was bound with that garland of lotuses. She was no ordinary Princess, no matter how much she had craved to be.

"No matter what you decide, I will always be by your side. You are not alone. Remember that." There was a twinkle in Krishna's eyes.

Shikhandini smiled gratefully at him. She wondered how he could be so sure the Maharathi would meet his end at her hands. But she knew he had already told her what she needed to know. She realized he was no ordinary being. Some things were best left unspoken.

***

Several days had passed since Krishna's visit, days when his words filled Shikhandini's thoughts. She debated the consequences, knowing the only person who would really suffer if she left was her son. But he was also too young to remember. Kush and Hema would give him a good life, the happy home and family she had dreamt for him. Perhaps Kush too, would eventually understand and accept Hema. If she left, they too would have a chance at happiness. In the end, she decided it was better if she left.

The first prahar had yet to begin when Shikhandini decided the time had come for her to leave Dasarna. Her heart as heavy as stone, she picked up the sleeping Kshatradeva and walked towards Hema's chamber. She knew Hema would be at her dawn prayers. Walking into the chamber, she looked around. It was the first time she had been there. It was modestly decorated but the walls were brightly coloured, reflecting Hema's nature. At the far end, on the wall facing east, was a small idol of Goddess Prakruti, the Goddess of her tribe.

Shikhandini walked towards the idol and bowed low, placing Kshatradeva at the Goddess's feet. The boy squirmed in his sleep at the sudden loss of his mother's warmth. Picking up the little boy once again, Shikhandini walked around the chamber. In one corner she found a cloth covered space. This was strange as there was no window. Shikhandini lifted the cloth to reveal a portrait. Tears sprang to her eyes as she realized it was one of her and Hema, from their days in Yakshavana. Hema had brought it with her after her marriage to Kush. Beside it was another, larger painting, of Kush and Hema's wedding ceremony. Shikhandini dropped the veil back.

She walked over to the bed. The first rays of light were making their way into the chamber. She knew Hema would soon be back. She had to be quick. As she looked at the note she had written, addressed to Hema and Kush, she suddenly realized this would be the last time she would see her child. She felt a pang of guilt; she was deserting him when he needed her the most. He would never know her. He would probably grow up hating her for having abandoned him. But she knew Hema would love him like a mother.

She held the little boy in her arms one last time, kissing his head gently, careful not to wake him. She felt her heart would shatter into a thousand pieces as she kissed his little hands, asking for forgiveness. Everything she had been through in her childhood; the greatest losses in battle, seemed nothing compared to the pain she felt now. She had never imagined how difficult it would be to part with her child. Kissing the little boy's head one last time, she placed him on the bed and covered him with a piece of her own clothing that she had brought along. It was to comfort him; assure him of her presence.

With that, she walked out of the chamber and out of the Prince's life.

***

When Hema returned to her chamber, she was surprised to find a fretting Kshatradeva on her bed. She looked around, hoping to find Shikhandini, but was disappointed to find the chamber empty. She picked up the crying child in her arms. It was then that she found the palm leaf note on the bed. Sitting down, she held the infant in her lap and opened the letter. A cold chill ran through her as she read. Picking up the child, Hema rushed to Kush's chamber. Tears filled her eyes and her legs trembled, threatening to give way.

"My Lord... Kush..." Her agonised cry echoed down the hallway.

It had been a long time since Kush had heard Hema call his name. He sensed something was terribly wrong and hurried out of his chamber. When he saw Hema hurring towards him, the child in her arms, her hair flying around her, he halted, standing still.

"What has happened?" he asked. His mind swirled with questions. Why was his son with Hema? Where was Shikhandini? Why was Hema crying?

Hema did not reply. With shaking hands, she held out the letter. Kush looked at her and then at the letter. It was only when he extended his hand to take it that he realized his hands were shaking. The same hand that had unflinchlingly killed foes in battle. He unrolled the letter and read:

Hema, this is probably the last time you and Kush will hear from me. I should have made this decision a long time ago but I did not want to deprive my son of what he deserved. But the time has now come and I cannot stay any longer.

I know what happened in our lives, was destiny at play and we merely victims. I have nothing against you or Kush. I also know no one else will give my son the love and care you will. I know you and Kush will make excellent parents. It is with this faith that I am able to leave him. I am aware he will never know me.

Hema, we all come into this world with a purpose. Some realize it early while others chose not to realize it at all. My case was different. I was fortunate enough to learn my purpose in life, but it came in guise of revenge. I have lived years in denial of my true purpose. I thought that if I refused to acknowledge it, I could live a normal life. But destiny had different plans for me. What happened in our lives was part of some great masterplan.

I have accepted my fate and I hope you will do the same. It is time you and Kush forgave yourselves and each other, and began a new journey. I am leaving a piece of my heart with you in the hope that you will be able to give him everything I cannot. Ayushman Bhava.

Kush's eyes glistened with unshed tears. His mind refused to accept he would never see Shikhandini again. Though their relationship had suffered, he had hoped that one day they could once again regain what they had once shared. But the letter extinguished the last ray of hope, leaving him in the darkness of despair.

"Kush…" Hema whispered. As though sensing the tension in the air, the little boy's wails had died down to silent sobs.

Kush looked at Hema. He had no words to describe his grief. There remained just one way he could atone for what he had done to Shikhandini – by giving their son all that his mother had desired for him. For the first time Kush reached out to comfort Hema, folding her and his son in his arms. Hema wept, overwhelmed by emotion.

Kush bent down to kiss the little boy's forehead, to hide his pain. Silently, he promised to protect his son till his last breath.

20
THE SCIENCE OF ILA

Although Shikhandini had lived in Dasarna for over a decade, she had never felt at home there. It felt as strange to her as when she had returned to Panchala. She felt relieved she no longer had to live there. She was free. Only the thought of her son Kshatradeva caused equal pain and guilt. She had given up her child in the name of duty. But knew she had done the right thing. Her son deserved a normal life and a family. She knew Hema and Kush would give him that. Dai Ma too, had promised to be with him for as long as he needed her. There was nothing to worry about, yet her mother's heart continued to grieve.

On reaching Yakshavana, she felt a sense of the past reclaiming her. Years ago, having lost the war against Dronacharya's pupils, she had left Panchala with shame and pain her only possessions. Krishna had shown her the way to her new life, bringing her to Yakshavana. Here, for the first time in her life, she had felt like she belonged. It was here that she had known what it was to have a family. She had come to Yakshavana a wanderer, in search of purpose. But today, she had come with a motive. She knew only Sthunakarna could help her to fulfill her purpose. She had to put an end to the atrocities of the Kauravas. Dharma had to be restored.

Her mind echoed Krishna's words as she walked into the village, glad the day had not yet begun. The first light of dawn was peeling away the darkness of night and somewhere in the treetops, she could hear the chirping of the birds. She smiled at the familiar sounds.

On reaching the Yaksha leader's house, she took a deep breath and stood wondering what to say. They were Hema's parents. She knew Sthunakarna and Yakshini had not approved of Hema's marriage to Kush. But they had been helpless before the King and Hema's wishes.

They had refused to participate in the ceremonies. A year later, when Hema had wished to visit Yakshavana, Sthunakarna had refused. Now, Shikhandini wondered if her return to Yakshavana would cause her foster parents pain. Standing at the threshold, dark thoughts clouded her mind. She turned to leave. She could not be the cause of further pain. They had suffered enough. But as she turned to go, she heard a familiar voice.

"Shikha, is that you?"

Guru Ma... Shikhandini turned and walked towards Yakshini, appearing through the veil of early morning mist that had formed around them. Shikhandini's eyes filled with tears as she embraced Yakshini, whom she loved like a mother. She had forgotten what it felt like to have her mother's arms protect her from the world.

***

"Shikhandini, my child, there is nothing in the world we can say to ease your pain. What our own daughter did to you was unforgivable. We are as guilty as her. It was done in ignorance," said Sthunakarna, folding his hands in a gesture of apology. Yakshini stood beside him, tears wetting her face.

"Guruji, no... All this is nothing but the game of destiny. I have forgiven everyone. Do not grieve. It was not your doing," replied Shikhandini holding Sthunakarna's hands in her own. He looked much older than he had when she had last seen him. His face had wrinkles and his hair was more grey than white. His eyes reflected his weariness. His once broad and taut shoulders stooped a little. But Shikhandini knew the Yakshas only aged in appearance, and not in strength or skill. He could still defeat a warrior half his age.

Shikhandini's words seemed to soothe them. She was surprised to learn that the events of the Dhyutsabha had reached Yakshavana and everyone sympathized with Draupadi. She recalled the Yakshas were influential people because of their skills. Skills that many considered divinely gifted. The Yakshas had their own ways to learning what was happening in neighbouring kingdoms. Shikhandi told Sthunakarna and Yakshini how the downfall of the Maharathi was no longer about avenging Panchala's defeat, but the restoration of dharma. She also explained to them her plight. Due to Hastinapur's patriarchal code, she could not participate in the Great War.

Sthunakarna knew what had to be done, but decided to wait, unsure if the time was right. "Shikhandini, we are with you. Whatever you decide to do, we will stand with you. We will take you to your goal. From now on our purpose will be your victory," he told Shikhandini. "We Yakshas would be honoured to be part of the Great War for dharma."

TWO WEEKS LATER

It was the the start of the second prahar and the sun was shining brightly above the Yaksha village. People were moving about, getting ready to start the day. On Sthunakarna's request, Shikhandini, Yakshini and Pashupathi had assembled at one of the discussion rooms of the Ayuralaya. When Sthunakarna entered, everyone rose respectfully to their feet.

"Pranam Guruji," said Pashupati.

Sthunakarna returned the greeting before settling down on one of the mats. Yakshini sat beside him. It was part of Yaksha culture to sit on the floor cross-legged during discussions and debates. It symbolized equality of the participants. Following the short prayer that was customary before starting anything important, Sthunakarna said, "Shikhandini, you are like my daughter. I have seen how unfair life has been to you. So it is for your sake that I have made this decision." Clearing his throat, he continued, "A decision which I hope will help you fulfill your goal. Rememeber I suggest this only in your best interests and because I believe it is what you desire."

There was a moment's silence as they all looked at each other.

"What do you have in mind, Guruji?" Pashupathi had been briefed about Shikhandini's life and the critical role he would have to play. Sthunakarna knew only Pashupati's knowledge could help them achieve their goal.

"I can only think of only one way to help Shikhandini reach her goal. We have to prepare her for the Great War," he said.

"They will never let her anywhere near the battleground, let alone participate in the battle," replied Yakshini. She hated the idea of Shikhandini fighting in the impending war, fearing for her safety. Everyone in Aryavrath knew the war was going to be the greatest bloodbath of the yuga. The Pandavas had vowed to avenge Draupadi's humiliation by slaughtering every single Kaurava Prince, all hundred of them.

"I know, Yakshini. But her role in the war is crucial. Without her, it will be impossible to defeat Maharathi Bheeshm. With him on the Kaurava side, the sons of the Late King Pandeshwar will be helpless," replied Sthunakarna, who had spent long hours analyzing the possibilities of the Great War.

"Guruji, is it not true that the Maharathi is not only invincible but immortal?" Pashupati voiced the question in everyone's mind.

"Yes, it is believed the Maharathi was blessed by his father with a boon. But the boon does not make him immortal; it allows him to choose the time of his death. No one in this world is immortal. Everyone has to return to Goddess Prakruti some day."

Pashupati had another question. "Guruji, is the prophecy about the Princess of Kashi being reborn as Shikhandini true? Do you really believe it?" he asked, clearly unconvinced.

"Pashupati, what I believe does not matter. What matters is what the Maharathi and the other warriors participating in the Great War believe. If the Maharathi believes in the prophecy, he will surrender to his fate. If not, he will accept Shikhandini's challenge to duel with him. We have to be prepared for either case," Sthunakarna explained.

"Even if we assume the prophecy is true, and Shikhandini can defeat the Maharathi, will the Pandavas and the other warriors permit her, a woman, to fight?" Yakshini knew that the fragile male ego was a greater challenge than any boon or prophecy.

"There is one way. But it will change her life forever. Shikhandini, it calls for a great sacrifice," Sthunakarna said, looking at Shikhandini, his eyes dark pools of sadness.

"I am ready to take any path, Guruji. I do not fear any challenge if it allows me to participate in the war. Guruji, there is nothing left for me to lose. The only thing keeping me alive is the fire within me to avenge my sister's humiliation and plight. What Guru Ma has said is true. No matter how good a warrior I am, I will never be allowed to participate in the war. All my strength and valour will be overshadowed by the fact that I am a woman," replied Shikhandini, citing the bitter truth embedded in every kingdom in Aryavrath. She wondered how many women who could have been great warriors, rulers or gurus, had been deprived by their gender.

"Shikhandini, you are right. No matter what you do or how hard you train, it will all be in vain because you are a woman," Sthunakarna agreed. "But there is a way you can change that."

Yakshini looked at her husband skeptically. Shikhandini's eyes never left her guru's face. She knew he was not a man of casual words.

"Thousands of years ago, our land was gifted with a new science. It helped those who felt trapped in the wrong body. While most people considered such people cursed, there was one extraordinary woman who decided to help them. This new science was named for her," said Sthunakarna.

"The Science of Ila," Pashupati murmured. He had heard about it from Guruji, and instantly understood what Sthunakarna was proposing. Gender transformation...

"Ila?" asked Shikhandini, turning towards Pashupati.

"It is an ancient science that existed in this land thousands of years ago. The knowledge of which was not lost, but buried over time," he replied, recalling what he had heard.

"Buried?" Shikhandini was intrigued. How could knowledge be buried?

"The Science of Ila was no ordinary science, Shikhandini. It was a revolution. It is believed that those who approached the masters of this science, were able to change their gender and live the life they yearned for. In fact, the name Ila came from the first person to use this science," said Sthunakarna.

"Who was he, Guruji?" asked Shikhandini, her mind whirling.

"It was not a he, Shikhandini, but a she. Ila was the daughter of Lord Manu, and a sibling of Ishvaku, the original forebear of Lord Ram's dynasty. Ila is also believed to have been the mother of Puruvaras, an ancestor of the present Hastinapur Kurus. There are many versions of Ila's story. Some believe she was a magical being who could change her gender as she wished, while others say she was cursed to live the life of an androgyn. Whatever the truth, the seekers of the Science of Ila regard her as a divine force."

Many people in ancient Bharat were benefitted by this science. Ila understood the plight of those unfortunates who had been born into a body they could not accept. But the majority of the Kings and tribal leaders, including the Yaksha leaders of the time, believed that such people were born that way for a reason. They had been cursed for their ill deeds in a previous birth to live like that. They regarded Ila as a dark science which opposed God's decision," said Sthunakarna, shaking his head sorrowfully.

"Is it really possible to change one's gender, Sthuna?" asked Yakshini, who did not find the idea realistic.

"Yes and no. Yes, because it has been done before, and no, because we can never prove it since both the science and its beneficiaries have been long buried and forgotten," he replied.

"Assuming we are able to bring the science back and Shikhandini is able to take advantage of it, will society accept her as a man?" asked Yakshini, her mind filled with doubt and worry.

"Ironically, though society pretends to be against the use of this apparently dark science, it has more often than not worshipped the Science of Ila and admired some of its early beneficiaries," said Pashupati, grinning wryly. He knew this would shock his audience.

"Beneficiaries of the Science of Ila...in Aryavrat?" said Shikhandini, surprised.

"Yes, can you guess who?" A small smile played on Pashupati's lips. It was exactly how his Guruji had introduced the topic to him years ago. Sthunakarna smiled, amused.

"I have never heard of anyone or anything related to Ila," replied Shikhandini positively.

"What about your name? How did you get it?" asked Pashupati.

"Ma once told me I was born after many years of prayer to Lord Shiva. My name is one of the thousand names of the Lord," Shikhandini replied, her voice cracking a little as she recalled her mother telling her the blessed story.

"That is true, Shikhandini, but do you not think it is unusual that Lord Shiva, the epitome of masculinity, was given a woman's name?" Pashupati asked, triggering fresh thought in everyone's mind. "Let us consider the more common name, Ardhanarishvara. Have you heard of it?"

Shikhandini recognized it from her childhood, when each day had begun with the recitation of the *Shivasahasranama*. "It is also one of the thousand names of the Lord," she replied.

"Yes, my child," Sthunakarna agreed, joined in the discussion. "Ardhanarishvara is a lesser known name of the Lord. In fact, it is not his name alone. It essentially signifies the union of Lord Shiva and his consort, Shakti and represents the synthesis of masculine and feminine energies. Both are inseperable in God and it is this combined energy without which the birth of *Brahmanda,* the Universe, would be impossible. But very few groups today regard this form of Shiva-Shakti as a true form. Society as we know it now is undoubtedly a man's world. Over time, female energy has become dominated by the male. It is no longer considered equal," said Sthunakarna.

Shikhandini nodded. Every woman knew the truth of this. It reminded her of Panchala, where girls were sent to separate schools, where they were taught to cook and sew, but never the use of any weapon. Whether in the palace or in thatched huts, it was always the male members of the family who had the upper hand.

"But how is Ardhanarishvara related to Ila?" asked Shikhandini.

Sthunakarna sighed, wondering whether he was right in having opened the discussion. "As the Science of Ila developed, the male dominant society of the time feared it would lose its dominance. With the use of Ila, the suppressed third gender began to rise. The science was so advanced that it became impossible to tell who had been born a particular gender and who had later been transformed using the science. This was not acceptable to many. Eventually, with the consent of all the major kings, sages and other learned men, the study and use of Ila was banned. The transfer of this knowledge was condemned. So, all we know about this science today is the name and the history related to it."

"How can we possibly find it then?" asked Yakshini.

"In the last fifty years, like much other revolutionary knowledge, the Science of Ila has resurfaced. Research and knowledge sharing about Ila is known to be taking place in several Ayuralayas, but in secrecy," said Pashupati quietly. "With Guruji's consent, my team and I can travel to these Ayuralayas to gather information. If we are lucky, we might even find one of the texts the masters left behind." Excitement made his eyes glitter.

"Yes, that is a good idea. Once Pashupati returns, we will know for sure if it can be done. I am sure it can. But before that, we must know Shikhandini's decision," said Sthunakarna.

Before Shikhandini could reply, Yakshini intervened. "It would be wise to give her time to understand the consequences of such a transformation. It is a decision that will change her life forever. Let us not be in a hurry to decide."

Everyone nodded in agreement.

"Guruji, it will take me a month to return from this expedition. That will give Shikhandini time to consider and gain a realistic perception of the Science of Ila, the process, its consequences, and limitations. She can then make her decision," suggested Pashupati.

Sthunakarna nodded in agreement. Yakshini was relieved the decision had been temporarily postponed. Shikhandini, on the other hand, was in a dilemma. Now that she knew there was a way to change her destiny, she was drawn to but feared the unknown. A storm raged in her mind.

***

"*Draupadi!*" screamed Shikhandini as she jolted awake, her heart hammering in her chest. It was the same nightmare she had every night since hearing about the Dhyutsabha in Hastinapur. Each time her hatred towards Hastinapur grew. She prayed for the chance to destroy her sister's abusers and fight for dharma. The warrior in her awakened as the nightmares reminded her of her duty. But the sister in her wept. No woman, commoner or Queen, deserved to be treated the way Draupadi had been. She longed to see her sister and share her grief.

The following day, when Shikhandini expressed a desire to meet her sister Draupadi, Sthunakarna agreed to help her. With the help of the Yakshas, she was able to trace Draupadi in a few days. The Pandavas had built a temporary abode in the forest of Kamyaka, on the banks of the river Saraswati. They had decided to remain there for a while before moving on. Kurujangala, a small village, was situated close to Kamyaka. Its people were devoted to the Pandavas. It was from these villagers that the Yakshas heard where the Pandavas were.

As the first rays filtered through the canopy of trees, Shikhandini left Yakshavana. She felt compelled to see Draupadi. But she promised Yakshini and Sthunakarna to return soon. Climbing onto Surya, with her sword at her waist, she left for Kamyaka.

When Shikhandini arrived, she was relieved to see a recently used pathway through the trees. She could hear the sound of a river close by and decided to follow the sound. Forest dwellers preferred to live close to water sources. It was also an easy way to navigate as the direction of the river was well known.

It took a prahar for Shikhandini to locate Draupadi's abode in the forest. When she did, she dismounted from her horse and walked forward, her eyes glistening with unshed tears. The last time she had visited Draupadi was in Indraprastha, when her sister had been as *Samarajni*, Queen of Queens, of Aryavrat. Today, she was a hermit.

"Didi…" whispered Draupadi, gazing at Shikhandini in disbelieving wonder. Like a child who has been separated from its mother, Draupadi ran towards Shikhandini, who engulfed her in her embrace. Holding on to Shikhandini, Draupadi wept.

"Shhh…I am here...with you..." Shikhandini comforted her.

Looking over Draupadi's bent head, Shikhandini's heart filled with misgiving. Behind them stood a temporary shelter, built of mud, sticks and stones. A log fence was the only protection the small hut had. Outside, there was a *chulah,* still smoking from having just been doused. From the charcoal residue on Draupadi's clothes, Shikhandini guessed she used it to cook.

"Didi, they took everything... my dignity, my pride, my position, Indrapastha!" Draupadi wailed.

Shikhandini knew there was nothing she could say to reduce her sister's agony. Her own heart filled with pain. Draupadi's once lustrous, long hair was threaded with silver, tangled and uncombed.

Draupadi noticed Shikhandini looking at her hair and said, "Didi, my hair is a reminder to my husbands of their vow. I will not tie it till I can wash it in Dushasana's blood! Every day, when they look at me, I want their hearts to beat with vengeance. I want them to realize their mistake in allowing Yudhistir to stake my honour in a silly game." Her red rimmed eyes reflected the fire within.

Shikhandini shuddered at the thought of her sister bathing in blood. She knew the Pandava brothers had been as much to blame as Duryodhan and Dushasana. Their thirst to win had made them desperate. In a moment of madness, they had forgotten every code binding them and staked their wife... Draupadi. Shikhanadini was no stranger to the knowledge that the pain caused by a loved one is far more agonizing than that caused by a foe.

"Draupadi, you *will* get justice. Those who have wronged you will be punished. I promise you that."

Draupadi nodded unconvinced. Had not her own husbands, valiant warriors all, failed her?

As the sun began to slowly sink below the horizon, Shikhandini took her leave. She knew the Pandavas would return soon. She feared she would be unable to hold her temper in check if she saw their faces. On her way back, Shikhandini ruminated on what she had to do. The storm that had raged in her mind seemed to have cleared after visiting Draupadi. Shikhandini felt ashamed at her own hesitation; she should have made the decision much earlier. Destiny had presented her with an opportunity to fight against injustice, for dharma. Her sister was but one of the victims of atrocities committed in the name of royal male privilege. Shikhandini vowed to put an end to it, beginning with the downfall of the Maharathi, the foundation on which the kingdom of Hastinapur stood.

A FORTNIGHT LATER

Shikhandini, Sthunakarna, and Yakshini had assembled once again in the discussion room of the Ayuralaya, this time on Pashupati's request. He had returned from his expedition in search for the Ila. He had spent weeks travelling to different Ayuralayas; studying and gathering information about the Science of Ila, to further Shikhandini's purpose. The Science of Ila was widely believed to be a magical transformation achieved after years of penance and prayer, or a curse of the Gods. Only a small group of learned people, who studied medicine and science, believed Ila to be a true gift of science.

"Pranam Guruji...Guru Ma. Pranam Shikhandini..." Pashupati said, entering. Placing his cloth bag beside him, he sat cross-legged, facing the others.

"Pranam, Pashupati. We eagerly wait to hear what you have to share with us," said the Yaksha leader.

A smile flitted across Pashupati's face before it became serious again. "Guruji, there is so much new learning that I wish to share with you. When I first began studying Shikhandini's case, I was not hopeful. But I saw it as an opportunity to learn something new and interesting. I began learning about the growth of the human body from the time it is conceived in the womb to the time it develops into a full grown adult. I visited several Ayuralayas in the snow clad mountains in my search. Some of the oldest *rishis* helped me gain understanding. Some had lived longer than a hundred years. They had a scientific explanation for every natural occurrance. Contrary to the popular belief, the rishis did not achieve their knowledge with just penance and worship. They studied hard, through years of experiments, recording their findings, to benefit future generations."

Sthunakarna nodded as he listened. He was aware of this.

"It was fascinating how the human body has been studied and carefully analyzed by rishis and rishikas, and medicine-men, over hundreds of years. The ancient medicinal texts written by them are invaluable. It was in one of them that I first came across *antahsraava*. Suddenly, everything seemed less impossible."

"Antahsraava?" asked Shikhandini, still skeptical about the possibility of such a transformation.

"To put it simply, they are messengers that relay messages from one part of the body to another," Pashupati explained. "These messengers tell the cells in the body when to grow, how to function, and when to die. Without them, it would be impossible for the body to function correctly."

"But how does this help Shikhandini?" asked Yakshini, struggling to understand the ramifications.

Pashupati smiled at her bafflement. "We have to go deeper into the behaviour of these messengers to understand how they can help us. Everything in the Universe is based on balance. Within the human body too, there is a balance, and antahsraava are no exceptions. One of the most important types is gender-antahsraava, responsible for regulating the growth of organs formed before birth, and the secondary characteristics that develop during puberty," he added. He paused briefly, waiting for his audience to absorb the information, before saying, "The gender-antahsraava in the body are male and female. Interestingly, the human body has both types, irrespective of gender. However, in men the male antahsraava dominate, and in women, the female antahsraava."

"You learnt all this from old texts?" asked Yakshini in wonder.

"Yes, Guru Ma. In fact, it is just one text that summarized all this information," replied Pashupati, clearly awed by such knowledge.

"Which text is that, Pashupati?" asked Sthunakarna.

Pashupathi opened the cloth pouch in which he carried all his important books and notes. Pulling a manuscript out, he passed it to Yaksha leader.

"*The Science of Ila...*" Sthunakarna whispered, moving his hand over the palm-leaf manuscript. He had heard of the existence of such a book but had never had the motive to seek it out.

"Yes, Guruji, *The Science of Ila*. It is indeed part of medical science and not magic," Pashupati stated.

Sthunakarna opened the palm-leaf book. Like all old texts, this too was delicate and broken in many places; some leaves were missing, while others looked like they had been eaten by insects. He passed the book to Yakshini and Shikhandini to take a closer look and appreciate the masterpiece.

"Unfortunately, we do not know who wrote it," lamented Pashupati.

Sthunakarna nodded. "Texts on Ila were written secretly after the ban on its usage; the knowledge transfered by rishis and rishikas, who wished to keep it alive. Afraid of being accused of treachery and killed, they wrote anonymously."

"But Guruji, why does the human body have both antahsraava if it only needs one kind?" asked Shikhandini.

"Ah yes... it remained a riddle for many years before we discovered the answer. The gender antahsraava are not merely responsible for the determination of gender. In men, a small ratio of female antahsraava is necessary for the correct functioning of the heart. While in women, the male antahsraava plays a vital role in building bone and muscle strength," explained Pashupati.

"So what do you suggest? What is our first step?" asked Shikhandini.

"Now that we know how these messengers work in the body, the next task is to find a way to increase the ratio of male to female antahsraava in your body," replied Pashupati thoughtfully, his mind already wrestling with the minutiae.

Sthunakarna looked up from his ruminations. "What do you think will be the immediate effect?"

"According to the book, the first signs are growth of facial hair and deepening of the voice. But we cannot be sure. We will only know once we begin," replied Pashupati.

Shikhandini wondered if it was really possible. It sounded like something in the magical realm. How could someone born a woman become a man? Yakshini too, turned away, unable to accept the idea of Shikhandini looking and sounding like a man.

"How long will it take to complete the process?" asked Shikhandini.

"It is difficult to estimate since we have never done this before. But it will certainly take several months before we see some real effects. The body does not appreciate intrusion. Changing the antahsraava balance changes normal functioning. The body will fight it initially. It will be a long process to adjust," explained Pashupati.

Fascinated by the book, Sthunakarna kept turning the palm leaf pages, trying to decipher the text, written in a language prevalent in the south – Tamil. As leader of his tribe, Sthunakarna had learned it a long time ago from his Guruji, who had explained that it was older than even Sanskrit, and the basis of communicating with many of the southern kingdoms. Many rishis used it to write texts meant to be read and understood only by wise men.

"Will there be any effects on her health?" asked Yakshini.

"That again is unknown to us, Guru Ma. Antahsraava therapy is not predictable. According to the text, they behave differently in different people. We will know only after we begin the process."

But Yakshini could not still her deep forebodings. "Even if her body reacts to the changes as expected, and she develops masculine traits, will she not still be a woman? Is it really possible to completely transform her?"

"You are right, Guru Ma. It is impossible to completely transform a body to the opposite gender. The antahsraava replacement process will only change her physical appearance and voice, nothing more."

"Hey Ram! So you are saying she will lead the life of an androgyn, neither wholly man nor wholly woman? What kind of terrible science is this?" Yakshini asked, her voice trembling with despair.

"Guru Ma, our knowledge of Ila is limited to this. We cannot help her transform completely. There could have been ways to do this, but over the centuries most of the information related to Ila has been lost. It is only possible to do this much with what we know."

"But how will this help her?" asked Yakshini.

"I think it will," Sthunakarna replied, closing the book.

Shikhandini looked at him in silent query.

"Before the battle begins, when the rules of war are written and sealed, not one of the Kings, Maharathis, Athirathis or Rathis, will think of adding a clause to ban the third gender from participating. In most kingdoms of Aryavrath, only women are disallowed from combat. There will be nothing to stop Shikhandini from fighting."

"It will be necessary to conduct the entire process in secrecy, and keep Shikhandini hidden until the war begins. If anyone gets even a hint of this, they will find a way to keep Shikhandini out of the battle," warned Pashupati.

Sthunakarna looked at Shikhandini. "The final decision is yours, my child. No one can make it for you." He placed a hand on Shikhandini's head in acceptance and blessing. "Whatever you decide, we will abide by."

Shikhandini knew the time for vaccilation was past. There was nothing left to think about. Her decision was made.

"But before you decide, there is one important thing you should know about this this process," said Pashupati quietly, his brow furrowed. "The Science of Ila as we know it today, is irreversible. Once the transformation is complete, you can never return to your old self."

Yakshini's eyes widened, her thoughts disturbed like a turbulent river. "Shikhandini, do not do this!" she pleaded. "We will find some other way."

"No, Guru Ma, there is no other way. We all know that. This is the only way," Shikhandini replied, embracing Yakshini.

She turned to face Sthunakarna. "Guruji, I am ready."

21
Lord Kuber's Wrath

"This is where you will live, Shikhandini," Sthunakarna said to her, pushing open the door of the thatched hut.

The hut was several yojanas away from the Yaksha village, but close to the Ayuralaya. The place had been chosen so the entire process could take place in secrecy, away from the eyes of the Yaksha village. Sthunakarna knew that even in his village there were people who believed the Science of Ila to be a dark art, practiced only by the evil.

Shikhandini looked around her. It was a modest dwelling with only the bare essentials. A *charpoy* stood along one wall, below a small window. In one corner was a small wooden stool on which an earthen pot, used to keep water cool, was placed. On the other side of the room, in the north-eastern direction, was a raised platform on which sat a small statue of Goddess Prakruti. Instinctively, Sthunakarna and Shikhandini knelt before the Goddess, touching their foreheads to the ground and praying silently to Mother Nature.

"This hut was used by Pashupati when he was undergoing the Sanjeevni therapy. He often says the Goddess' presence gave him the strength and courage to deal with the pain and loneliness," said Sthunakarna. Shikhandini nodded silently.

"We will begin exactly a fortnight from today. Till then, we will use the time to study and understand the nature of your body. We will use samples of your blood to understand its reaction to different medicines," Sthunakarna explained.

Shikhandini simply nodded in response. Questions swirled in her mind, but she did not doubt her Guruji.

"Shikhandini, my child, I know this is difficult; probably the toughest challenge of your life. But I want you to know I am proud of you for having made this decision. We all are. You are among the rare few who are willing to make a great personal sacrifice for the greater good. If destiny has brought you to this threshold, I am sure it also has a vital place for you in the Great War."

Shikhandini recalled Krishna's words: *The purpose of your life is not just vengeance on those who have wronged you and your loved ones. It is to restore dharma in this great land. The decline of adharma will be impossible without your participation in the Great War.*

She smiled at Sthunakarna. They understood each other. But she remembered someone she had made unhappy with her decision. "Guruji, is Guru Ma still upset about this?" she asked.

"Yes, but she will slowly learn to accept. Do not worry about her."

"I hope she does, for I cannot do this without her, Guruji," said Shikhandini softly.

***

Six months had passed by since Shikhandini first stepped into the small hut. After the initial tests and study of her blood and Antahsraava behaviour, Pashupati and his team at the Ayuralaya had successfully created a therapy course. With their advanced knowledge of *Rasashastra*, he and his team had successfully replicated the serum the ancients had used as an antahsraava changing therapy – a critical step in gender transformation.

The serum had to be administered into Shikhandini's bloodstream at scheduled intervals. To do this, they had created a palm-sized cylindrical glass tube, framed in *tamra*. The serum was filled into the tube through the rear end, in the prescribed dosage. A pushing decice helped to push the serum into the tube. The front end was sealed, except for a tiny opening to which a thin and sharp needle was connected. Causing negligible pain, the needle would create an inflow into Shikhandini's arm. Using gentle pressure, the serum would be pushed into her bloodstream. Pashupati was convinced that direct inflow into the bloodstream would make for quicker results.

In the time these developments were taking place, Shikhandini had only two visitors – Pashupati and Sthunakarna. She longed to see Guru Ma, who was still unhappy with her decision. Finally, Yakshini could no longer hold back from seeing her daughter. Eavesdropping on Sthunakarna and Pashupati's conversations, she had wondered if she was failing in her duty to support her daughter in the greatest challenge of her life. When she heard Sthunakarna mention the first stage had been completed, she made up her mind to stand by Shikhandini, even though she did not agree with her decision.

As Yakshini stepped into the hut, she tried not to see the transformed Princess. She had visualized her daughter's physical transformation from the descriptions she had overheard, but nothing had prepared her for what she saw.

"Guru Ma," she heard a hoarse, slightly familiar voice say.

"Shikhandini!" Yakshini gasped, turning around. Time seemed to cease in that moment as Yakshini stood speechless. A part of her mind marvelled at the ingenuity of the therapy her husband and Pashupati had formulated. It was beyond her wildest imagining. But another part of her mind cried in pain as she realized what the therapy had done to her beautiful daughter.

"Guru Ma, do not cry," whispered Shikhandini as she came forward.

The change in her gait did not go unnoticed. As Shikhandini stood at arms length from Yakshini, the fine traces of transformation became evident to her. Shikhandini's once rounded face now had an angular jawline covered with the shadow of hair growth. The softness of her facial features was gone. Her hairline had slightly retracted, unveiling a broad forehead. Her posture was more masculine, owing to developing muscles. Her shoulders were broader and her hips narrow and taut. Her arms were muscular.

But what surprised Yakshini the most was Shikhandini's voice. Had she not heard it herself, she would never have believed such a change was possible. She suddenly recalled a conversation she had had with Pashupati, about how the antahsraava would slowly change her voice, making it more masculine.

"Guru Ma..." Shikhandini whispered, unable to hide her uneasiness from Yakshini's loving gaze.

"Shikhandini, I did not mean to make you conscious. But this..." Yakshini found it hard to speak. She looked into Shikhandini's eyes, hoping to find some comfort there.

"I know, Guru Ma. But this is how it is going to be after this," replied Shikhandini.

Yakshini sat down on the charpoy, her head in her hands, trying not to weep. Shikhandini sat down beside her, patiently waiting for Yakshini to speak.

"Are you happy?" Yakshini finally asked. When there was no response, she rose to leave. "I thought so…" she murmured

"My happiness does not matter, Guru Ma. This is the purpose of my life. This is what is meant to happen. If my sacrifice brings good to this land, then I am ready to do ten times more without any regret," Shikhandini said to Yakshini's retreating figure.

TWO DAYS LATER

The residents of Yakshavana looked up in awe at the magnificent bird that flew above their leader's house. The bird looked like a pigeon, but was larger and spotless white. Its eyes sparkled in the sunlight, resembling the ruby that hung on a chain on its breast. It was a messenger bird.

On hearing the commotion, Sthunakarna and Yakshini rushed outside. The bird swooped down and dropped a message scroll at Sthunakarna's feet. Before he could pick it up, the bird had flown away on its return journey to its owner.

"Is the Lord visiting us, Guruji?" asked a Yaksha, eyeing the message Sthunakarna had just unrolled.

Reading it quietly, Sthunakarna nodded. "Yes, he is." He cleared his throat and made an announcement: "The Lord has decided to pay us a visit in the coming days. We must make preparations. Let Yakshavana be decorated like never before. A grand feast shall be held to celebrate his coming. You are all exempted from your usual tasks to prepare for the Lord's visit to our humble village."

There was clapping and cheering at the news. The people milled around chattering, wondering why the Lord came, noting tasks to be undertaken. They began to disperse, planning for the big day.

Inside the house, Yakshini asked her husband the question that had been troubling her since hearing of the Lord's visit. "Do you think he knows about Shikhandini?"

Sthunakarna shook his head reassuringly. "Only you, I and Pashupati know. No one in Yakshavana knows. It would be impossible for the news to reach the Lord."

"What about the people in the Ayuralaya? They surely sense something with all the unusual medicines being prepared there in the last two months," Yakshini reasoned.

"I trust Pashupati and his team. They have been sworn to secrecy. You know it as well as I that under no circumstances will a Yaksha betray his word."

"Sthuna, it is as you say, but we cannot deny that our people fear and worship the Lord above all."

Sthunakarna nodded, knowing what she said was true.

A WEEK LATER

There was an air of excitement and anticipation in Yakshavana. The villagers had spent days decorating the village to welcome their Lord. It was the first time he would grace them with his presence. The inhabitants of Yakshavana had only heard about his greatness, but never seen him in person. When the sound of the conch echoed through every house, finally announcing his arrival, the Yakshas hurried out to to welcome their Lord.

Pashupati, who had grown up listening to stories of the Lord, stood mesmerized as he watched the Yaksha King emerge from the forest. First, a group of foot soldiers who functioned as guards made their appearance. Then a row of men on horseback moved towards the village, scanning the place with practiced eyes. Behind them was the Lord, on his magnificent elephant. Like his messenger bird, the Lord's elephant too, was spotless white, and unusually large. Its wide ears flapped and the long white tusks, polished with coconut oil, gleamed in the sun.

When the Lord descended from his elephant, the entire population bowed in respect. He was a short man with a protruding belly. His pale skinned face flaunted a long moustache. His torso was barely visible under the layers of gold he wore. He greeted his people with folded hands and a smile.

"Pranam, My Lord. I hope your journey was comfortable," said Sthunakarna, placing a garland of marigold around his master's neck.

"Pranam, Sthunakarna," replied Lord Kuber, looking into the Yaksha leader's eyes. After a brief pause he said, "You have been wondering about the reason for my sudden visit."

Sthunakarna stood in respectful silence.

"It has been brought to my notice that there has been a violation of the Yaksha code, here in Yakshavana," said Kuber, raising his voice so everyone could hear. Turning towards Sthunakarna, he asked, "Is it true you have begun using our knowledge and resources to practice the dark art?" he asked, looking directly into the Yaksha leader's eyes.

"I have not, and never will, encourage any kind of practice of the dark art, my Lord," replied Sthunkarna.

"Then what is it that I hear? Sthunakarna, tell me that what I have heard is untrue, that you have not permitted the practice of Ila in Yakshavana," said the Lord in a low voice meant only for the man he addressed.

Sthunakarna stood mute, unable to lie. Kuber understood his silence.

"What were you thinking, Sthunakarna? How dare you break the law?" Kuber roared. The Yakshas who stood in their vicinity trembled in fear as Kubera's voice echoed through the gathering.

"I have broken no law, My Lord," said Sthunakarna clearly, unflinching before the Lord's anger.

Kubera took a threatening step forward as the others moved back several paces. "Speak! What do you have to say?"

"Ila is pure science. It is not a dark art. It is meant to help people, like other medical knowledge. It was banned in ignorance...by Kings and leaders who did not understand it," Sthunakarna said.

"The Science of Ila was banned for a reason!" Kuber growled, forgetting that he was raising his voice against the tribe leader of Yakshavana, who, for the villagers, was next only to the Lord. "Who are you using it on?" he demanded.

Sthunakarna stood in silence. He could not betray Shikhandini even for the Lord.

"Answer! Who are you using it on? Who is this person who has led you to disregard the laws of your own people?" he growled. His eyes fell on Yakshini. She stood as silent as her husband, eyes fixed on the ground.

"Go, search the entire village! Bring to me any new face," Kuber ordered his guards.

Quickly, Kuber's men spread through the village, entering every house, looking for unknown faces. Sthunakarna and Yakshini exchanged a glance, relieved that Kuber's men would not reach Shikhandini's hut.

"My Lord, we have searched every house in the village. There is no suspicious person here," one of the guards informed the Lord, running back to where he stood under a spreading Banyan tree.

Kubera looked disappointed. His anger flared once again when he saw the flash of relief on Sthunakarna's face. "You leave me with no choice, Yaksha," he sighed, shaking his head. "Unlike you, the laws of the Yakshas are to me above all."

With a stern look on his face, the Lord said in a voice every man, woman and child in the village heard, "I, Kuber, King of the Yakshas, hereby banish Sthunakarna from the clan."

A collective gasp of horror rushed through the gathering like wind through a field of wheat.

Kuber continued inexhorably, "He is no longer your tribe leader. He and his family will leave this village before sunset. A new tribe leader will be appointed in his place."

Turning away in the tense silence, Lord Kuber walked towards his elephant, his eyes smouldering. Immediately, the beast fell to its knees, to allow him to ascend. Despite his bulk, Kuber sprang nimbly onto one of the tusks and regained his seat atop the elephant. As the people of Yakshavana watched, the cavalcade disappeared into the forest as quickly as it had come.

***

"How did the news about Shikhandini reach the Lord? No one but us knows about it. And how does he know about the Science of Ila?" questioned Pashupati, his voice agitated.

"He is the Lord, Pashupati," replied Sthunakarna calmly.

"How can you be so calm, Guruji? He just took away everything you have worked for all your life!" asked Pashupati, frustrated and angry.

Yakshini put a hand on his shoulder. "Pashupati, my husband has fought all his life to help the people of Yakshavana. Becoming the tribe leader was never his goal. The people of Yakshavana love and respect him for his deeds, not because he is their leader."

Pashupathi nodded slowly. It was the truth. "Forgive me, Guruji, I spoke in haste."

"Pashupati, I feel guilty for having kept this secret from the Lord. But it was for the greater good. Sometimes, life demands sacrifices so you can be part of a bigger task."

"But what are we going to tell Shikhandini?" asked Yakshini, recalling the Lord's order to leave the village before sunset. "She will be devastated to know the Lord punished you because of her."

"She does not need to know."

"But she will know when we tell her we have to move."

"Yakshini, the Lord has banished us from Yakshavana, not the forest beyond the borders of the village. The Ayuralaya and Shikhandini's hut are outside Yakshavana," Sthunakarna reminded her.

"So you and Guru Ma can stay outside the village and still take care of Shikhandini," said Pashupati, relieved.

Yakshini and Sthunakarna nodded.

THE HOUR BEFORE SUNSET

"Pranam, Sthunakarnaji," said Dundubi in greeting. He was one of the eldest members of the Yaksha clan. A man of medium built, with widely spaced eyes, his bushy moustache was more white than black.

"Pranam, Dundubiji, please sit down." Sthunakarna helped the old man onto a low bench. "What brings you here?" he asked.

"I come on behalf of the people of Yakshavana, My Lord. We have decided together, to help you in your difficult time. Just outside Yakshavana, in the direction of the sunrise, we have begun building a house for you and your family. We wish you to remain close to us. Without you, Yakshavana would be like a body without a soul. Accept this humble request, Sthunakarnaji," the old man said with folded hands.

Sthunakarna looked at Yakshini, and then smiled at the old man. "My humble gratitude, Dundubiji. We will forever remain indebted to you and the people of Yakshavana for this kindness."

"My Lord, we do not believe you would ever break the Yaksha law," responded the old man, shaking his head.

Sthunakarna smiled sadly. The blind trust his people had in him was unsettling. He wanted to explain to them how Ila was not a dark art but a form of science. But he also knew he could only do so after Shikhandini had completed her purpose.

"The villagers and I are not sure what the Lord meant by saying you have allowed the practice of the dark art, or what the word Ila means.

But what I know with the certainty of my years is that you would never do anything to harm our people. If you have broken a law, it would have been for a good cause, for the good of the people."

"Dundubiji, I promise that when the time is right, I will explain everything to you and the people of Yakshavana," Sthunakarna vowed.

22
THE TRANSFORMATION

Several months had passed since Kuber's visit to Yakshavana. Sthunakarna was no longer the tribe leader. He and his wife now lived in the small house outside the village that the villagers had built for them. Though he was not their leader, the people of Yakshavana still treated him with respect. The new Yaksha leader, Bhupati, also consulted him before making decisions about the village.

Shikhandini still lived in the hut, far from Yakshavana. Her presence and the use of Ila for her transformation, remained unknown to people of Yakshavana, who believed Lord Kubera had fallen prey to the whispered words of one of Sthunakarna's rivals in the clan.

"Shikhandini, now that we have completed the first stage of your transformation, I think we can start the next and final step. It is for you to decide. We will do it only if you are ready," said Sthunakarna.

Sthunakarna, Yakshini and Shikhandini had gathered once again in the Ayuralaya.

"What is the next step?" asked Shikhandini.

"*Shastra Chikitsa*. It is an operative procedure that was first invented to help patients with serious ailments. It is a way Vyeds could treat problems related to the internal organs, by either removing or fixing the tissues of the affected part," Pashupati explained.

Despite her resolve, a shudder went through Shikhandini's frame.

"In your case, we will be using it to remove tissue." Pashupati paused, hoping he would not have to explain further about the surgical procedure needed to transform the upper part of Shikhandini's torso. It was an essential step to transform her from woman to man. "It is an important and necessary step for your transformation, Shikhandini.

Once completed successfully, there will be no reason for anyone to object to your participation in the war."

Sthunakarna knew the myth of the Yakshas possessing magical powers to transform humans was more convincing to outsiders than the real truth of their advanced knowledge of science and medicine.

"Is it really possible, Pashupati?" asked Yakshini, still unhappy with the transformation idea.

"Yes, Guru Ma, it is. For the last few decades, Maharishi Ved Vyas and his disciples have been working on this new branch of medical science. It is called *Shastra Chikitsa*. Several patients who had lost all hope, have been gifted a new life because of shastra chikitsa. In fact, I have even heard of birth stories, where a surgical procedure was performed to save the life of the unborn child."

"Did the mother survive?" asked Shikhandini, recalling the loss of her first child in the birthing chamber at Dasarna. At the time, she had not known such a science existed. But the memory of losing her first child had clawed at her mind during the last days before her son was born. It had felt like a rebirth.

"Yes, both mother and child were in good health after the shastra chikitsa," replied Sthunakarna on Pashupati's behalf. He remembered hearing about it at the time. It had been a great achievement and saved both mother and child.

"But will it not be painful, tearing open the skin and treating the inner organs? Will there not be the risk of losing the patient because of loss of blood?" Guru Ma asked, her anxiety evident in her tone.

"We do not know all the details yet, Guru Ma, as Maharishi Vyas's principal disciple, Pavki, is the only one who can perform this shastra chikitsa. We will send for her once we decide to go ahead. She will explain everything to us."

Shikhandini had already made up her mind. She was ready to move forward with the shastra chikitsa.

A WEEK LATER

"Pranam, Shikhandini," a soft voice said.

Shikhandini folded her hands in greeting. The voice belonged to a middle-aged woman, dressed completely in white. She wore a *janeu* across her torso and had a u-shaped *tilak* on her forehead. It was years since she had spoken to anyone other than Sthunakarna, Yakshini or Pashupati. Shikhandini suddenly felt conscious of her appearance, wondering if the woman knew about her. Then she realized that only people who knew would come here.

"This is Pavki, Shikhandini," said Sthunakarna, introducing the newcomer. "She is here to help us with the next step."

Pavki smiled warmly at Shikhandini. Having heard the story of Shikhandini's life and transformation, she knew what to expect. Shikhandini was everything she had imagined – the perfect combination of Shiva-Shakti, the androgynous form that combined both the masculine principle of strength and the feminine principle of wisdom. She looked at Shikhandini in admiration.

"I will go and arrange for Pavki's stay. Meanwhile, you two can get acquainted," said Sthunakarna, breaking Pavki's chain of thought.

Shikhandini shifted uncomfortably under Pavki's gaze. She felt conscious of how she looked to others. Her face now resembled that of a man, with a sharp jawline covered in slight stubble. Her body, however, was neither completely man nor woman. Her shoulders were broader than before, her hip narrower. Her breasts had reduced considerably due to the antahsraava replacement medicines that had been injected into her bloodstream, and her body looked more male than female.

Recognising Shikhandini's discomfort, Pavki averted her gaze. "Do not concern yourself, child. Of all people, I cannot be the one to make you uncomfortable. It is just that you are so beautiful! I have read about the Science of Ila, but never in my wildest dream did I image to see it realized before my own eyes! You look divine."

Shikhandini sighed, letting the tension ease from her body.

Sitting down, Pavki asked Shikhandini to narrate her experience with the therapy in detail. Opening a palm leaf book and her ink pot, and taking a bird feather from her sling pouch, she prepared to write.

Noticing Shikhandini's uncertainty, Pavki began to worry. She wondered if Shikhandini was being forced into this. Then she shook the thought from her mind. Sthunakarna would never do that.

"You do not seem happy. Is there a problem, Shikhandini?" asked Pavki, concerned.

"No, no...I am sure. But the thought of what comes next scares me," Shikhandini confessed. She felt guilty of being afraid; she was a Kshatriya. Fear was akin to cowardice.

"I know it can feel overwhelming, especially with the antahsraava changes and anxiety about the future. But the next step is essential. Without it, you cannot prove to the world that you have transformed into a man," explained Pavki.

Shikhandini nodded slowly. "Is it really possible for someone to completely transform into the opposite gender through shastra chikitsa?"

"At this point in time, no. But I have read that, several centuries ago, before Ila was banned, there were several cases of complete transformation. While most people believe Ila to be a form of dark science, where the transformation is magical and has nothing to do with medicine, it was in reality a boon to people who were trapped in wrong bodies. It gave them a chance to live as they desired. But, people who underwent such transformations were considered to be cursed or possessed by evil spirits."

"So what happened?"

"The Science of Ila perished. With no one to pass on the knowledge over the centuries, it died a slow death. If you ask me, it was a great loss to medicine," Pavki replied sombrely.

"If it was possible then, why not now?" asked Shikhandini, glad to finally meet someone who had the answers to her questions.

"We no longer know how. Most of the information related to Ila was destroyed over the centuries, following the ban. It is only in the last few decades that we have learned about partial transformation – enough to prove to the outside world. The success of your transformation will open new possibilities. You could be the reason for the rebirth of Ila," Pavki added, her deep eyes giving Shikhandini the motivation she lacked.

"What if I do not make it?" asked Shikhandini, uncertain.

"You will. You are a strong woman, Shikhandini. When I first heard your story from Pashupati, I felt in awe of you. I know how difficult it can be to leave your family, especially your child, to serve a greater purpose. What you have decided to do is a great thing, Shikhandini. I feel honored to be a part of your story," said Pavki, taking both Shikhandini's hands in her own.

***

It had been more than six months since Pavki's arrival in the Yaksha village. During this time, she had prepared Shikhandini mentally for the shastra chikitsa to be performed on her. Pavki, a specialist, knew the success of the shastra chikitsa depended as much on the patient as on her. The patient had to be as strong mentally as physically to bear the pain and shock.

The shastra chikitsa was to be performed in a secluded room in the Ayuralaya. Apart from Pavki and her team, all others, including Pashupati and Sthunakarna, were asked to leave. A suitable time was set, based on the position of the stars and planets in the sky. All the doors and windows had been sealed shut from within to avoid intrusion. The place had been cleaned with natural disinfectants to avoid infection during or after the shastra chikitsa. Small oil lamps were placed at suitable distances to provide light. One of Pavki's assistants held a specially designed torch to provide light during shastra chikitsa. It was a thick wooden rod with a small fire at the tip. The tip was covered by glass, except at the top, from where air entered to keep the flame alive. It could be brought close to the patient, providing visibility without risking accidental fire.

"Ready?" asked Pavki, a small smile of encouragement on her face. Two of her assistants stood by her side, ready with the knives and blades needed for the shastra chikitsa. Suturing material made of animal skin and sterilized needles were also kept ready. A bowl of hot water and a pile of clean rags lay on the table beside Shikhandini.

Shikhandini nodded in reply. She, who had never known fear, was experiencing it for the first time. It was not the fear of death, but of dying without having fulfilled her purpose on this earth. She was aware that shastra chikitsa had its own grave risks. There was no guarantee it would succeed. There were cases when the patient had never woken up or recovered. But she knew there was no other way. It was a gamble she had to take.

Pavki and her assistants recited a short prayer before beginning the procedure. Shikhandini shut her eyes and waited for the first sting of pain. One of the assistants began to apply a thick paste on Shikhandini's upper torso. It was to ease the pain.

The paste was one of Pavki's innumerable gifts to the field of medicine. A pain-numbing medication, it was meant to effectively block pain signals from reaching the brain. It helped patients bear the excruciating pain they were subjected to during surgical treatment. It was because of this paste that many of the shastra chikitsa earlier thought to be impossible to perform, had become possible. But the medicine had its limitations. It did not completely block the pain but reduced it. Its effects did not last long. Though effective on first application, its efficacy reduced quickly over time, compelling the *chikitsak* to finish the procedure as quickly as possible. There was also the possibility of the patient losing consciousness from the pain.

"I am going to start now. Be strong. We are with you," said Pavki, signalling her assistant to hand the knife. It was slender blade, as thin as the edge of a leaf. It had been designed especially for shashtra chikitsa procedures by Pavki's team.

As the knife cut through her skin, a familiar sense of throbbing pain hit Shikhandini. It reminded her of the numerous battle scars she carried on her body. The pain was bittersweet. This transformation was no less of a battle; the cuts of the knife on her torso similar to those of the sword. It had been several years since she had last held a sword. She wondered how long it would be before she could hold one again.

As the minutes passed, the pain began to rise. Sweat broke out on Shikhandini's forehead and her hands balled into fists.

"I know this is painful, Shikhandini. And I know you are doing your utmost not to give up. I am proud of you," Pavki whispered as she continued to cut through the layers of skin.

Shikhandini did not respond. The pain was now intense as the knife penetrated to the tissues of her bosom. The numbing medicine Pavki had applied could no longer control the terrible pain. Involuntarily, tears sprang to Shikhandini's eyes and her body began to shake. She prayed for the pain to stop. She moaned, biting on her lips to suppress her screams. Time and again she experienced short pulses of bone-cracking pain rise up her spine. It was nothing like she had ever experienced. The pain she had endured in childbirth seemed nothing compared to this.

"It will be over soon, Shikhandini. The pain will subside. Just hold on a little longer," Pavki said quietly, her voice a soothing murmer in Shikhandini's ears.

Two of the assistants held Shikhandini in place as she began to shake and tremble, as if with the ague. They watched admiringly as Shikhandini refused to scream or beg Pavki to stop. Shikhandini lost all sense of place and time, her mind filled only with one name , one image...Krishna...

When Pavki began to extract the tissues from Shikhandini's bosom, Shikhandini's eyes rolled back in their sockets. She let out a sharp cry, unable to bear the tormenting pain. In a delirium of pain, she called to Krishna to save her. Her breathing slowed, her body stopped shaking, and her fists opened. Her body could fight no more.

"Shikhandini, wake up!" Pavki urged, trying to keep her patient conscious. One of the assistants placed a wet rag on Shikhandini's burning forehead. "Shikhandini, we are almost finished. Do not give up now. Remember why you chose to do this. You cannot give up after coming so far. Wake up!" Pavki knew Shikhandini had not heard her; her body too tortured to hear or understand.

Shikhandini found herself drowning in darkness. She had lost all sense of where she was. There was peaceful silence all around her and the pain seemed far away. It was as though her soul was trying to break all connection with her body and merge with the darkness. With each passing second, Pavki's voice seemed to fade further.

Uddhiran, one of the assistants, shook his head in disappointment. He had far seen too many cases where the patient became unconsciousness, never to return. He waited patiently for Pavki to examine Shikhandini and make a declaration.

Pavki was in a dilemma. She was almost at the end of the shastra chikitsa and knew that if she could bring Shikhandini back to consciousness, the chikitsa was likely to succeed. But the chances of that looked bleak. Shikhandini's pulse was faint and thready, her breathing shallow. They were losing her and there was nothing they could do. It was over.

In that moment of defeat, as Pavki looked up, something unexpected occured. Dispelling the eerie silence, the faint sound of the flute filled the chamber; a mesmerizingly sweet sound that was not mere music but a message of healing. It was as though someone was telling Shikhandini not to give up; that she was not alone; that this suffering would end soon. From deep within the darkness, Shikhandini instantly recognised it as Krishna's flute, the one he carried tucked into his waistband. He had kept his promise to stand beside her.

As Shikhandini listened intently, the pain flooded her body once again, and she began to gasp for breath. Slowly, her breathing eased and her pulse returned to a stronger beat. Pavki noticed the changes, and knew consciousness had returned.

In the next few minutes, the procedure was completed and the wounds stitched, covered with healing medication, and bandaged.

Pain still ravaged her body. Pavki administered a herbal potion to help Shikhandini sleep. She would have to wait for a few more hours before she could declare the operation a success.

FIVE WEEKS LATER

It had taken many weeks for Shikhandini to heal completely. For the first two weeks, she had been confined to her bed, with only Pavki and her two assistants allowed to visit her. After the wounds had begun to heal, Pavki permitted Shikhandini to move around in the hut, and then outside it. The fear of infection or the stitches breaking faded away. Finally, Pavki told her it was time to look at herself.

It was the moment of truth. Shikhandini quietly told Pavki she wished to do this alone. Pavki understood and left with a reassuring smile. During the transformation, Shikhandini had been advised by Pashupati not to look in the mirror. He knew that seeing each step of the transformation, incomplete in itself, would leave her overwhelmed. There were times she would appear androgynous, and this could cause depression and trauma. But now that the shastra chikitsa had been successful and the transformation completed, Pashupati had placed a full-length mirror in the hut.

Standing in front of the mirror with her eyes closed, Shikkandini's hands trembled. It was the first time she would see herself in years. She knew what to expect, but she also knew no one could be truly prepared. She felt relieved to be alone. Holding her breath, she opened her eyes.

In that moment her life changed forever. Seeing her reflection in the mirror, she stood spellbound. Although she had seen her body change, it had been gradual, allowing her mind to absorb and accept the changes. But she had not expected anything like what she now saw. In the mirror she saw a man who looked several years younger than she in fact was. Her slightly plump cheeks had given way to a strong jawline. Her smooth flawless skin was now covered in fine hair. Her once waist-length tresses barely reached her shoulders. Her arms felt hard and muscular. Her shoulders looked broader than she remembered. As her hand went over her torso, her hard chest and taut stomach felt foreign. Only her doe-eyes were unchanged, reminding her of who she had been.

Shikhandini moved her palms over her face, absorbing every detail. Tears welled in her eyes as she realized how close she had now come to achieving her goal. The last few years had been excruciating painful, both physically and mentally. But she knew she had been prepared to pay the price.

For a brief moment, her mind wandered to Kush. How would he take this transformation? Would he be proud or cringe in disgust? She smiled wistfully. He had his new family. Sadness filled her heart as she thought of her son. She knew she had arrived at a point from which there was no turning back. Even if she survived the Great War, she would never be able to return to her family. She would never again be a wife or mother.

***

Three years had passed since Shikhandini's decision to transform herself. It was nothing less than a rebirth. For three years she had spent every day building her physical strength. With unfaltering discipline and practice, she had sculpted every inch of her body to match that of a male warrior. While her chiselled torso and muscular arms spoke of her will and determination, the innumerable scars on her body reflected her pain and sacrifice.

Though physically transformed beyond recognition, mentally Shikhandini remained in a tristate. Sthunakarna, aware of this, decided it would be best if she was given a new identity. It would help her leave her past behind and focus on her future. He arranged a naming ceremony. Like other important life events, it was held at the temple of Goddess Prakruti, outside Yakshavana. A small group, consisting Sthunakarna, Yakshini, Pashupathi, and Pavki and her team, gathered at the day and time appointed by Yakshavana's only astrologer. In the first hour of the second prahar, Shikhandini was to receive her new name.

Dressed in a dhoti and angavastram that loosely hung from her left shoulder, Shikhandini sat cross-legged before the Goddess, a garland of aromatic flowers around her neck. Yakshini placed a tamra plate of rice grains in front of her. Saying a prayer, she placed a saffron tilak on Shikhandini's forehead.

"Shikhandini, this day marks the new beginning of your new life. You have been reborn; a boon that few in this mortal life receive. You have been given a second chance, to leave behind the darkness of your past and walk into the bright sun of the future. May you fulfill the purpose of your life. Vijayi Bhava!" Yakshini placed a hand in blessing on Shikhandini's bowed head. Having witnessed her unwavering will to achieve her goal, Yakshini had slowly come to terms with her transformation.

The naming ceremony was one of the few rituals where the mother took center stage instead of the father. As per Yaksha tradition, the mother held her child's index finger and traced the new name in the rice on the thali. So Yakshini sat down beside Shikhandini and held Shikhandini's forefinger. Together, they traced the name. In the plate, the word shone, the burnished metal reflecting the light from the lamp in front of the Goddess.

Shikhandi...Shikhandi...Shikhandi... Yakshini whispered the name thrice in her child's ear, completing the ceremony.

***

"Shikhandi, this is your first real fight. Your performance today will reflect the training of the past three years," said Sthunakarna as he threw a sword at his opponent. Shikhandi caught it with ease.

Sthunakarna and Shikhandi stood in the flat area outside Yakshavana which was used for riding, battle training, ceremonies and festivities. Today it was surrounded by Yakshas who had come to watch the duel between Sthunakarna and his new student. None had recognized Shikhandi, and Sthunakarna took this as a good omen. Had the Yakshas recognized him, they would have known Sthunakarna had permitted the use of Ila. The people, who had remained loyal to Sthunakarna despite Kuber's allegation, would have been left heartbroken. It would also have make Shikhandi's life a living hell. He had lived for years in hiding. It was time he came out and lived like a normal human being.

As Shikhandi hesitantly lifted the sword, he found his body reverberating with a new energy, stronger than before.

"On guard!" called Sthunakarna.

"On guard!" responded Shikhandi in a thick, hoarse voice. Even after all this time, his voice felt strange to his ears. He shook off the thought and took up position. He had to win.

The audience hooted and clapped when the swords clinked together. Shikhandi used one sword, following Sthunakarna's instruction. His ability to use two swords simultaneously would have certainly given him away.

Sthunakarna, though twice Shikhandi's age, was agile and moved swiftly, escaping the blows his opponent rained on him. Shikhandi already had a few shallow cuts on his arms. Sthunakarna was not making this contest easy. Shikhandi did not wish him to. Sthunakarna, noticing Shikhandi's wavering concentration, took the opportunity to disarm him with one clean blow to the centre of his blade. Shikhandi bent to pick up his sword. Immeditaely, Sthunakarna placed his own blade on Shikhandi's neck. Shikhandi knew the fight was over. Had it been on the battlefield, he would have lost his head. Removing his sword from Shikhandi's neck, Sthunakarna moved away. Shikhandi rose to feet, his face reflecting his disappointment in his own performance.

"Let us try again," Sthunakarna said, his voice unemotional.

Shikhandi nodded and took position again. This time, he planned his moves carefully. He knew what to expect.

Circling with his sword above his head, stretching low with his left arm and leg outstretched, Sthunakarna gained momentum. Shikhandi did the same. They looked like mirror images of each other. Once again their swords clashed. This time, the spectators noticed Sthunakarna had lost his balance slightly. Regaining it quickly, Sthunakarna smiled at his student approvingly.

The duel went on for several minutes with neither side faltering. Finally, Sthunakarna said, panting a little, "Shikhandi, this fight cannot last forever." He had decided to use his characteristic move.

Shikhandi realised what Sthunakarna planned to do, and moved to counter attack. If executed well, he could disarm his opponent and win. He watched his Guru with rapt attention. Without warning, Sthunakarna executed his masterstroke. With his right foot stretched back and his body leaning forward, his spine almost parallel to the ground, he stretched forth both arms. Suddenly, Sthunakarna rose, jumping high and spiralling in the air, his sword raised high above his head. Shikhandi ducked low, his right knee on the ground, his sword horizontal, withstanding Sthunakarna's mighty blow. The spectators watched in awed silence.

Shikhandi pushed his Guru away with all his might. Before the Yaksha could steady himself, Shikhandi attacked in a wheeling motion, his right hand gripping his sword, his left arm outstretched. He delivered several blows one after the other, not allowing his opponent a chance to counter. With one last blow, Sthunakarna's sword was flicked from his hand.

Sthunakarna rose, a smile on his face, eyes gleaming with pride. Shikhandi bowed low before him.

"May you be victorious in all your battles, my child. Vijayi Bhava!" the Guru said in blessing.

23
Kurukshetra

Thirteen years had passed since the fateful day of the Dhyutsabha in Hastinapur. The Pandavas had spent twelve years in exile, wandering through forests, living the live of simple mendicants. In the thirteenth year, they lived in disguise, taking various positions in King Virata's kingdom. Yudhistir put his gaming skills to use as the King's chess companion; Arjun, disguised as a eunuch, taught dance to the Princesses; Bheem used his skills in gastronomy as a cook in the royal kitchens, and Nakul and Sahadev used their mastery of horses to find postions in the royal stables. Draupadi was handmaiden to the Pricesses, doing their hair and dressing them in the way she once had herself.

When the Pandavas once again entered Hastinapur, having completed the terms of their exile, to ask for Indraprastha to be returned, Duryodhan denied having made any such promise. Left with no choice, Yudhistir, the eldest Pandava, declared war against Hastinapur. The drums of war sounded across the length and breath of Aryavarth as Kings, Princes and warriors chose sides. Alliances were formed and preparations made. Every kingdom, big and small, made haste to be part of the Great War least history forget them.

Draupadi chose the auspicious day for the commencement of the Great War. Commanders and Kings of both sides convened to discuss and agree upon the rules of engagement. Kurukshetra, land of the Kurus, situated between two rivers Saraswati and Drishadvati, was chosen as the field of battle. It was believed that Lord Parashuram had himself stepped onto this land to end evil and restore dharma in Aryavartha, thus giving the palce its name – Dharmakshetra, Field of Righteousness. The greatest war of the yuga was to be fought there, three days later.

On the first day, warriors from all over Aryavrath were present. Every significant kingdom in the country had joined with either the Pandavas or the Kauravas. With the Pandavas stood Magadha, Dwaraka, Matsya, Kekaya, Pandya, Kashi and Mathura, forming the seven *akshauhinis* of their army. A much stronger force of eleven akshauhinis stood on the Kauravas side, with Anga, Kalinga, Kekaya, Sindhudesa, Avanti, Gandhara, Bahlikas, Mahishmati and others. One akshauhini consisted of twenty thousand rathas or chariots, twenty thousand elephants, sixty thousand horses and one hundred thousand foot soldiers. From the numbers, it was clear that no matter which side won the war, Kurukshetra would soon turn into an ocean of blood and tears.

While Maharathi Bheeshm led the Kaurava army, Dhrishtadhyumna, son of King Drupada of Panchala, and Draupadi's brother, was appointed Senapati of the Pandavas. The Kaurava army stood facing west. The advice Arjun received on the battlefield from his charioteer, Lord Krishna, now forms the Song Celestial, the *Bhagavad Gita*.

When battle finally commenced, Maharathi Bheeshm, believed to be invincible, tore through the Pandava army, wreaking havoc wherever he appeared. Among the Princes slain were Uttar and Shveta, sons of King Virata. The Kauravas won the day. With the blowing of the conch and the setting of the sun Kuruksketra red, battle ceased.

On the second day, the Pandava army entered the field in hopes of reversing the losses they had suffered the previous day. Arjun challenged Maharathi Bheeshm to a duel, which went on for many hours. Guru Dronacharya battled Dhrishtadhyumna. Prophecy said he was destined to be the cause of Guru Drona's death. The Guru, however, defeated the Prince of Panchala and it was only by Bheem's intervention that Dhrishtadhyumna was saved. The troops of Kalinga had engaged with Bheem, losing their lives en masse.

Satyaki, a powerful Yadava-Vrushni warrior on the Pandava side, killed Maharathi Bheeshm's charioteer. With his charioteer dead and no one to control the horses, Bheeshm drove away from the battlefield. At the end of day two, the Pandavas were victorious, having subjected great losses on the Kaurava army.

As the third day of battle began, Maharathi Bheeshm arranged the Kaurava army in the *Garuda Vyuha* or Eagle formation. Bheeshm rode in the vanguard while Duryodhan's forces protected the rear. The Pandavas countered this by using the *Chandrakala Vyuha* or Crescent formation, with Bheem and Arjun heading the right and left points, respectively. Both sides faced large losses by the end of the third day.

The war went on... Blood and death followed the men into their dreams in an inexhorable march of destruction. Some days the Pandavas were victorious, on others the Kauravas took the day. Following every defeat, warriors on both sides fought with renewed vigour to avenge their losses. The war seemed to stretch into eternity, with no beginning or end...

On day nine, the invincibility of Maharathi Bheeshm was the evident cause of Kaurava victory. Krishna, overcome by anger and frustration, decided to kill him himself, but was stopped by Arjun, who reminded Krishna of his vow not to raise his weapon in the war.

"Krishna, as long as Maharathi Bheeshm is on the battlefield, we cannot win this war," cried a distraught Draupadi. She sat with her five husbands and Krishna in one of the rescue tents at the far end of the battlefield, where the wounded soldiers were being treated. Outside were the burning pyres of the dead. The battlefield was a bone-chilling sight, where death seemed to hide in every corner.

"I know, *sakhi*," replied Krishna, addressing her as friend, "we have to find a way to defeat the Maharathi or he will destroy our army."

"How is that possible, Madhav? Pitamaha Bheeshm is invincible. He was blessed with a boon by his father, the Late King Shantanu. There is no way to defeat him," said Arjun, who could not accept the thought of eliminating the Maharathi.

"Yes, Arjun, it is true that only he can decide the time of his death. Until then he is invincible," replied Krishna, carefully choosing his words. He did not wish to upset Arjun at this critical juncture by declaring the Maharathi's invincibility to be a myth.

"We must find a way to force him to surrender," said Bheem, contemplating solutions.

"Pitamaha will never do that. He has vowed to remain loyal to the throne of Hastinapur; to protect it to his last breath," declared Arjun.

"There is only one way to make the Maharathi drop his weapons," said Krishna softly.

Every eye turned on him.

"What do you suggest?" asked Yudhistir.

"We must remind him of his other vow – the promise he made to Princess Amba," said Krishna, a faraway look in his eyes. "We will have to bring your sister Shikhandini onto the battlefield," he said, looking at Draupadi.

The story of Shikhandini, believed to be Princess Amba in her previous birth, was known to everyone. Krishna's words reminded them of the vow the Maharathi had taken in the presence of the Lords Shiva and Parashuram – if he ever faced the Princess in a fight, he would surrender and wait for death at her hands.

"But she is a woman, Krishna. Women are not allowed to fight," replied Yudhistir, recalling the rules that had been read out and agreed to before the commencement of the war. Yudhistir persisted in upholding the rules of the battlefield.

"Yes, women are not permitted to fight, but Shikhandini is..." his words faded away. The day had finally arrived, he thought.

"What do you mean, Krishna?" asked Bheem, confused.

"You will all see for yourself tomorrow," replied Krishna smiling.

***

The boy ran towards the man with dagger in hand, determined to kill the beast who had destroyed his family. The man was a foot taller than the boy and several times stronger. But the boy knew that if he did not kill the man, Gandhara and his dead parents would never forgive him. Above all, he would have failed himself.

"Leave my sister alone, Bheeshm!" he yelled, his recently broken voice hoarse and rough.

"I cannot do that Prince Shakuni. I have promised to take her to Hastinapur. It is an order from the Queen," replied the Maharathi, urging Princess Gandhari onward.

"No! Stop!" shouted the boy, hurrying after the retreating figures. The boy winced each time he lifted his right foot. A sword had cut through the skin and muscle, reaching the bone. He would limp for the rest of his life. "Do not walk away, you coward! Turn and fight."

The Maharathi did not stop, walking swiftly away from the Prince. As they walked, the Princess sobbed quietly, looking around the once beautiful palace that was now in ruins. Everything the beast touched had been wrecked. The mutilated bodies of soldiers lay everywhere, making her cringe. The palace, once her home, resembled a graveyard. There was nothing she could do to reverse the destruction. She had surrendered to her fate. Suddenly, something flashed through her mind and she stopped walking.

"What?" asked the Maharathi, looking over his shoulder. The Princess was now several feet behind him.

"I cannot leave my brother here," she said sternly, her piercing grey eyes boring into his.

"He is the Prince of Gandhara. We cannot take him with us"

Gandhari gave a bitter laugh "Prince of Gandhara? What have you left for him to rule over? This?" She pointed to the lifeless corpses and smouldering ruins, wondering how many more dead she would have to see outside the palace grounds.

The Maharathi turned in silence to look at the Prince, limping after them, leaving a trail of blood from his wounded foot. The Maharathi was amused by the boy's courage. The youngster's eyes held no fear, only rage.

"If you want me to come with you and marry your nephew, you will have to take him with us," said Gandhari. "Or you will have to kill us both here."

On another occasion the Maharathi would have appreciated her courage. He had always admired women who could speak for themselves. But not today. His mind was fatigued, his body exhausted. The struggle to fulfil his vow to uphold the throne of Hastinapur was taking a toll on him.

The boy stopped. His face looked dazed and pale; only his light eyes glowed like opals. Slowly, he crumpled to the ground.

Walking swiftly back to the boy, the Maharathi picked up the limp form, still clutching his dagger. The boy was unconscious, probably due to loss of blood. The Maharathi carried the boy to where Gandhari stood like a statue. "If we start now we can reach Hastinapur by the last prahar," he said.

She followed him out, leaving behind everything she had ever known.

THE KAURAVA CAMP, END OF THE NINTH DAY

"How is that even possible?" asked Duryodhan angrily when he heard of Shikhandini's return as a man.

"It is said she spent many years in severe penance, renouncing food and water to please the gods. Sthunakarna, a Yaksha tribe leader with magical powers, pleased with Shikhandini's devotion, granted her his manhood so that she could participate in the war and fulfill her life's purpose by killing Maharathi Bheeshm," Shakuni, the Kauravas' uncle said, telling them what he had heard from his loyal messenger, who had heard it at the Pandava refugee camp.

"Nonsense! That is impossible. How can a woman turn into a man?" growled Duryodhan, annoyed by his uncle's irrational explanation.

"Have you not heard of the powers of the Yakshas? They are magical beings. If they are pleased, they can grant you anything. On the other hand, they can also destroy you if they wish to," said Shakuni, his light grey eyes staring into Duryodhana's coal black ones.

"I am sure this must have been that cunning Krishna's idea. Only he would have thought of something so wicked," added Dushasana.

"Yes, looks like he has been plotting against us for several years," said Shakuni, limping towards a vacant seat. Once the Prince of Gandhara, Shakuni was an intelligent but devious man. His hatred for the Maharathi had grown over time. He lived to destroy Hastinapur the way the Maharathi had destroyed Gandhara. He had been the one to carefully sow the seeds of hatred towards the Pandava brothers in his nephews' minds at an early age. He was the mastermind behind the Great War.

"She was born to kill Maharathi Bheeshm. There is no denying that. Destiny somehow finds it way, my friend." Karna's voice broke into Duryodhana's thoughts and brought Shakuni out of his dark reverie.

"Whose side are you on?" hissed Duryodhan.

Karna chose not to reply. Having always believed in the path of righteousness, he did not like Duryodhan's ways, he was bound by his loyalty. When everyone else had humiliated him, calling him low cast, it had been Duryodhan who had risen to his defence, making him King of Anga. Karna would remain loyal to the Kuru Prince to his last breath. Helpless to turn the course of destiny, he watched Duryodhan and his brothers' wrong doing, knowing the time would come when fate would play a hand.

But Karna yearned to prove he was the better archer by defeating the Pandava Prince Arjun, who was regarded as the greatest archer in Bharatvarsha. But Maharathi Bheeshm refused to let Karna fight in the war. Duryodhan, knowing the Maharathi was the supreme warrior, aceeded to this. So Karna waited patiently. He knew the day would come when he rode into battle.

"Yes Uncle, this has to be Krishna's idea to destroy us. Without Pitamaha, we are doomed," said Dushasana.

"No, Dushasana," replied Duryodhan with uncharacteristic calm. "If something does indeed happen to Pitamaha, Karna will take over as Senapati. He will lead us to victory."

Karna smiled. It would finally be his time.

***

On the tenth day of the Great War, an air of sadness and despair shrouded Kurukshetra. The day had come. Maharathi Bheeshm's end was at hand. It was a day of grief and anguish for the Kauravas and Pandavas alike. The Kurus were all children in the presence of the Pitamaha. The thought of his death was unbelievable.

"Today the Kaurava army has but one goal – to keep Shikhandi away from Maharathi Bheeshm," Krishna warned as he drove Arjun's chariot towards the centre of the battlefield.

Arjun nodded in sombre silence. The first rays of the sun were dispelling the morning mist, reflecting off the armour of the men as they faced each other across the narrow aisle of dusty ground.

Yudhistir held up his hand and said, "As you might have heard, we have appointed a new Senapathi – Shikhandi. If anyone wishes to object, this is the time to speak, or forever hold your peace."

Each day, before hostilities resumed, both sides were dutybound to inform each other of any changes they had decided to make, in accordance with the codes of war.

"It is your right to do so, Prince Yudhistir," replied Dronacharya, on behalf of the Kaurava army. "We are ready to fight."

Guru Dronacharya and Maharathi Bheeshm had discussed the clauses of the code. To Duryodhan's anger and dismay, they had concluded that the code was not violated by Shikhandi's participation. He was no longer a woman. He was an athirathi, a warrior of the second highest rank. It made him eligible to fight.

"*Shank Nadh*!" Yudhistir ordered the conch blower behind him.

The sound of conches being blown on both sides indicated the start of yet another day of merciless conflict.

With singleminded focus Shikhandi rode in his chariot towards Bheeshm, who had been placed at the rear of the Kaurava army. The

Pandavas rode alongside, tackling every obstacle in the way. Within minutes every warrior was engaged in a duel with someone of the same warrior rank from the other side. Shikhandi found himself riding alone towards his destination. A chill ran up his spine as his heart ponded in his chest. He was at the threshold of his life's purpose. All the sacrifice and pain had been for this moment. He knew that if he succeeded today, his name would be forever known as the warrior who overcame every obstacle to restore dharma.

It was Dronacharya, the honourable Guru to both the Pandavas and the Kauravas, who first stood in Shikhandi's way. To his eyes the Guru appeared pale. Though he had fought the war with vigour, his eyes betrayed his emotions. Shikhandini wondered if he, like the Maharathi, was bound by his word to remain on the Kaurava side. He recalled hearing that Dronacharya had a fatal weakness – his beloved son Ashwathama. The Guru was helpless in his unconditional love for his son. Ashwathama was one of Duryodhan's closest friends from their days at the gurukul.

"If you wish to reach the Maharathi, you will have to fight me first," declared the Guru. His wrinkled skin, white mane and hooded eyes disguised his great strength. Shikhandi knew that defeating him in a duel would be as difficult as defeating the Maharathi himself. Although tempted to fight him and prove himself to the most respected teacher in Bharatvarsha, Shikhandini knew it would exhaust her, leaving her vulnerable when facing the Maharathi.

As though in answer to her thoughts, a clear voice said behind her, "Guruji, you will have to pass through me to reach Shikhandi."

Dronacharya smiled. "It will be an honour to duel with my best student, Arjun," he replied.

"We must move, Shikhandi, the second prahar will soon come to an end," said Nakul, slowing his horse next to Shikhandi's chariot. Shikhandi nodded and followed him towards the Kaurava army. As he passed by, he saw the familiar sight of mutilated bodies lying in pools of blood. Above them, crows and vultures flew in circles, waiting for the sun to set so they could begin their feast. Somewhere near the horizon, she saw *daivasthras* rocketing into the sky, bombarding the enemy troops. Scores of lives were lost in moments.

Her mind swirling with thoughts, Shikhandi charged through the enemy lines, swords swinging in both hands, cutting through everything that came in his way. On either side of him rode Nakul and Sahadev, each bearing deep cuts on their arms and faces. Arjun was the last of the Pandava brothers to join in flanking Shikandi, riding his chariot with Krishna at the reins. From the faint smile on his face, Shikhandini inferred the had defeated Dronacharya, but the Guru still lived.

As the six of them tore through the *vyuha* of the Kaurava army, wreaking havoc as they crossed each level, Shikhandi finally caught sight of the Maharathi's chariot. The time had come.

***

As death stared him in the face, the Maharathi recalled his wrong actions of the past. He thought that now he would finally be free of the shackles of the vows that had bound him to the throne of Hastinapur all his life.

"Before you kill me, I wish to ask forgiveness, my child," said the Maharathi, standing still.

Shikhandi lowered his sword, confused. He looked around at the Pandava brothers; each had lowered his weapon and stood with hands folded respectfully. Instead of the anticipation of victory, there was the darkness of sorrow on their faces. Unshed tears filled their eyes as they witnessed their granduncle's vulnerability.

"What I did to Amba, Princesses of Kashi, was wrong. I had no right to attend the Princesses' swayamvara uninvited, and take them forcefully to Hastinapur. I had no right to separate Amba from the man she had chosen. It was because of my blind loyalty to the throne of Hastinapur and my inability to see right from wrong, that Princess Amba had to suffer. Forgive me, my child."

The Maharathi like many others was a firm believer in prophecy. He strongly believed that Shikhandi was the reincarnation of Princess Amba, who had vowed before surrendering herself to the burning pyre, to return and avenge her humiliation. Shikhandi wondered if she was the only one who still doubted the prophecy. All her life she had attempted to recall some incident from Princess Amba's life that she had not heard about from her father or grandfather. But she had never been able to do so, and so the question remained unanswered.

"Will you forgive me, my child?" the Maharathi repeated, his words pulling Shikhandi from her thoughts.

She stood rooted to the spot as the Maharathi's eyes bored into his. His eyes softened a little at the Maharathi's confession. He wondered if he was doing the right thing. Who was he to slay the Maharathi? Lowering his sword, he took a step back.

Dropping his sword, Bheesma walked towards Shikhandi and knelt before him. Arjun and the other Pandavas averted their eyes, unable to watch his humiliation.

"I do not ask you to spare my life, Shikhandi. I only ask for your forgiveness so that I can die in peace. Without your forgiveness the blemishes on my soul will follow me into lifetimes to come."

Uncertain what to do, Shikhandi joined his hands and nodded, granting him absolution. The sight of the proud Maharathi, the most powerful warrior in the Kaurava army, on his knees before him, brought tears to Shikhandi's eyes. He wondered if a man capable of such humility could indeed be as sinister and ruthless as he was made out to be, or whether he, like so many others, was merely a pawn of destiny.

Rising, the Maharathi composed himself. Shikhandi's forgiveness made him feel lighter. He knew there was only one other thing to do. As a Kshatriya, who had lived every minute of his life with dignity, wished to abide by the laws of dharma and fight to his last breath.

"As a Kshatriya and Senapati of the Kaurava army, my dharma does not permit me to surrender. Therefore, I challenge you to a duel," he declared, his deep voice like a clarion call to battle.

Shikhandi looked towards Arjun's chariot, where Krishna sat watching, reins in hand. His eyes revealed nothing. His face was calm and indifferent, as though aware of what was to transpire. She recalled him saying to her: *The purpose of your life is not revenge, but the restoration of dharma. The Maharathi's death is inevitable in the war of dharma.* With a slight nod, he signalled to Shikhandi to continue; what he had to do had been ordained.

"I accept your challenge, Maharathi Bheeshm!" said Shikhandi, picking up his sword and raising it to the sky. *Har Har Mahadev!*

Har Har Mahadev! repeated the Maharathi. He waited for Shikhandi to land the first blow, holding his sword in a defensive posture. He observed how Shikhandi's eyes reflected the sun slowly rising in the sky. The Pandava brothers had thrown off their grief and now stood behind Shikhandi, urging him to battle and victory.

Shikhandi raised his sword, chanting a silent prayer to Goddess Prakruti. Then he rushed towards the Maharathi, holding his weapon high above his head in an attempt to attack Bheeshma diagonally across the torso, ripping off his armour. With the armour gone, Shikhandi knew the fight was half won. But the veteran warrior knew better. He countered the strike, throwing his opponent off balance. Shikhandi stumbled a little before regaining his balance.

The duel continued with neither side faltering. Shikhandi knew he was tiring and would not last another hour of the punishing fight. Each time the two swords clashed in mid-air and then returned to the ground, a cloud of dust rose, momentarily blinding them. Shikhandi had managed to cut through the Maharathi's armour, leaving a deep gash on the Maharathis right arm. Shikhandi himself had several cuts across his torso. She could not but marvel at the Maharathi's immense strength. He was almost four decades older, but several times stronger.

Amidst the cloud of dust that surrounded the duo, a third silhouette became visible. As the dust settled, the Pandava brothers saw that Shikhandi was fighting Maharathi Bheeshm and Prince Duryodhan simultaneously.

"Prince Duryodhan, step back! Do not violate the codes of war," warned Maharathi Bheeshm, as Shikhandi's sword missing him by a hairsbreadth.

"I will not let him kill you, Pitamaha! Your life is more important to me than any law!" Duryodhan roared, using his mighty mace to crush Shikhandi.

When Bheeshm saw that Duryodhan would not heed his warning, he signalled to Bheem to step into the fight.

"Duryodhan!" Bheem, who had been waiting for this moment, charged towards his cousin, mace upraised. He was a fearsome sight.

The other Pandavas and Krishna stood still, witnessing the two duels – one a swordfight, the other with maces.

When Bheeshm saw that Shikhandi was using only one of the two swords he was famed for, he feared his opponent was not giving his best to the fight. The Maharathi wanted him to use every last iota of his strength and skill.

"Shikhandi, use both your swords!" he called, swinging his own weapon in a circle that was almost invisible to those who watched.

Shikhandi countered each strike but his agility was as nothing compared to the Maharathi. The air resounded to the clinking and clashing of their swords. With each blow from the Maharathi's sword, Shikhandi found himself moving back a step. His arms ached from the impact of the blows that reverberated from the blades into the shafts.

Now that the Maharathi had himself permitted the use of two swords, Shikhandi felt relieved. He was one of the few warriors who could use both swords with equal skill. Pulling out his second sword, he crossed the swords in front of him to reduce the impact of the blows. But the Maharathi gave him no opportunity to attack. Helpless in the face of his overwhelming skill, Shikhandi could only defend himself.

As his chest began to heave with exhaustion and sweat soaked through the red cotton band he wore round his forehead, Sthunakarna's words suddenly echoed in his ears: *Let the opponent think he is winning. Let him exhaust himself. Keep calm and wait for the right moment. Sooner or later his strength will fade and then you will have your opportunity.*

Just then, the clouds seemed to shift in the sky above them. Shikhandi mumbled a prayer to Goddess Prakruti, asking for strength. All the while she kept steady, countering and ducking the Maharathi'a attacks.

Another hour passed before Shikhandi finally saw the Maharathi begin to slow. His blows, though powerful, were not as frequent. His eyes looked glassy with fatigue and his breathing more laboured. Shikhandi knew his turn had come. Moving his swords from the sides to cross infront of him and then back again, he gained momentum. As they rotated, he moved with slow strides towards the Maharathi. Flashes of the past filled his mind – Draupadi's agonized cries, Princess Amba's vow as she entered the pyre, the Pandava brothers as they stood by helpless to protect their wife's dignity, Sthunakarna's sacrifice so she could fulfil her goal. Each memory seemed to have a physical reaction in her body as energy rushed up her spine. To those who watched, he appeared to be Kaal, the harbinger of death.

But the Maharathi was undisturbed. He rushed towards Shikhandi with his sword. He knew his time had come but he would fight to the bitter end as the warrior code dictated. The momentum of Shikhandi's blades was fierce. When they came into contact with the Maharathi's sword, the impact was several times stronger than it would have been with a single sword.

In a lightning move, the Maharathi's sword was flung from his hand. Like Shikhandi, he too, never used a shield. He had never needed it. In that split second, Shikhandi attacked him, catching him defenceless. A deep gash formed in the middle of his torso and blood oozed from his stomach. With hands outstretched, as though welcoming death, the Maharathi collapsed, his old and injured body hitting the ground. Time seemed to stand still on the battlefield of Kurukshetra.

"Pitamaha!" cried Bheem and Duryodhan in unison, rushing towards their grandsire, their duel forgotten.

The other Pandavas too, rushed towards the fallen Maharathi. Krishna descended from the chariot he was driving.

"Pitamaha…" whispered Arjun, holding the Maharathi's hand. Tears wet his face. Carefully, he lifted Bheeshm's head onto his lap.

The old warrior smiled, extending a hand to wipe away the tears from Arjun's face. "There is nothing to be sad about, my son. It was destined."

Nakul and Sahadev, the youngest of the Pandavas, began dressing the Maharathi's wound, trying to staunch the flow of blood.

"I have one last wish, my son," said Bheeshma to Yudhistir. "I promised my father that I would not accept death until I saw righteousness and truth ascend the throne. I cannot die until I see for myself that Hastinapur is in your hands."

Yudhistir nodded, his face a mask of sorrow. Where was the joy in victory he wondered, if all it brought was pain?

"Arjun, you must do one last thing for me," said Bheesma.

"You have but to ask, Pitamaha"

"I wish to spend my last days in this dharmakshetra. I wish to witness all the destruction and death I have caused. Use your arrows to make me a bed here and then lay me on it so I can repent for all my sins before I depart this life."

24
THE END

Following the Maharathi's downfall, Guru Dronacharya was appointed the new Senapati of the Kaurava army, and Karna entered the war, to Duryodhan's great joy. Shikhandini continued to stand by the Pandavas.

It was now the eleventh day of the war. Dronacharya planned to capture Yudhistir and hold him hostage. This would leave the Pandavas weak and helpless. The Pandavas used all their strength to shield their King. They were successful for most of the day. Finally an hour remained for the sun to sink below the horizon marking the cessation of the day's hostilities.

Shikhandi was on foot. He had just beheaded a soldier who had deliberately stabbed a horse – an inhuman and unforgivable violation of the war code and Kshatriya dharma. As he stared down at the headless body lying in a pool of blood, he suddenly felt someone's presence. Whirling around with sword in hand, he stared at the man behind him.

It was only when the man looked into Shikhandi's eyes that he realized who he was. "Shikhandini…" he whispered, standing frozen like a statue.

"Kush…" Shikhandi instantly regretted having spoken. There was nothing left between them but pain.

Around them the sounds of battle seemed to die into silence.

"You look…so changed..." Kush murmured, struggling to find the words. His heart thudded painfully in his chest. Was this man his beautiful wife; the woman he had loved unceasingly?

Shikhandi merely nodded. He had long overcome all consciousness about his appearance. He was what life had made him.

"Father!" Shikhandi heard a voice call urgently. Kush quickly caught the sword thrown to him.

The youth had assumed his father had dropped his sword in the melée. Now, pulling his second sword from its scabbard, he rode back towards the enemy lines, slaughtering whoever stood in his way. Kush and Shikhandi took shelter behind an overturned chariot.

"Is he...?" Shikhandi asked, unable to take his eyes off the charging figure with sword in hand. He had no doubt who the youngster was, but he wanted to hear it from Kush.

"Yes, he is our son."

Shikhandi's eyes glistened with tears of pride and joy. He had left Dasarna believing he would never see his son again. God had granted him this final boon.

"He has inherited your traits. His swordsmanship is exceptional. It was his decision to fight in the war. Draupadi's sons are his friends," explained Kush.

"Does he...?" asked Shikhandi hesitantly, his voice dying away.

"No…" Kush replied, understanding what Shikhandi yearned to know. "He thinks Hema is his mother."

Shikhandi blinked back the sudden rush of tears. He was relieved to know he would never have to face his son or embarrass him, nor would he have to explain anything. To his son he would just be Shikhandi, a figure of lore and legend. His heart yearned to embrace his child, to ask forgiveness for having abandoned him during the most crucial years of his life.

"After you left, Hema looked after him like her own son. We do not have any children of our own. Kshatradeva is our only child" said Kush. There was no hint of loss or sadness in his eyes. "Shikhandini, will you ever be able to forgive us?" asked Kush.

Shikhandi seemed lost in her memories but Kush's words brought her back to the present moment. "I forgave you long ago, Kush. I hold no bitterness in my heart against you or Hema. My decision to leave Dasarna was not because of your betrayal." Kush winced at the word she had used.

"No Kush, I left Dasarna knowing you and Hema would give our son everything he deserved, everything that I could not. My trust and faith in you enabled me to take such an irretrievable step." For the first time, Shikhandi smiled.

Kush nodded, feeling bereft once again. "Shikhandi, I want you to know that I will always stand with you and fight for you until my last breath. I did not keep the promise I made when I married you, but I will keep this one to my last breath."

***

In the next eight days, Kurukshetra saw the death of great warriors on both sides. But the incident that enraged the Pandavas into making them fight with renewed purpose was the death of Abhimanyu, Arjun's son. The courageous young warrior had been killed in the most insiduous way. Trapped inside the *chakravyuha,* he had been attacked by several warrior sat the same time, in violation of the codes of war. Abhimanyu had fought valiantly until he was brutally killed.

This was soon followed by the death of Anga Raja Karna, the only warrior whose death was mourned on both sides of the battlelines. Shortly before his death, Kunti had revealed the truth about his birth. The fact that he was her eldest son, left the Pandavas shattered. Arjun had killed his own brother.

With the downfall of the Maharathi, and the death of Karna, Dronacharya and Duryodhan were the last ones left to steady the Kaurava army.

Yudhistir, known never to speak anything but the truth, finally broke his vow. Krishna convinced him that Dronacharya's death was inevitable for the greater good. The news of Ashwathama's death was thus delivered to the Guru by Yudhistir, who forebore to tell him that it was not the Guru's son about whom he brought such dread tidings, but an injured elephant of the same name. Drowning in sorrow at the thought of losing his only son, the Guru lost his fight with Dhrishtadhyumna, Prince of Panchala. He died never knowing his son still lived. Yudhisthir had withheld the truth.

It was not long before every one of the ninety-nine Kaurava Princes had been put to an end by Bheem. The *Madhyama Pandava* had thus kept his vow to annihilate them. Only Duryodhan remained. Finally, he too, was swept up in the whirlwind. His death was the most cruel of all. In a mace fight, Bheem broke every bone in his body. The once proud and arrogant Kaurava Prince lay in the mud, unable to rise, waiting for his soul to escape his body.

With Duryodhan's death, the eighteen-day bloodbath finally came to an end. But there was no joy or celebration anywhere. Kurukshetra had turned into a graveyard, decorated with the bright light emitted by the funeral pyres of thousands of men. The river of blood was replaced by a, flood of tears. The wails of widows and orphans rose to the heavens.

Royal mothers, watching helplessly on both sides of the Kuru divide, saw their sons perish. Subhadra, Arjun's wife, lost Abhimanyu; Kunti her firstborn, Karna; Hidimbi, Bheem's wife, lost their son Ghatothkacha; and Gandhari, proud mother of a hundred sons, lost them all.

The Pandavas emerged victorious in the Great War, winning back Hastinapur, Indraprastha, Anga, and all the other kingdoms that had once been under the overlordship of King Shantanu. Yudhistir was soon to be declared King of Aryavrat. But the war had first to be declared to have ended before the bedraggled remanants of the two armies could leave the battlefield. The Pandavas, with Draupadi, walked to the scene of so much carnage, wondering what had been the purpose of it all. Draupadi's eyes glittered with unshed tears. She had kept her word to wash her unbound hair in Dushashana's blood to avenge her humiliation at his hands. But dead men tell no tales and the act of revenge had been but a hollow act.

***

In the darkest hour before sunrise, when the Pandava camp slept the sleep of the weary, a shadowy form flitted from tent to tent till he arrived at the one he sought. Oblivious to danger, the five sons of Draupadi slept peacefully, knowing the war had ended and good times were about to begin.

"The war is not over, my brothers. I have lost everyone – my father, my friend, my kingdom. It is time you too, felt the loss of those you love most," the man murmured, peering through the flap at the five sleeping figures.

He slid behind the sleeping guard and with one clean stroke, slit the man's throat. One by one, he killed every guard around the tent, and then entered. It was pitch dark inside, but he could not miss the silhouettes. He felt enraged at the sight of his enemies sleeping peacefully. Pulling out his sword, he slaughtered all five. As the blood of each splattered his face, he let out a bitter laugh. His purpose was served. He had fulfilled the promise he had made to his dying friend Duryodhan.

Suddenly, Shikhandi appeared like an apparition in the tent. He saw the rictus grin on Ashwathama's face; his hands and sword covered in the blood of Draupadi's sons. "Ashwathama, you coward!" he yelled, horrified by what he saw.

"Shikhandi..." Ashwathama hissed his name like a curse. "I was waiting for you, Princess of Panchala, or should I say Prince?" laughed Ashwathama.

Shikhandi pulled out his sword. "Fight, you coward!" he challenged.

Ashwathama held up his own sword, ready to do battle. "I should have killed you the moment you set foot in the battlefield. You are the reason for our defeat. The cause of Duryodhan's death. Had you not mortally wounded Maharathi Bheeshm, Bheem would never have laid hands on my friend. You filthy eunuch!" Shaking the blood off his sword, he walked towards Shikhandi, his bloodshot eyes glared at him like a predator.

Shikhandi knew he had to be alert while fighting Guru Dronacharya's son. He was known to be an excellent warrior. Some even believed him to be invincible.

Ashwathama's sword missed Shikhandi's arm by a hairsbreadth as he moved reflexively away. Every nerve in Shikhandi's body was alert as he fought for his life. Ashwathama attacked again, this time aiming at Shikhandi's thigh. He was fighting dirty. Now that his father was no longer alive, he had no reason to follow the rules of combat. Shikhandi countered with his sword.

Ashwathama fought like a man possessed. Shikhandi, on the other hand, had been caught off guard. Time and again he glanced to where his nephews lay lifeless. He wondered what Draupadi would do when she returned. Shikhandi wished he could die before he had to witness his sister's agony.

"I will not spare you, you filthy eunuch!" roared Ashwathama as he charged towards Shikhandi. The time for codes and fairplay was long gone. He knew he had to finish Shikhandi before the others arrived.

"Fight, you coward!" Shikhandi yelled.

As their swords clashed again, Ashwathama pulled out a dagger from his waistband. Shikhandi, eyes on his sword, did not see the weapon in his other hand. She raised her sword high to behead him in one clean strike.

Ashwathama, son and pupil of the great Guru Dronacharya, was an experienced warrior. He sensed her intent and immediately countered it with his own sword. Then, without a second thought, he plunged his dagger into Shikhandi's stomach. He twisted the dagger, lacerating Shikhandi's gut. Pulling it out, he turned and fled.

***

Blood oozed from Shikhandi's stomach like sand in an hourglass, reducing time. He knew this was the end. The prophecy had been served but he still had questions before he left the world. Clutching his stomach, he tried to move. Who was he looking for? He did not know. Weak from exhaustion, his vision began to blur. As his body slowly collapsed, he waited to feel the mpact of his head hitting the ground. But the jolt did not come. The hard ground was replaced by something familiar and comforting. Slowly, he looked up. *Krishna...*

Laying Shikhandi down gently, Krishna knelt beside her. Looking into Shikhandi's pain filled eyes, he smiled. Shikhandi tried to say something, but his voice was inaudible even to his own ears. He clutched her stomach in mortal agony, hoping to stem the blood. He needed a little more time.

"Shikhandi..." Krishna called, even though no words left his lips. His deep-set eyes bored into Shikhandi's, as though reading his mind.

"Why?" Shikhandi asked, speaking the language of the eyes. He realized he did not need his voice to talk to Krishna.

"Your time has come, Shikhandi. This is the end of your suffering."

"What wrong did I do to deserve such a life?"

Placing a hand on her head, Krishna replied, "God gives the toughest challenges to his bravest soldiers. No one would have been able to accomplish what you did. The reason for your birth was not to seek your grandfather's, King Drupada's or Amba's vengeance. It was to restore dharma. Having eliminated the Maharathi from the war, you served that purpose."

"But why me? Why did I have to be a part of this? Why did I have to be the reason for the Maharathi's death?"

"This Great War was fought to restore dharma. It began to avenge a woman's humiliation, while so-called wise and righteous men stood by as mute witnesses. The war was begun by a strong-hearted and valiant woman, and only one who shared the same inner power could bring it to an end. Who better than you Shikhandi?"

"But he was a good man, the Maharathi. Why did I have to be the cause of his death?" Shikhandi recalled his visit to the place on the battlefield where the Maharathi lay helpless on the bed of arrows Arjun had made in accordance with his wishes. Guilt filled Shikhandi as the Maharathi's face flashed in his mind.

"Death is inevitable Shikhandi. It is written even before one is born. Our time here is limited. His time had come; you only did what you were destined to do. Caught in the shackles of his own words, he lived his long life protecting the throne of Hastinapur, trying to hold the family together. All his life he abided by the laws of dharma, which were dearer to him than his own life. But when fate placed him in the position of mute witness on the fateful day of Draupadi's *vasthraharana*, he began to die from within. He was aware that all his good karma, everything he had earned by living a righteous life, was washed away in that one day when he chose not to help Panchali. Each day after that he prayed for death to release him."

Was that why he had been able to defeat the Maharathi? Because he had desired to end his life, Shikhandi wondered? Drenched in his own blood, too numb to move a muscle, he was grateful to have Krishna by his side. His presence alone made death less painful, a threshold he had to cross. Images flashed before his eyes of the little boy who had often visited him in his childhood whenever he was sad and lonely; the stranger who saved his life and showed him the path to Yakshavana; the sound of the flute during the painful shastra chikitsa in Yakshavana. The truth struck him like a flash of lightening on a stormy day. *Was Krishna indeed Lord Vishnu himself?* He stared at Krishna, eyes wide with wonderment.

Krishna smiled enigmatically. "Perhaps it is so. But that depends more on you than me. What is God to you?" he asked. "God resides in all of us, Shikhandi. Some just realize it earlier than others. We are all tiny sparks of the holy flame that burns for eternity, abundant in energy, imperishable. We all borrow a small portion of that energy in order to do our karma in the mortal realm. But one day we must return what is borrowed. Then we merge with the *Ekam*, the One God, the holy flame. I am Vishnu, as are you, my child. We are all a significant part of him."

Shikhandi forgot his pain. Fear left his being as Krishna's words filled the gaping hole in his heart, satiating his soul. For the first time in his life, everything seemed right. His life no longer seemed unfruitful. He felt content, for he had played a vital role in the war of dharma. His eyes shone with tears of gratitude as he smiled at Krishna. Peacefully, he sank into the darkness.

Glossary

Bharatavarsha	Land of Bharat, modern India
Adharma	That which is not in accord with dharma; wrongfulness, unrighteousness
Akshauhini	Battalion of 20,000 chariots, 20,000 elephants, 60,000 horse and 100,000 foot soldiers
Angavasthram	Long rectangular cloth worn draped over the shoulder
Antahsraava	Hormones
Antariya	Lower garment made of cotton or silk. The dhoti and lungi are evolved forms of this.
Apsara	Celestial singers and dancers of unmatched beauty.
Ardhanarishvara	One of the names of Lord Shiva meaning *ardha* (half), *nuri* (woman), *Leshwara* (God). Composed of Shiva and his consort Shakti, this form represents the synthesis of masculine and feminine energies.
Aryavart	Land of the Aryans or 'abode of the noble/ excellent ones'
Ayushman Bhava	A blessing meaning: May you live long'
Bansuri	Flute
Brahmanda	Universe
Chakravyuha	A multi-ringed defensive formation used in battle, named for it's disc-like structure
Chikitsak	Medical practitioner; surgeon in this context
Chulah	A small earthen stove used for cooking

Daiva Astras	Powerful weapons governed by specific dieties
Dharma	The eternal and inherent nature of reality, regarded in Hinduism as the cosmic law governing right behaviour and social order
Digvijay Yatra	A expedition of expansion undertaken by a King/ Prince to conquer other kingdoms
Gajra	Garland worn in the hair or around the neck
Gopuram	Monumental ornate tower at the entrance of a Hindu temple
Guru Dakshina	A tradition of repaying a teacher/guru after a period of study or completion of education
Gurukul	A traditional school where students live near their guru, in a simple way, as his/her family
Gwalas	Cowherd
Ischa-Maran	A boon whereby a person can choose his time and place of death. Such a person is considered immortal.
Janivara/Janeu	Sacred thread worn by students to mark their status as seekers of knowledge
Jyothishi	Astrologer
Khagolashatra	Astronomy
Padmasana	A seated crossed-legged yogic posture with the feet placed on the opposite thighs
Panchabutha	Five great elements said to be present in the universe, including the human body
Panchakarma	A five-stage detoxification treatment in ayurveda
Panchayat	Village council
Parajay	Defeat
Pativrata	A woman who is devoted to her husband
Prahar	Sub-division of time; about three hours
Prasadam	Consecrated food offered to a deity and consumed by worshippers as food blessed by God

Purana	Ancient Sanskrit writings on mythology and folklore, of varying dates and authorship
Purohit	Priest
Pushpakavimana	A flying chariot
Rahu	One of the two shadow planets generally considered to be malefic in nature
Rasashastra	Branch of Ayurveda dealing with mineral and inorganic drugs for therapeutic use
Rathi/Athirathi/Maharathi	Different warrior ranks
Rudraksha	Seeds traditionally considered holy and used as prayer beads in Hinduism
Senapati	Title denoting Military Commander or General of the Army in ancient India
Shastra Chikitsa	Surgery
Shastras	Ancient writings, often considered sacred
Shiva-Sahasranama	Recitation of the 1000 names of Lord Shiva
Shloka	Sanskrit couplet containing 16 syllables.
Smrithis	Literally 'that which is remembered'; a body of Vedic writing usually attributed to one author but constantly revised, in contrast to Śrutis, that are were authorless and transmuted verbally over generations
Suryanamaskars	Salutation to Lord Surya or the Sun God
Swayamvara	A grand ceremony in royal families where a Princess chose her future husband from among eligible suitors, who often competed in contests for her hand.
Tama	Copper
Tilak	A vertical mark worn on the forehead indicating the movement of an individual's thoughts towards spirituality
Trishul	Trident held by Lord Shiva and other dieties
Uttariya	Cotton or silk shawl for the upper body
Vignyana	Science

Vijayi Bhava	A blessing: 'May you be victorious'
Vyed	A medical practioner of Ayurveda
Vyuha	A battle formation
Yagya	Sacrificial rite performed before a sacred fire
Yantra	A device used in scientific study
Yojana	Measurment of distance in ancient India
Yuga	An age

Acknowledgements

A debt of gratitude to Chandralekha Maitra, and everyone at Leadstart Publishing, for their belief in this project.

To my friend Karthik Rao, for his enthusiasm and unflagging effort.

To my dear friend, Aparna Shastry, for her constant support and encouragement.

To my friend, Abhishek Kalkeri, for being my prime source of information on various topics.

To my dear friend, Sunitha K, for her insightful inputs, and putting up with our lengthy discussions.

To my friend and well-wisher, Aurobindo Jay, for believing in this project despite his dislike of fiction.

Last but not the least, I would like to acknowledge with gratitude, the support and love of my parents – Ramachandra and Rekha Shenoy. They kept me going. This book would not have been possible without them.

Wish To Publish With Us?

We are always keen to look at interesting content across genres. Please email your submission to: **submissions@leadstartcorp.com**

The submission should include the following:

1. **Synopsis**

   A summary of the book in 500 – 1000 words. Please mention the word count of the manuscript.

2. **Sample chapters / Poetry**

   A couple of chapters from the book; these need not be in order, just send the best two chapters of the book. Or a few poems if the same is a collection of poetry.

3. **A Note About The Author**

   An interesting note about yourself (about 200 words).

4. **Additional Information**
   - Target audience
   - Unique selling proposition
   - List of illustrative content (if any)
   - Other comparative titles
   - Your thoughts on marketing the book